killingsuperman

MARY-ROSE MACCOLL's first novel, *No Safe Place*, was runner-up in *The Australian* Vogel Literary Award and was published in 1996. *Angels in the Architecture*, published in 1999, was shortlisted for a Ned Kelly Award. MacColl lives and writes in Brisbane.

killingsuperman

MARY-ROSE MacCOLL

ALLEN&UNWIN

First published in 2003

 This project has been assisted by the Commonwealth
Government through the Australia Council, its arts
funding and advisory board.

Allen & Unwin
83 Alexander Street
Crows Nest NSW 2065
Australia
Phone: (61 2) 8425 0100
Fax: (61 2) 9906 2218
Email: info@allenandunwin.com
Web: www.allenandunwin.com

National Library of Australia
Cataloguing-in-Publication entry:

MacColl, Mary-Rose, 1961–.
  Killing superman.

  ISBN 1 86508 998 2.

  1. Fathers and sons—Fiction. I. Title.

A823.3

Set in 11.5/14pt Adobe Garamond by Asset Typesetting Pty Ltd
Printed in Australia by McPherson's Printing Group

10 9 8 7 6 5 4 3 2 1

When I was a child,
I spake as a child,
I understood as a child,
I thought as a child;

but when I became a man,
I put away childish things.

— The Apostle Paul's letters to the Corinthians

chapter**one**

Later, I might think of the way each event leads to the next and the next and eventually to you, but right now I'm not thinking at all. I've woken feverish and thirsty in a strange bed, with nothing familiar except my travel-clock on the table on one side and Emily's face on the other. Everything else — the bed, the room, the wooden window frames to the lightening sky outside — looks strange and new.

I reach over to touch Emily's cheek and notice my fingers mid-air are trembling. Then I remember. Emily's involved. She's a liar, like you're a liar. I turn away and get up from the bed. Emily shifts position, taking over my space now as if I'd never been there. I steady myself against the wall as I head out to the little kitchen. It looks as if it's been burgled in the night, with saucepans, plates and wineglasses abandoned where they were used. I take the roasting rack from the sink and put it on the floor. I can still smell the rosemary and garlic that filled the little apartment with anticipation of a lovers' feast yesterday, when Emily and I were lovers; they smell like defeat now. I put my head under the tap. The icy water feels true on my flushed face and scalp. I take a long drink, rub my clipped hair with the nearest kitchen towel to dry it, discover too late the towel's covered in gravy. I wash my hair again, shake it dry, grab my coat from the table and stumble down the narrow stairs and out the door.

Emily picked the apartment on the Internet. It's in an old stone building, in the medieval part of the city, she said. Niçoise authentique, she called it. It will be so perfect, she added, qualifying the superlative which I didn't bother to correct because at that time everything about her was so perfect I didn't care. We'll shop at the markets on the Cours de la Saleya, she said. We'll drive the corniches and head for Monte Carlo to make our fortune. She talks of these towns as if they're completely familiar to her. That's Emily all over. Five minutes in a place and she's a local. She's an endless optimist, too, assuming the best, never caring for disappointment until it slaps her in the face. I'm the opposite; I plan for the worst so I'm never disappointed.

I was optimistic about Emily, though; my mistake. Last night I told her we're finished. We'd had too much wine for that kind of talk, but I don't know how to go on from here. I spent all my forgiveness on you. And now, to find that Emily's involved. I don't know how to accommodate that. I don't know how to reframe it, as Dr Bain would have me do. Emily's put me back into your frame, you at the centre, me the radius at any given point, just like old times.

Outside on the street everything but the baker is closed. Yesterday, I bought warm mountain bread, ordering by pointing. What's the word for mountain again? Montagne? It doesn't sound like bread. I took the bread back up to the apartment and made coffee and took it in on a tray with some strawberries. I might have done the same today. If it had been something else, anything else but you, I might have gone back to Emily and said sorry, as if it was my fault. I don't mind taking the blame. But you. I'm not sure I have that sort of courage.

I turn out of the Rue de la Place Vielle where we're staying and into the Rue Droite, which will take me to the fish markets. I look up at the silver sky and see that a gold jet has left a pink jetstream like a tow-rope on the coming sun. Straight ahead of me is the narrow cobbled path that leads up to the Château with its layers of ruin — an ancient Greek fortress, a Roman temple, and on top of these an 11th century Catholic cathedral. Everyone's conquered Nice. On the spur of the moment, I turn away from the markets, away from the ruins and towards the sea, where the jetstream points.

At the water's edge, the Promenade des Anglais is like a carnival in the evening, everyone slow with too much food and fun, the light soft. Two lovers use a pair of blue beach chairs as a bed, her on top, his fingers worming up her skirt from behind, revealing black underpants. They're smoking as they kiss; it looks like steam. If you were up here with me, you'd make a joke. Thunder-thighs, you'd stage-whisper, loud enough for them to hear.

Embarrassed, I look away down the beach towards a group of fishermen who pull in the night's catch from a little red boat. An authentic French beach scene, Emily would say in the American travelogue voice she uses. I turn to walk the Promenade like the other authentic people do, towards the pink Hôtel Négresco which looks anything but authentic in this French pixie light.

An old woman in yellow bathers with a matching cap, robe and towel catches my eye. She has the mauve hair of a grandmother. She moves slowly down the pebble beach past the fishermen. They call out to her in throaty French, but she ignores them. She drops her robe and towel and stumbles over the shoals. She's as clumsy as a seal on the shore, and as graceful once in the water. She flips over. I watch her slow lovely backstroke.

They're like a relay team, from the jetstream to the lovers to the fishermen, the old grandmother and then to you. I could easily have missed you, a man down on the beach, fifty metres from where I stand, leather-tanned body painted with white dick togs, just like the thousand old men who haunt these beaches. This man looks towards the water in the way you used to, one hand shielding his eyes from the nonexistent glare, as if we're in bright Australia and not soft France, the other hand clutching a towel like it's a little boy's hand. This man's shoulders are rounded, just like yours; a life of asthma. He shakes the towel gently, as if pulling on the boy's hand, pointing out the rip that makes swimming dangerous. Danger is my middle name. I was young enough to believe you when you said that.

Clark, they called you, didn't they? After Clark Kent, after Superman. That's what they told me. That's what you told me. You could swim faster than men half your age.

'I'm not a poser, but…' you'd say. You could run like the wind and your eyes were sharper than a hawk's. A hawk's. 'X-ray vision,' you said, your eyes were that good. 'You will believe a man can fly,' we'd recite together, me with the accent. And your hearing? God, your hearing was bionic. 'Bi-onnic,' you said. The forward scout. I so much want to be cruel to you but find it exhausts me.

The man on the beach turns his head my way, and automatically my heart punches at my ribs. I know you wouldn't recognise me now anyway; it's been close enough to twenty years; but I feel exposed up here on the Promenade, like a butterfly pinned to a display board. The man takes a step towards me, then stops, turns back to the Mediterranean, as if hesitating about what to do. 'He who hesitates is lost.' That was one of your sayings. The man turns again, sure now, and starts reeling in that radius, pulling me back. He swings his right arm forward in the way you used to, a brief flick of the wrist so we see the Rolex Oyster watch, and takes up that unmistakable confidence of gait. He moves from the hips, legs forward, arms swinging, head high, and I know that marching that soldier's march towards me is my soldier father, who I haven't seen since I was fourteen, and at whose funeral I couldn't cry because I was so sure you weren't dead.

chapter**two**

Last night the wind whistled through the tiny gaps between the closed windows and their frames. I'd been startled awake by Emily's cry. 'Scott, you're hurting me!' I was hanging on to her, like I used to when we first met. I blinked hard and tried to let her go.

I have a theory. Everyone gets one good thing in their life. Maybe only one. One lucky break, one chance, in my case one encounter, that can change everything. That was Emily, or so I thought. She was my one good thing. So let me leave this beach and you. Let me soothe myself awhile and think of Emily, sweet Emily, before I knew the truth.

It was a Monday in September just six months ago; it seems like longer. Two of our reference librarians had phoned in sick. The senior of them, June, our longest serving staff member, was sure to be genuinely ill. June was old-school conscientious, but more than that, it was

Matthew's birthday. Matthew's a file restoration technician who's been with the Archives nearly as long as June, and every year she brings in a chocolate cake, his favourite, for morning tea. He takes no notice of her efforts, despite the fact she doesn't cook cakes for the rest of us. On his fortieth birthday, I commented on how nice it was of June, hoping he might say something. Instead, June said, with considerable feeling, 'What if I didn't do it?' and left the room. Matthew looked at the floor. The next year, we had the usual chocolate cake, and I didn't make comments.

The other librarian who called in sick was Alison, our most recent appointment. Alison was a new graduate with both ears pierced in more places than I could count without looking obvious. She was abrupt in her responses to questions when we interviewed her for the post. Understandably, I suppose, June hadn't wanted to appoint her. I'd insisted. Something about Alison reminded me of my sister Stella when she was younger, and I wanted to give Alison a chance. So far she hadn't worked out well. I was relieved June wouldn't be there to roll her eyes as she told me Alison was sick, again. Alison was probably taking the day off after a big night, and tomorrow I'd feign concern when I asked her how she was feeling. I've always thought it's better to take people at their word in the hope they might start telling the truth.

When the reference manager told me we'd be short-staffed, I offered to cover the front counter myself. In their annual performance feedback, my staff say I'm a good manager who pitches in when needed. I always feel a little dishonest, because the truth is I like working the counter; in the midst of the centimetres of paperwork I process each week, it reminds me what we're here for — to help people by finding out what they don't know.

When we opened at nine, a woman around my age came through the double doors, followed by an older university professor I knew was doing a study on dead Queensland poets. The woman stopped at the directory panel. The professor walked towards me, probably assuming I'd help him, since his search was sure to be complicated and his patience was sure to be limited. I asked the other attendant, a junior, to look after the professor and I walked around the counter and over to the woman. 'Can I help you?' I said.

Most of our clients come from what we used to call the general public and what we now refer to in our strategic plans as 'stakeholders' or 'the wider community'. Whatever you call them, when they come into the State Archives they're mostly looking for personal history, often in the form of a past secret. The rest are researchers. I can usually tell the moment someone crosses our threshold what they're after. I picked the woman for the first category, personal history, some sort of past secret, but a fairly distant one. She was interested rather than life-and-death committed to finding out some truth. She didn't look worn down enough to be carrying the pain of her own secret.

We keep secrets of every kind in the Archives — the truth about births, deaths and marriages, records from police, hospitals, the courts, government departments, schools and universities, and anything else anyone cares to send us. If an event happened, it's probably recorded and we've probably got the record. And if we haven't, I can probably get it for you without too much trouble.

Archives work is tricky. A few years ago June gave an adoptee access to birth records which meant he could find his birth parents. In doing so, June crossed a line we shouldn't cross. The adoptee's birth father, now in his seventies, was furious when his secret son turned up on his doorstep. The father made a complaint to the Minister, and there was an inquiry that came down the line to me. June denied the charge, of course, but our secured records are in closed repositories that are impossible to access without card identification, and reference staff must be accompanied by a security officer, so I knew who it was. I pretended I didn't, though, drafted an apology to the old man and backed my staff member. I said it was an error. I pointed to our outstanding service record (as demonstrated by the customer feedback which rated us at four point two or above on every point of the five-point scale) and asked that we be given the benefit of the doubt. I knew it wouldn't happen again, I said. Frankly, if I'd been in June's position, I'd probably have done the same.

The woman who'd arrived when we opened had bright green eyes that rested on me and then took in everything else in the reading room quickly before coming back to me. Her eyes were incredibly expressive. If she were an operating theatre nurse on one of those television programs, with a mask and cap covering the rest of her face and head, you'd know the exact moment they lost the patient, just from the look in her eyes.

'I'm searching for a record of a death,' she said,

tilting her head and returning my smile with a quizzical smile of her own.

'Do you have a name and date?'

'Do you have to be a relative?'

'Not at all,' I said. 'As long as what you're looking for is on the public record, we can find it for you.'

Her eyes flicked to my ID tag and back to my face. For a moment she looked confused. 'What if I am a relative?'

'We'll give you a discount.' I felt like showing off, something I don't often do. She smiled.

I ushered her to the counter and remained on the client side next to her, reaching over to grab a pen and notebook from the desk. I felt awkward for some reason, as if my arms and legs had suddenly grown a foot. I was poised ready to write down the name and when she didn't offer it, I wrote, 'Dead?', and underlined it. She stood close; I could feel the warmth she radiated. Too much damp heat, my sister Stella would have said in her Chinese-herbal period. The young woman's hand rested on a leather satchel slung over her shoulder but the strap kept slipping down her arm and when she pulled it up her elbow bumped me in the ribs as if she was making a joke I wasn't getting. She wore straight denim jeans and a purple long-sleeved T-shirt. My grandmother would have called her womanly, which meant she had broad hips and large breasts. 'Do you have a name?' I said.

'What's your name?' she said. Her eyes move from my face to my ID tag again and back to my face.

'Scott Goodwin. I'm in charge of information.' I'm in charge of information; I sounded like such a jerk. The counter attendant who was helping the professor was watching me, perhaps hoping I'd offer to swap. I pretended I didn't notice.

'Jack Duval. That's my father.'

'And you want to know if he's dead?' I said, matter-of-factly.

She chuckled. 'No, he's been dead for years. I want to know what records you have about him.'

'He's your father?'

'Yes.'

I figured I was right; past secret, long time ago, not too painful. I walked around and behind the counter and logged into the system. I found a J M Duval in an Australian Associated Press database. She confirmed this was Jacques Michel Duval, her father. From there I located birth and death records. Jack Duval had been a newspaper photographer who'd died in Lebanon in 1976. I told my client I could put her onto someone in Foreign Affairs who could help her further.

'Can you get things from the Army?' she said suddenly.

'Kind of. We have access to most Commonwealth databases, but the armed services are a law unto themselves.' Earlier in the year I'd helped a widow get access to records relating to her late soldier-husband's exposure to chemicals in the Second World War. It took all my research skills and months of patient work, doing my best to use the State's Freedom of Information legislation. Quite frankly, from what I could see, the legislation made information harder, not easier, to come by. But eventually we got what we needed. The news about her husband probably wouldn't give the poor woman compensation according to her lawyer, but at least she knew he got sick for a reason. She had someone to blame. We all want that. My section received a commendation from our Minister for that job. 'Come down to my office and I'll show you what we have.'

We didn't need a private interview. The woman's request for information about her father was straight-forward, I could have continued using the counter terminal, and I probably should have referred her on in the first place. Instead I decided to fill out a request form which we use for complicated searches. It would give me her name and phone number which, while not ethical, was something I wanted. While not ethical, was something I wanted — can you believe me? 'Was your father in the services?' I said on the way to my office.

'No, he was a photographer, working for Reuters, but he also did some media liaison work for the Australian Army in Asia,' she said. 'So I thought you might have some of their records. All I really need is a copy of his birth certificate but I'll take whatever else you've got.'

She walked in front of me but didn't know the way and had to stop for directions. I kept bumping into her. When we reached my office she went in ahead of me. I stood at the door, seeing the little room as she might: the seventies pine desk and credenza, the empty in-basket, full out-basket, my hard black briefcase. Vinyl chairs and green carpet completed an image that yawned dag dag dag at me. The only cheerful note was a corkboard behind the desk which was covered with photographs I'd taken and quotes I'd collected. It wasn't enough. I wished I'd taken up the department head's offer of a refit the year before.

After surveying the office I started to think about its occupant, me, as my visitor might see me, fitting right in with the decor; tall, skinny, short-sleeved blue-checked business shirt, Santa-red bow tie, grey shorts with black socks and beige Rockport shoes, gold-rimmed glasses that died with John Lennon and cropped curly blond hair. I had an urge to offer an explanation. I'm not really as much of a dag as I look, I'd say. I walk to work from the city and that's why I wear the shorts, and the bow tie doesn't get in the way when I'm dealing with fragile material. It was weak, I knew. On weekends, I'd tell her, I'm stylish. But she'd be a fool to believe me. And she didn't look like a fool.

The woman had sat herself down on my side of the desk by this time, and she leaned forward as if she was about to start work. I grabbed a form from the credenza behind her, put it onto a clipboard with a twang, and went round her to sit in my visitor's chair. I should have swapped places but I didn't and then it was too late. I rested the clipboard on my knee so she couldn't see it, then filled it in on her behalf. She fidgeted with my desk calendar.

Her name was Emily Duval, she said when I asked, and Emily Duval was thirty, just turned. She was a freelance journalist. 'Marital status?' I said, pretending to get ready to tick something.

'You're inquisitive for an archivist,' Emily Duval said. She was single. 'Inquiry is my business.' I felt silly.

I was making the questions up as I went. I thought she must know. 'We collect data on what sort of people use our services.' She smiled but didn't volunteer more.

'Are you vegetarian?' she said. From the desk, she'd picked up a card from a vegetarian restaurant. The restaurant was actually owned by the mother of one of the girls in the office. I'd never been there. I never went to any restaurants.

'Sort of,' I lied. I don't lie as a rule, I'm kind of strict about the moral point, but I had a hunch Emily Duval wouldn't be the type to like a big clumsy meat-eater, and I wanted Emily Duval to like me more than I cared about the truth.

'Me too,' she said. 'Vegan?'

'Ovo-lacto,' I said, recalling a conversation with the staff member whose mother owned the restaurant.

'What's that do?' She pointed to the computer terminal on my desk between us which I had to swing around to the visitor side to use.

'It's our records system, which is how we'll find information on your father. We can access just about anything from here.'

'Including the Army?' she said.

'Depends,' I said. 'So much information is hidden.'

'You can say that again,' she said. She looked at me with a peculiar intensity and, just for a moment, I was filled with shame. I couldn't say why. I turned away and waited for the feeling to pass.

Emily Duval was rooting through my out-tray, each piece of incoming correspondence now marked with my neatly penned instruction to the administration officer, initialled and dated in the bottom right-hand corner, then squared off with the rest of the pile.

I didn't seem to be able to tell Emily Duval to stop. 'So how does someone like you get into a job here?' she said.

'How do you mean?'

'I expected to find some old fuddy-duddy flipping through dusty books.'

'There's plenty of fuddy-duddies here if you know where to look,' I said. 'In our book restoration area, the exhibits and workers are about the same age, and both are older than the dinosaurs.'

'So, how did you end up here?' I was relieved she'd stopped sifting files on my desk. She was making a mess.

'I got a job operating the photocopier after I finished school. I was good at photocopying so they kept me on.'

'What sort of photocopier?'

'A Rank Xerox 9400 Deluxe,' I said with an American accent, quoting the old Xerox brochure. 'The most efficient multiple copier to hit business. The quality of offset printing without the mess. As a matter of fact, I still have my key operator's certificate.'

'So, you came to operate the photocopier and stayed?' she said.

'Kind of. My boss took a shine to me.' When I was still at school, John Neumann had helped me to find my father's birth and death records. He saw that, like him, I was a thorough researcher. When we finished he told me to give him a call if I was ever looking for work. After I got out of the hospital, I contacted him. He'd given me not only a job, but a chance to study and time off whenever things got too much, which they did periodically.

Mr Neumann never once questioned me on my sometimes lengthy absences. 'Eventually, I did history and librarianship at uni. When the boss retired, he recommended me for the job. And here I am.' Neumann had left two years before.

'That's a great photo,' Emily Duval said. She was looking past me at a shot I'd taken of new red leaves on a rainforest tree. One of the leaves was about to lose a drop of moisture which had caught the light rather well. 'Did you take it?' I said yes. 'Where?' I told her the name of the national park. I couldn't help feeling she was running my interview rather than me, but I didn't particularly want to get back in control either. 'I've never been there,' she said. 'I'd love to go, though.' She smiled.

I told her our paper files were stored at our new offices out at Runcorn and she'd have to come back the next day for the birth record she wanted. They could have faxed the records to me at West End, but I thought if she had to come back I'd see her again. Tonight, I'd work up the courage to ask her out. I'd practise a few times so I could sound cool, and then tomorrow, I'd casually suggest coffee and a movie. But she looked so disappointed when I told her she had to wait a day that my nerve failed me. I said I could get some basic details from her father's birth and death certificates on-line while she waited. Her name kept going through my head as we spoke. Emily Duval. Duval, Duval, Doo-Vall.

Emily Doo-Vall was getting up out of my chair to leave. I stood too. I wanted to suggest the movie. I took a breath to speak and let it out.

Then she said, cool as a cucumber, 'There's a new

vegetarian restaurant at Teneriffe, a kind of Asia meets California in Brisbane. I don't suppose you'd like to try it?'

'Well, I'd love to try that restaurant with you, Emily Duval.' I had no idea what Asia meeting California would be like, and I didn't much care. My grin must have been a mile wide. 'How about tonight?' She couldn't, she said, she had a deadline, so we arranged to meet that Friday. I felt great. She asked me out, on a Friday, when everyone had someone to go out with. Later, Emily denied that she was the one who asked me out. It was mutual, she said. Her selective bloody memory. Not that it mattered. That's the thing about Emily's lies. They're not about the important things, or at least I didn't think they were. On these, I believed, she was scrupulously honest.

After lunch I took a taxi to a department managers' meeting in the city. Nick Cave's 'Into your Arms', came on the radio. It made me think Emily and I were fated, and perhaps we were. On the Friday, she came along Edward Street and crossed diagonally to our meeting place. We'd agreed to catch the Citycat ferry together to New Farm and walk around the river past the Powerhouse Theatre to Teneriffe. She saw me and walked shyly, stooping and grabbing at the leather satchel over her shoulder, waving with her other hand. She was wearing slacks and a red shirt. I said, 'I didn't think you'd show up,' then wished I'd been more cool.

'Here I am.' She was grinning. We both were, like we had a secret the other pedestrians didn't know.

'Look, I haven't been completely honest with you,' I said. I was still smiling, finding it hard not to. We stood on a crowded street corner, late afternoon, the sun behind me, soft gold on her face. Her green eyes were on fire and I could see patches of red in her hair. I said, 'I'm not really vegetarian. I just said that to make you like me.'

'Neither am I,' she said. 'Fancy a steak?'

chapter**three**

We walked along the river towards the Story Bridge to a restaurant Emily knew called e'cco, which was fully booked except that they'd just that moment had a cancellation, which meant they could fit us in. Emily said it was meant to be. She ordered field mushrooms on toast followed by lamb fillets. I said I'd have the same. Then she started on the wine list, saying she knew nothing whatsoever about wine, so I offered to take over since she'd done the food. She was impressed with my suaveness, she said, when she heard me ordering a wine called Devil's Lair. I wasn't sure if she was kidding. I'd never have called myself suave and in truth I had no idea what I was ordering. It was just that the name appealed to me.

Emily said she'd grown up in Brisbane but was restless to see the rest of the world. 'I was born in Europe, you see; and I feel so parochial here.' She sounded like a

teenager acting like a grown-up. 'My dad took me everywhere when I was little. He had a great life.'

'He probably wanted to be more settled,' I said. 'You
always want what you don't have.' I'd lived in half a
dozen cities and towns in Australia, and I liked that I'd
stayed in one place for so much of my life now.
'Brisbane's a good city, and it's safe.'

'What do you mean by safe?'

'I don't know, small without being claustrophobic.
Friendly.'

'To me then, safe is claustrophobic. I think it's
unreconstructed. Did you grow up here?'

'No. My father was in the Army, so we moved round.
We came here when I was a teenager and ended up
staying.'

'Did your dad get out of the Army?'

'No,' I said, more loudly than I'd intended. 'He died.'

'I'm sorry,' Emily said.

'It was a long time ago.'

'How did he die?'

'He was asthmatic. So, where would you go
overseas?'

'Asthma. How old was he?'

'Forty. Tell me where you'd travel overseas.'

'That's young.'

'Asthma's like that,' I said. 'Anyway, tell me about
where to travel.'

'Oh, I don't know, all the ordinary places, London,
Paris, Rome. And I'd really love to see the south of France.
That's where my family's from. Côte D'Azur. Nice.'

'Matisse's old haunt.'

'Yes,' she said, surprised I knew this. 'There's this chapel I want to visit that Matisse designed.'

'La Chapelle du Rosaire in Vence.' My accent was better than my comprehension. I'd failed French at school but was good at mimicry, so I sounded good even if I had no idea what I was saying.

'That's it. How'd you know?'

'When I was at school, I saw a documentary about Matisse's life.'

'Apparently he was ill and the nuns from the convent in Vence cared for him. That's why he did it, as a gift for their healing him. It would be great to see.'

I can't remember everything we talked about. I know Emily managed to extract more of my life story than I generally shared with anyone. I'd been cautious since the hospital. You never knew what people really wanted when they asked questions about your life. I was always on my guard.

'Okay, let's do previous relationships,' Emily said suddenly. I grimaced. 'We may as well get it over and done with. If I'm going to spend the rest of my life with you, I need to know something about what you'll do wrong.' She smiled.

'The rest of your life? You make quick decisions.'

'I know what I like,' she said, and grinned. I couldn't tell if she was serious.

'I might be crazy.'

'But it just might be a lunatic I'm looking for,' she sang, off-key.

'Okay, past relationships. I was married for five minutes,' I said. She looked surprised. 'Yes, one of many

impulsive acts of my early twenties that drove my poor
mother to despair. The others I'll tell you about when
I know you a bit better.' I was trying to sound flippant,
but the look on Emily's face told me my voice was
betraying me.

When I didn't say more, she said, 'And the marriage?'

'Oh, you want details. Well, Cecilia worked in the
snack bar at uni. I used to buy dinner there before classes.
The biol sciences refec.' Emily nodded as if she knew the
place. 'Opposites attracting, I suppose. I'm quiet, and
I thought Cecilia was the kind of girl I needed. She was so
full of beans. It brought me out of myself a bit.

'She said she liked that I always ordered the same
thing. I think she thought it meant I was dependable,
which was her first mistake. In the end, I think that was
the only good thing she could remember about me. Not
much of a basis for a relationship from her side, I suppose.'

'What did you order?'

'A hamburger with chips and a Coke.'

'At least it was balanced.'

'We had interests in common as well. She used to
read, I read. We both liked movies. I wasn't ambitious,
though, and Cecilia was. She was saving up to open her
own dress design shop. We married after about a semester
of hamburgers. She left me six months after that.'

'That's it?'

'Pretty much,' I said.

'Can't be that simple. What went wrong?'

I didn't know. Or didn't want to know. When
I thought about Cecilia, I felt vaguely ashamed, as if I'd
been dishonest marrying her in the first place. I'd done it

simply because it was a normal thing to do, and I wanted to be normal more than anything. We bought a little house in Coorparoo, with money we borrowed from her parents, and set out on a new life that was nothing but a chimera. 'Partly, she was wrong about me being dependable. And maybe we didn't have as much in common as I thought,' I said to Emily Duval. 'She said I was over-emotional. I have a hunch I'm not very good with women.' Cecilia left me a week after I told her about what had happened with my father. She said the two things were unrelated. At the time, I believed her.

After Cecilia, there had been two girls, hardly definable as girlfriends, neither of whom stayed around more than a few months. The first said I was dull, in the heat of a moment, but couldn't bring herself to unsay it when the moment cooled. The second didn't say anything. She simply stopped returning my calls. I gave up on relationships in my mid-twenties and decided to be a loner for the rest of my life. I spent my spare time at work, surrounded by things that followed a natural order. It became a kind of haven.

Emily asked a lot of questions, and although I found them nerve-wracking at first, she had a way of bringing out the best in me. She made me feel better than I am, I'm sure. When she asked me what I was good at, I talked about work and people's right to information about themselves. At the end of the night, I realised I'd talked the whole time. I was surprised I found out so little about Emily. Generally I was the listener with people. I apologised for being such a bore, but she said I hadn't bored her at all and looked as if she meant it.

'So, relationships,' I said. 'What about you?'

'I'm not great on relationships,' Emily said. 'One serious, almost marriage, but he was gay, followed by spectacular catastrophes including one married man and two first dates I'd prefer to forget. Actually, I'm one of those *Women who Love Men who Don't Love Women*, I think. I always seem most attracted to the ones least attracted to me.'

'So, if I want you to like me, I should pretend I don't like you?'

'I guess,' she said, 'although maybe I'm tired of knocking my head against a brick wall.'

'Good,' I said, surprising myself with my forthrightness.

After dinner we walked back to the city and Emily's car. At my suggestion she drove us up to Mt Coot-tha, where boys from my school had taken their girlfriends in their fathers' Volvos on Saturday nights. They'd tell stories about it on Monday mornings. Sitting there on the top of the mountain with Emily, surrounded by the lights of the city, the moon coming up over the black snake of the river and a cool breeze in from the north, I felt like I was a boy again, with all the choices those boys in their fathers' Volvos had.

We were kissing, the kind of kisses that are going somewhere else, when I heard a tap on Emily's window. I saw the outline of a police officer's hat. Emily was adjusting her shirt and winding down her window. The policeman peered at Emily and then over at me.

'Everything all right here?' He took a long sniff as Emily replied yes. 'Been drinking tonight, Miss?'

'I had wine with dinner,' Emily said, wiping her mouth.

'How many?'

'Two glasses —' she checked her watch — 'about four hours ago.' It was after one am. I felt I'd landed with a thud back on the earth. I was squinting into his flashlight. I couldn't see his face.

He put the flashlight aside. 'You came up here to look at the view?'

Emily nodded. 'We're astronomers,' she said. I elbowed her as surreptitiously as I could. I didn't think it was a good idea to joke with police officers. I didn't think they were selected for their sense of humour.

'Oh yeah,' the policeman said.

'We're studying the constellations,' Emily said.

'I see.'

'Dr Scott Goodwin is from Houston. He's a rocket scientist.'

The police officer got down on his haunches. 'We've had one or two problems with cougars up here, Dr Scott Goodwin,' he said to me. 'So take it easy.'

Emily laughed. 'We'll let you know if we see one. Thanks for the warning.'

'You two are a bit older than my normal clientele, if you don't mind my saying. Don't you have a home to go to?' He waved back to his partner in the car.

'Our home's the night sky,' Emily said.

'Well, you can stay here if you like, but this is our last run. You might not want to be around once the younger kids start up here. They're more into loud music and fights than the night sky.' We thanked him and sat in silence, nervousness abating, as he returned to his car and they drove off.

I didn't look at Emily. 'I don't want to go home alone,' I said, finally.

'Why would you?' she said. 'I'll come with you.'

chapterfour

My sister Stella used to say I was like someone walking through life with a blanket over my head. There's joy, she'd say, in her post-therapy voice. It wasn't until I met Emily that I knew what Stella meant. I remember one afternoon, on the way home from work, early for some reason, I went to collect the mail from my post office box in West End. I didn't feel that familiar disappointment about what I found. When I turned around, I saw a group of kids in blue uniforms and sunhats waiting to cross the road. When the light changed, they moved like a big uncoordinated caterpillar around a teacher. I had a strong desire to go with them. I smiled and watched as they disappeared up Vulture Street.

Emily brought an abundance to my life that I believed could change anything. It could even change me, or at least something that had been wrong in me. I found myself sleeping through nights and waking feeling refreshed. You don't realise you're not doing that until you start doing it again. We ate in, cooked, drank wine, explored parts of Brisbane I never knew existed; the Northey Street organic food markets, the Citycat ferry up and down the river, New Farm Park where we had picnics on a few Sundays. It was like a new city I'd never known, and mine was like a new life.

Emily even found uses for my herbs. 'Why do you grow them if you don't use them?' Emily asked early one morning when I was trimming the flowering heads from my basil.

'I like watching them,' I said. She thought this was hilarious and kept repeating it for days afterwards.

The first morning we woke up next to each other, I felt a million dollars. Not that we had great sex. We didn't have any sex at all. We arrived home and stood in the kitchen talking. When we finally went to bed, it was more by osmosis than design. Later, Emily said it was because it mattered so much. I liked that she said that. Emily wore a pair of my pyjamas which were too big. After I turned off the light, she asked me to open my eyes while we kissed, which made me cross-eyed. At some stage we both fell to giggling, and then talked until the sky started to pale. She made me feel that everything I said was important. She ended up falling asleep on my shoulder and I lay there for a long while listening to her slow, even breaths and thinking how light she felt on me.

She insisted on cooking breakfast that first morning: bacon, eggs, toast, sausages, tomatoes, mushrooms, orange juice and coffee. We had to go to the shops to buy everything except fresh parsley for the mushrooms;

I grew enough of that to open a parsley store. But I didn't even have bread. It was a fine, warm September day and after breakfast Emily said, 'Let's go to the beach.' I don't know if I'd told her the night before about swimming, or if it was coincidence, but just before she said it, I'd been thinking that I'd love to go swimming with her. I hadn't been in years.

That morning, for the first time in my adult life, or at least since Duntroon, I left a mess in the kitchen. I'd become pretty obsessive about tidiness. Not to the point of colour-coding pegs with washing, but not that far from it either. 'Bugger it,' Emily said when I started clearing things away. 'Can't we do it when we get back?'

'Yeah,' I said. 'Why not?'

Emily drove an old Peugeot fast and thoughtlessly. She seemed to be doing about ten things at once, in addition to driving, like putting on her seatbelt or fiddling with the radio and checking her mirrors. I didn't feel safe with her but when I asked her to slow down, she did.

Emily's idea of the beach was a three-hour drive to Byron Bay, taking the scenic Numinbah Valley route into New South Wales past Mt Warning and the little village of Chillingham. When we got to Byron, it was as hot as summer. We parked at Watego's beach and walked up towards the lighthouse, turning off before the final climb and heading down to a little cove where we were alone except for surfers a long way out from the point. I played like I had when I was a boy, diving into waves, body-surfing and digging my feet into groggy sand. In the afternoon we drove back to town and parked under a stand of pines across the road from the main beach hotel.

We walked along the water's edge while the sun set behind the trees. We found the creatures you find when you have the time, washed up jellyfish and bluebottles and pipi trails in the sand. Emily talked to a fisherman about what he was catching and said hello to everyone like we were locals. She collected one shell and one stone to add to her collection at home.

When we stopped to watch the sun set, Emily stood on tiptoes and whispered, 'Tonight, we'll make love on the beach.'

'I think I'd prefer a hotel,' I said. She looked disappointed. 'The sand …,' I offered, although I knew I sounded unadventurous.

After dinner we went back and lay on the beach. I watched the moon pull the stars across the sky while storms flickered a long way out to sea. 'So, tell me about your family,' Emily said. 'We've been together twenty-four hours and I know nothing about you.' It occurred to me then that I'd been in the water all afternoon and hadn't thought of Dad once.

'You can talk,' I said. She didn't respond. 'My family. My father's been dead for years. I already told you that. My mother's a biologist. She and I have lunch once a week and she tells me I look thin. I have one sister, Stella, who lives in Canada now. She's a nurse.'

'That's it?'

'Stella comes home to visit and shakes her head and says, "What are you doing with your life, Scott?", to which I respond, "I'm all right," but it's not the sort of question you can answer successfully.'

'Sounds like the sister from hell.'

'She's all right. She just worries.'

'Why?' Emily turned onto her side and propped her head on her hand to watch me. I remained on my back, turning my head to look at her. Her eyes were bright in the moonlight. 'What's to worry about?'

'I had some trouble when I was growing up. Stella had to look after me. It's a hard habit to break.'

'What sort of trouble?'

I looked up at the sky. I could hear people laughing a long way away. I was surprised at how emotional I still felt after all the years that had passed. 'I was in a psych hospital,' I said. 'I don't usually even tell people.'

When I told people about the hospital, their voices got louder, as if I was deaf as well as mad, but Emily's voice remained soft. 'Ah, the quote on the wall at work.'

'Which quote?'

'R D Laing: schizophrenia is a sane response to an insane world.'

I was surprised she'd noticed, let alone that she'd remembered. 'I like that quote, but it's not the full story.'

'So, what's the full story?'

I didn't answer at first. 'I got into drugs a bit when I left school. Nothing major but when my dad died, I kind of lost the plot. It's hard to explain. He died.' I made myself count stars.

'You must have been close,' she said.

'It's complicated.' I wanted to say more, but something stopped me. After Cecilia left, I decided that if I met a girl I was serious about, I'd be honest with her at the start. I'd have no secrets about what had happened and what I'd done. She could take or leave me on that basis. Just not yet. 'Actually, the reason they sent me to hospital was so I didn't get charged. I broke into someone's house.'

'Why?'

'I'll tell you one day when I know you better,' I said.

'And your dad was in Army Intelligence?' I nodded. I didn't remember mentioning this. 'Tell me about him.'

'No,' I said. I leaned over and kissed her forehead. 'Let's go.'

We tried four hotels before Emily found the one, an eighties imitation hacienda that I was sure would serve soft toast in little paper bags and weak coffee for breakfast. Emily said we'd be able to hear the waves from our room, and in the morning the ocean out the window was the first thing we'd see. It was perfect.

We undressed quickly and climbed under thin crisp sheets. I felt a little nervous; it had been a long time. I didn't look across at Emily, not until we'd pulled the covers up over us and she took my face in her hands and looked into my eyes in silence. I felt scared and excited at the same time. I kissed her lips lightly and leaned over her to turn out the light. A sheen from the moon, almost full, turned her skin alabaster. She was lying on her back with her arms stretched above her head like a Venus. Her beautiful eyes were wide and true. I closed my own eyes and, with my fingers, traced the line of her body, from her hips up to the tips of her fingers and back to her shoulder blades. The skin was soft and cool like she'd just come out of the sea. I kissed her breasts. The soft pale nipples went hard under my touch. Kneeling up beside her, I ran my hand over the curve of her belly, the inside of her thigh, calf, ankle, to the tips of her toes. I leaned over and kissed her on the mouth again. I kissed her belly and moved further down, using her sighs to guide me. When she pulled me up to kiss her on the mouth again, she guided my penis inside her. She sighed and I came almost immediately. Afterwards, embarrassed, I said I was sorry and offered to try again. She took over, pulling me across the bed, folding me in her limbs. We made love slowly this time, with her in charge.

Afterwards, I was the one who cried, my tears surprising even me. Going crazy has a way of shaving off layers of your self, or false selves, as Dr Bain called them. False or not, when they're gone, you're naked. Often, especially in the beginning, my emotions were right there on the surface for anyone to see. I lacked the defences other people had. But when I cried in Emily's arms that night, quietly at first, and then noisily like a kid, she didn't seem to mind or even need to know a reason. Not that I'd have had a reason I could give her. She just held on and said nothing.

I fell asleep with the sound of the sea in my ears and the taste of Emily in my mouth. I woke when the sun first peeked in the bottom of the window and Emily was walking towards the bed with weak coffee and toast in paper bags on a tray. 'I think I love you,' I said when I saw her.

She shook her head and put the tray down on her side of the bed. 'How'd you sleep?'

'Great. I think I love you.' I rolled over to face her. We ate our toast and drank our coffee and agreed to go get the papers and have a good coffee somewhere. Instead, we had sex.

'Tell me about your dad,' she said afterwards. She was lying in the crook of my arm, snug as if she'd been made for the spot. 'Something happened, didn't it?' I was going to say I don't want to talk about it. 'My father died when I was four,' she said. 'So I know what it can do to people.'

'What did he die of?' I said.

'He was in the Middle East covering the UN Peacekeeping Force. He was shot by UN troops by mistake.'

'Is that why you're trying to find records of him?'

She looked confused at first and then shook her head. 'No,' she said. 'I just wanted to get his birth and death certificates for patriality, so I can work in the UK. His mother's family was English.'

Emily told me that in dreams, sometimes, she talks to her father. She's wearing a white communion dress with knee-high white socks, black shiny shoes, and her feet don't touch the ground. They're at a café and her father lights up a cigarette. It's a golden afternoon and Emily says she feels beautiful in the dream. It's like she imagines heaven to be.

'Do you remember him?' I asked her.

'Oh yeah,' she said. 'He smoked Camels, and the smell is unmistakable. So I remember that. I remember the packets too, and the way he'd flick a cigarette out onto his palm and line it up on a table to pack the tobacco down. He was a big man, or maybe it was that I was so small, but I can remember him arriving home, ducking under the door, and scooping me up in one hand. I know I adored him. Everyone tells me that.'

'Must have been hard to lose him so young.'

'That's the funny thing. I remember him being there, but I don't remember losing him. I don't remember loss. I'm sure I've become a different person because he died but I'm not sure I'm a worse person. Sometimes I think I'm better. I used to feel ashamed for thinking that.

'When I see pictures of him with me, I'm like this baby doll. Maybe if he'd lived I'd be a spoiled brat.' We lay there for a while in silence. 'Your turn,' she said.

'Let's get some coffee first,' I said. 'This is going to take some time.'

She shook her head. 'I can wait.'

'Okay. My father died,' I started, 'or at least that's what everyone said. But I didn't believe it. I still don't.

'But let me start before that. Let me ease myself into this. Let me start on the last day I saw him alive.'

chapter**five**

That day, the last day I saw my father alive, he called me at four-thirty am to go to swimming training as usual, I told Emily. I was fourteen going on fifteen and mornings were hard, especially in the winter. He called me a second time from the kitchen. I knew better than to risk a third call. He couldn't abide selfishness, not in anyone.

Every morning was a struggle. I had this routine; envisaging swinging my legs around, standing up, pulling up my togs and tracks, grabbing goggles and towel, walking across the cold floor. My coach used to call it 'envisaging the win'. I had to envisage the training. Hell, I had to envisage the getting out of bed.

The car was warm by the time I got in. He talked. He couldn't stay for training that day, he said, because he had to finish off something at work. He didn't say what it was. I had to start thinking about my turns, he said. That's where I was losing time. I had to use my brains, not my brawn. He had sayings like that. Stella used to make fun of him about them, not to his face of course. I didn't talk much in the mornings. He always woke with shining eyes, and he liked to chat, changing subjects constantly. I just had to listen and add the occasional acknowledgment to let him know I was paying attention. He didn't like it if you didn't listen to him. And it wasn't that what he said wasn't interesting. He just said so much of it.

My coach was Jack Rebo, who in those days worked out of the Newmarket pool which was close to our place. Dad had picked Rebo because he'd trained just about every Australian champion of the seventies. He wore sandals, even in winter, and when you pulled up after a sprint, the first thing you saw were these big blue toes, followed by his big head leaning over you frowning, or his hand ready to shake yours. Although Rebo wasn't normally shy, I'd noticed he was quieter when Dad was around. Lots of people were. Dad took up space, and he didn't like shy people. He said they wouldn't let you know them, which was a form of selfishness. When people would describe me as shy, or reserved at least, I used to wonder if it meant I was selfish too. Dad felt Rebo didn't push me hard enough. But I liked Rebo, and three years was the longest I'd been anywhere. I wanted to stay in the squad.

Everything was changing that year. We were shifting again, which was nothing new. The Army moved us round every couple of years. But this was a short-notice posting back to Melbourne, where Dad's unit had its headquarters. We'd only found out the month before. Dad said he wanted me to stay at the mess in Brisbane with him until after the State swimming trials. 'Do him good to be with some guys,' he told Mum. She didn't reply, which meant she didn't like the idea. Mum didn't want me to have anything to do with the Army. 'Sweetheart?' he said. 'I was talking to you.'

'I was thinking,' she said. In Dad's plan, Mum would go down to Melbourne with Stella, and they'd find a house and settle in and we'd follow soon after. Mum didn't tell Dad what she was thinking, and he moved on to something else.

I was changing too, that year. I'd grown tall suddenly, and my hair, which had been a bit wavy, went curly like it is now. I fancied I looked like a lean, blond surfer. For a while I wore board shorts over my Speedos, but Mr Rebo said they weren't streamlined enough. I couldn't get used to my new self. I kept touching the places that were different. I remember I found this muscle under my arm and down my side one morning that felt like the start of wings. I was sure it hadn't been there the night before. I felt I wasn't me anymore, but I wasn't someone else yet either. Mum said I was growing too fast, having waited so long to start growing at all. I'd been little in my class every year until then, and slight like Dad. He wasn't as tall as me, even then. But it's funny; in my memory, he's always been much taller.

I remember details of that morning as if it was yesterday, Dad's voice a little rough and strained from sleep, the smell of polish on our shoes. Normally we both packed our uniforms in the car the night before. After training, we had Weet-bix together at the pool, and Dad dropped me at Marist Brothers on his way to the base at Enoggera. That morning he was already dressed for work. 'How's your time on the fifty free?' he asked me when we were pulling up outside the pool.

'Twenty-eight three,' I said.

'Record's twenty-five four. You're miles off. I want to see twenty-seven by the end of the week,' he said. 'You hear me?' I didn't answer, so he repeated the question.

'Yes sirree,' I said. He looked at me to check I wasn't being smartarse. He couldn't stand anyone making fun of him.

When he said goodbye he asked for a hug, which was unusual. We hugged quickly, me leaning in his window, and he headed off without saying more.

Mr Rebo stopped me during the warm-up laps, waving the guys behind me on. 'I've been thinking maybe you should take a break,' he said. He'd crouched down to the pool which must have taken considerable effort for the big man. He spoke quietly so the other guys didn't hear on their turns. Behind him the sun was coming up through the middle of a ghost gum. Steam came off the water, and earlier we'd been entertained by a family of ducks who overshot the creek and accepted the pool as a substitute. They'd been fished out by swimmers. I looked up at Rebo's red face. 'I mean, you've got the body shape and your style's all there,' he said. 'But you're not enjoying it.' A kookaburra let out a long laugh, as if Rebo was being funny. 'Are you?' Rebo smiled as much as he ever did, a kind of crushing of his facial features, and crouched there a moment more, waiting for me to respond.

I figured this was one of Rebo's training strategies. I'd noticed he had these books on the front seat of his car

lately, *Everyone Wins* and *TA for Sport*. He used to try
things on us too, but he never sounded like he believed
they would actually work. The month before, he'd given
us special waterproof pens and pads for us to record our
overall goals and training objectives. We didn't have to
show him if we didn't want to, he said. I looked to the other
end of my lane with what I felt was determination, and I
nodded as if I knew that what Rebo really meant was that
I should try harder, not that I should give up. But later,
I wondered if he saw that I lacked the kind of drive other
guys in the squad had, the kind of drive Dad had. Dad
made Olympic class in swimming. I didn't think I'd ever
do that. You need more than strength and style. Maybe
Rebo knew that at some level, I wasn't cut out for it.

To be honest, I probably hated swimming, or at least
I hated training, but I couldn't say that, not even to
myself. If you'd asked me, I don't think I'd have had any
idea what I liked and didn't in those days. Dad was like
this megaforce in our lives, mine and Stella's and Mum's,
and I didn't let myself have thoughts that might be
different from his. Stella managed him better than me by
making fun of him behind his back, but I couldn't do
that. I just went along with everything he said.
Sometimes I felt like I was acting all the time. Here's
Scott the swimmer, Scott the student, Scott the kid. I felt
I wasn't really real, and perhaps Rebo could see that. I
didn't take him up on his offer, Dad would have killed
me if I had, but for the rest of the session I found myself
feeling light and breezy without knowing why.

At school that day I got an A plus for an assignment
in history, my favourite subject. I'd half-decided I

wanted to do an arts degree when I finished school. I was
good at finding things out and I knew history would suit
me. I also knew it was going to cause trouble in the
family, because Dad wanted me to follow him and his
father into the Army. Dad thought history was pretty
useless compared to real life. He'd been in Vietnam, and
that was history in motion, he said.

My history teacher in Year 10 was Mr Maitland. He
wasn't the sort of teacher you'd normally give the time of
day; greasy hair, dirty glasses and a limp from childhood
polio that guys would walk along behind him imitating.
But I liked him. I didn't have many friends at school
anyway, so I didn't have to go along with a peer group.
I was pretty quiet mostly, and Maitland had a way of
directing a question to me if he knew I'd want to answer
it. He and I used to argue, which I liked. He never lost
his temper. He was always respectful of my views, and I
found his views interesting.

Maitland was one of those people who believe that
big institutions can be identified and held responsible
for their actions. Looking back, he was the original conspiracy theorist, I suppose, but this was post-seventies
so there were plenty of conspiracies to be found if you
looked, especially in a place like Queensland before
the Fitzgerald Inquiry. When the government sacked
the state's electricity workers, Maitland joined the
protests. A kid in my class had to leave because his
father, an electrical linesman in his fifties, had lost his
job. Maitland said the government was corrupt and
evil. Maitland was arrested, of course — protest
marches were illegal in Queensland — and one parent

wanted him removed from the school. This was another thing I liked about him. Mum and a few others had written a letter to the principal supporting him. Maitland stayed.

Maitland believed individuals were culpable. On wars, for example, his position was that every soldier had a responsibility to conscientiously object. I thought he was wrong about that.

'If they all did that,' I said, 'who'd be left to fight?'

'No one, Scott. That's my point.' Sometimes he was a bit of a smartarse.

Normally Dad didn't come to afternoon training. I caught the school bus from Marist Brothers to the pool, and Mr Rebo dropped me home afterwards. Mr Rebo's daughter Jennifer was in the squad, and I sat in the back with her while Mr Rebo talked to us about our goals and objectives. Jennifer was the same age as me. She never made faces the way I would have done if Rebo was my father. She didn't have that sort of sense of humour. Once I would have said she was dumb, but really she was just kind. We picked Mrs Rebo up from Mount Saint Michael's, where she was the librarian, and Mr and Mrs Rebo talked in the front, which left Jennifer and me to ourselves. A lot of the guys in the squad wanted to date Jennifer, and she could have been one of those real bitches to a guy like me. I wasn't the best swimmer or anything and I was a bit of a dag. But she was always nice. We hung around together a lot that year.

That afternoon Dad showed up and I was disappointed I wouldn't get to go home with Jennifer. I didn't say anything to Dad, not just because I didn't want him to know about Jennifer, which I didn't, but also because he didn't like it if you didn't appreciate what he did for you. I said I was glad he was there. And maybe because he was there, I swam harder and did a new personal best which I'd been waiting to crack for over a month. I took three seconds off my four hundred freestyle. Mr Rebo couldn't believe it, and for once couldn't contain his joy. His eyes were all crinkled up and he was actually giggling as he said to Dad, 'You ought to come more often, Allan. He's a mighty young man, all right. What do you reckon?' I was still in the pool and Mr Rebo reached down and put his hand on my shoulder and then ruffled my hair. My grin must have been as wide as the Amazon when I looked up towards Dad. His face was unreadable. He looked at his watch and said we needed to get home.

He was quiet in the car too, and at first I figured I must have got something wrong in my stroke. 'If my times stay like this, I'll make the team,' I said carefully. He didn't respond. 'Dad?'

'Sorry, what did you say?' His tone was flat; always a warning.

'I reckon I'll make the state team. Four thirty-nine, pretty bloody good.' My voice was breaking and kept failing me. I repeated the sentence.

'Yeah, but Neilsen's your man.' Stephen Neilsen had been the youngest member of the Australian squad two years before when the Commonwealth Games were held in Brisbane. His four hundred was still five point three seconds faster than mine, a huge margin I had no hope of closing in the short term.

'Rebo reckons I'll take him next year.' Neilsen was one of those guys who developed early, big, with flipper feet that could power him through the water. I was still growing and had a way to go to catch up with him.

'Fuck Rebo. What would he know? You could do it this year if you worked at it,' Dad said. 'If you cared less about sleeping in and more about your stroke. Swimmers swim.' Swimmers swim, runners run, fighters fight. His sayings. He didn't speak again until we'd pulled into our driveway. Then he said, 'I'm going away tomorrow. You knew that, didn't you?'

He didn't get out of the car so I didn't either. 'But you'll be back for state trials?' I said.

'You won't need me there.' He opened his mouth as if to say more, but closed it again. He stared at the garage doors. Finally he said, 'Look at that time you just did. You're on your way. Last thing you need's me. You got Rebo.' His tone was ice-cold. His hands gripped the steering wheel as if he was still driving. His knuckles were white. I figured Dad saw Rebo's hand on my shoulder. I'd reacted badly, smiling instead of ducking away, which is what Dad would have expected. Dad didn't like me to be friendly with Rebo, or with anyone he didn't like for that matter. Mostly that meant anyone outside the Army, and quite a few in the Army as well. Dad had strong views about people. He reckoned you could tell the measure of a soldier within five minutes, just from the way he stood and walked. That afternoon I was relieved it wasn't something I'd done wrong in swimming which was impossible to fix. I thought it was recoverable as long as I played my cards right. 'Yeah, but he doesn't know what he's talking about,' I said. 'You're the one who swam for Australia.'

I can't be certain whether I remember what happened next or I've made it up subsequently, but when I recall the scene now, there are tears in Dad's eyes that weren't there in my initial remembering. I don't know when I started to believe there were tears, but when I think of him now, I see him turn to me and I see tears brimming in his eyes. He tilts his head and he puts his hand up and strokes my cheek, then pulls away and wipes his eyes. His cheeks shine where he's smeared the tears, like glitter. I wish I knew if this really happened, or I've imagined it.

He said, 'I've done my best. You're all right now, kiddo. You really are.'

It was the last thing he said to me. He got out of the car and went inside. He ate dinner, went to bed, and got up at three to go to the base. He'd gone by five when I woke late to ride my bike to training. But I must have replayed it in my head a million times. I thought he was talking about swimming, a pep talk ahead of the trials. 'I'm the best dad at the pool, the best dad in the world, and don't you kids forget it,' he'd say to Stella and me as he handed us an ice cream after a swim. And I thought he was the best dad in the world. He stayed in the pool with you for hours. He threw you up in the air and caught you, while other dads smoked cigarettes or read their stupid papers in the stands. He raced you, and never let you win for the sake of it. 'I'll never let you down,' he said. 'You believe me?' If you didn't answer yes straight away, he crouched down and took the ice cream and teased you until you did. 'Where I come from, blood runs thicker than water, and you kids are blood. I'd kill for you.' He hugged us tightly. 'If anyone ever hurt you, I'd kill them. Simple as that.'

I believed him absolutely when he said he'd kill anyone who harmed us. I'd seen him kill an animal myself, and he did it without hesitating. It was our first and only hunting trip, my eleventh birthday present. We camped out overnight and in the morning, I spotted this kangaroo. 'Good boy,' he whispered when I pointed. He moved forward on all fours, quickly disappearing into the long grass. When he appeared again, up on his haunches, much closer to the kangaroo, like they were a pair, I was surprised at how far he'd travelled. He took aim. I watched the kangaroo. I couldn't believe he'd actually shot it, even after I heard the report. It had looked so solidly calm in the mist and when it fell I thought it must be shamming. But Dad was a marksman, which is one better than a first-class shot, and he'd killed the kangaroo outright.

He called me twice and we walked over to the kangaroo together. It had a joey in its pouch. I vomited my bacon and eggs. We didn't eat the kangaroo. I don't know whether that was because of my vomit or because we were never planning to and kangaroo's a beast you kill but don't eat. It's not something we discussed in advance, killing, it just sort of happened, and it wasn't something we discussed after. I never went with him again. But on that morning we were together, I could see I'd disappointed him. He shook his head and said, 'Jesus, you got a long way to go, kid. You need to be tough. One day you'll have to kill a man. You just do it, Scott.' I said yes sir, because I was frightened he was going to make me kill the joey.

chaptersix

The sun was streaming through the window onto the end of the bed where I'd been sitting. I'd moved onto the floor in the far corner of the room. I could hear a lone swimmer in the hotel pool outside.

'How old did you say you were on that trip?' Emily said.

'Eleven,' I said. Emily started getting up to come over to me. 'No,' I said. 'Stay where you are.' It came out more like an order than I meant it to. 'It gets harder to tell soon. Let me finish the story without you doing anything, or I'll stop.' She nodded and sat back down on the bed.

Dad used to travel with his work, I told Emily, maybe two or three times a year. To be honest, I didn't really know much about what he did. He was in a unit called S-12 which had been set up in the seventies to deal with terrorist attacks. Or at least that's what the Minister for Defence said when questioned in Parliament. I've since found out through Archives that S-12 was gathering intelligence on other armies in the region rather than on likely terrorists. They used to run these joint training exercises with Indonesia and Malaysia. S-12's role was to spy on our neighbours, although no one would admit publicly to that, even now.

Growing up, I'd always assumed that Dad's work was dangerous. When he was away, I'd be on edge, especially if he'd hugged us really hard and tongue-kissed Mum for ages to say goodbye. Mum never seemed to worry about him like I did and Stella says she doesn't remember him saying he was going on secret missions to other countries, but I'm pretty sure that's what he told me. It was one of those things I was sure he'd said even if I couldn't recall a specific instance of him saying it.

Sometimes he talked about death as if he knew he was going to die and that made me think his work was even more dangerous than he could let on. He took risks, swimming out too far in the sea, working on fuel lines in cars or on live electrical connections in the house. He'd always tell you what he was doing. Doing something stupid, he called it. I worried about him. Stella said he did it for attention. Superman, my arse, she said. That was his nickname at work, because he'd been so fit. Superman can still drown, Stella said. But I don't think Stella was right, or not completely right. I don't think it was attention he wanted. Mum didn't like him talking about death. She told Stella she thought Vietnam had made him morbid.

Once, I heard him tell Mum that it was better she didn't know exactly what he was doing. 'The only way I can be sure you'll be safe if something happens to me is if you don't know what I'm doing.' I was in my room with the door open a crack. They didn't realise I could hear.

'Don't give me that nonsense again,' Mum said. 'I'm not stupid, Allan. Just tell me what's going on.'

'Nothing. I've got work to do, that's all,' he said, pausing between each word. I imagined he was facing her, his arms slightly out from his side, his hips forward. 'As I said before, it's one weekend and I'll be back first thing Monday.' He'd smile.

'I'm not an idiot.'

'Just don't worry about it, darling. I'm here when I'm here, but I have other responsibilities. You knew that when you married me.'

'Well, I am worried about it, *darling*. I have a right to know,' she said. She paused between each word, imitating Dad, which was a dangerous strategy.

Mum talked too low for me to hear then. I caught something about Melbourne, and Grandad, then I heard Dad's voice, much louder: 'I'll do what I fucking well like.' Their bedroom door slammed and his bare feet pounded down the stairs. That night he was crawling. He told Mum how great the dinner was, which was nonsense because it was curried chicken, which he hated, and he asked her would she like to watch something on television, which he never normally did. Mum wasn't having a bar of it, answered his questions and stuff, but didn't talk other than that. I knew it was something serious between them, but I didn't know what.

When Dad was away, we never knew exactly when he was coming home again. One afternoon he'd walk in, just like that. It was always when someone was home, usually all of us, and I sometimes wondered if he timed it purposely. In the Brisbane house, he'd stand in the doorway with the sun behind him. He'd step up in front of the sun, put his bag down carefully on the kitchen floor, side-bending and holding his hat so it didn't drop off, and he'd hold out his arms for Mum and us. He'd be wearing combat fatigues and his big boots, and he'd look as if he'd been plucked from the jungle, dusted off and dropped back in the city. Later in the day he'd shave and shower and come out bright as anything and say he felt brand new.

Mum got a letter of acceptance from the university the first week Dad was away. She wanted to go back to finish the biology degree she started before she and Dad were married. She seemed surprised they'd let her back in to uni. She said they'd even give her credit for some of her earlier studies and they had a special scheme for women who wanted to come back to study after having kids. Mum was amazed they even thought about her. I asked her what would happen about the posting to Melbourne, and she said she and Dad hadn't talked about it yet. I wasn't even sure she'd told him she'd applied.

Stella had started at the QIT in the city doing medical laboratory science that year, and she took advantage of Dad's absence to stay out late. She wasn't allowed out past nine-thirty pm when he was home. Usually Mum and I went out together to get takeaway Chinese or pizza. That was something you couldn't do when Dad was home. He didn't like takeaways. 'You don't know what you're eating,' he said. 'That's the point,' Stella said, but he didn't get it. His sense of humour didn't include irony, and although he could be sarcastic, that was never funny.

I remember the evenings with Mum when Dad was away that time, the ease of time passing, the gaps in our conversations and room for both of us. Mum and I were the quiet ones in our family, so when it was just the two of us, we had enough space to talk for once. With Stella and Dad around, neither of us could get a word in.

I told Mum about Jennifer Rebo, that I thought I liked her but I wasn't sure.

Mum always knew what you were saying even if you didn't say it. 'Why don't you tell her you like her?' Mum said. 'I think you'll find most girls prefer the honest approach.'

I think I blushed. 'Then she'd know.'

Mum nodded. 'Yes, and isn't that what you want? It is, isn't it?' She scrunched up her nose. 'She's a lovely girl,' she beamed, as if I'd announced my engagement.

'The thing is, I'm not sure I like her in the way you like girls,' I said. 'I just want to hang around with her. Is that normal?' Guys in my class talked about things they'd done to girls and I didn't even understand the words they used. I was still a kid, or I was in-between being a kid and growing up. I wasn't quite sure what I wanted to do with Jennifer Rebo.

'Normal? Of course it's normal,' Mum said, sounding bossy all of a sudden. 'You'll meet lots of girls you like, but you won't always feel that zing with them.

You probably won't feel a zing about someone until you start to love them.' Now I knew this wasn't true. If by zing she meant sex, I'd got a stiff dick from rolling around the grass with our dog after a walk. While I loved Duchess, I didn't want her to be my girlfriend. In fact, I think it was more the smell of cut grass.

'Dad says there are girls you play with, and girls you marry, and they're different,' I said. 'Maybe Jennifer's one of the ones you marry, not play with. And the ones you marry, you don't feel like playing with.' When Dad told me the facts of life, he made it sound like a threshing machine in good working order. Mum gave Stella the love stuff. I got the mechanics. That was Dad all over.

'He didn't really say that?' Mum said. 'Sometimes I can't believe that man. Let me tell you right here and now, when I met your father, we wanted to play with each other, that's for sure.' I had an image of my parents out of control on the grass, followed by our dog Duchess. I was relieved it disappeared quickly. 'Sometimes it drove us crazy.'

'So how did you know he was the one?'

'Maybe he wasn't. Maybe I should have played with him and married one who wouldn't fill your head with rubbish.' She looked towards the open window dreamily, then frowned as if concentrating on a difficult puzzle. 'He asked me to dance,' she said. I started a scowl. 'No, I'm serious. This was Toowoomba in the sixties, don't forget, so his competition was the locals who drank beer on the verandah and came inside to ask if you wanted to go for a spin in their cars. Then there were the other Army boys. Most of them were more interested in fights than anything else.

'Your dad was different. He went to dances to dance, not to get drunk or beat people up. I liked him right away. And do you know something? I think he was the happiest person I ever met. He really was. And boy, could he move. We were groovy.' Mum often used words she thought we'd like, which was embarrassing since they'd gone out with the dinosaurs, but I didn't mind when it was just her and me. 'He had so much energy for life. He loved every minute of his days, simple as that. I never met anyone else quite like him.'

She smiled. 'He didn't ask me to marry him. He said it as a statement. Did you know that?' I shook my head, even though I'd heard the story at least twice before. 'A statement. It was three months after we started going together. We were on a picnic with my youth group. After lunch he and I lay down together under the fig tree at Grandad's place. He looked at me and said: "I want to marry you." We were both so young. I was still at school and he hadn't even finished his apprenticeship.' Dad had joined the Army at sixteen as an apprentice fitter and turner. He hadn't moved to Infantry until he was called up for Vietnam. 'But Grandad put his foot down. He said we couldn't get married until the following year. But then your father was posted to Albury, and it just made us miss each other madly. I started at university, but I knew what I wanted. First visit home we made Stella, and Grandad had to go along with us getting married.'

In my favourite photograph of Mum and Dad, they're dancing, Mum in Dad's arms, leaning back. It's after they were married, when they were posted back to Toowoomba. They used to go out every Saturday night.

Gran looked after baby Stella. In the photograph you can just see the top of Mum's head, the tip of her nose, her chin and then her long neck. Dad's leaning forward and looking at Mum, not the photographer. He's more filled out than he was in later pictures, and he's smiling with his whole face, as if Mum's just told him the most enormous joke. I've never seen him smile like that in real life. The picture was in the *Toowoomba Chronicle* with a little story about families and the Vietnam War. Dad was about to leave, I guess. For years we had the clipping. I don't know what happened to it. Mum was pregnant with me, although neither of them knew it. One of the things I like is that I'm in the photo, in Mum.

'And you've never looked back,' I said to Mum.

'No,' she said, but her dreamy eyes were gone.

The phone rang and Mum went to answer it. At first I thought it might be Dad and I walked back towards the kitchen. I could hear Mum laughing and chatting. From the doorway I saw her in an easy chair with her feet up on the windowsill, playing with the phone cord. She turned and shook her head at me. Mum had started a drawing class that year, and when Dad was away she talked on the phone to her classmates. Once she showed me some sketches she'd done which looked wild. When I said as much, I could see it disappointed her. 'No,' I said, 'good-wild not bad-wild. They're fantastic.' I meant it. I was amazed I could know Mum so well and yet not know this whole side of her. She'd always seemed so calm and in control and yet here were these drawings that were so out of control. Now when I think of them, I think of Mum as someone I didn't really know at all.

A few days after our talk I arrived home from training to find two books on my desk, one about puberty
and what happens and the other about relationships and
love. I read them both, and liked them, although I didn't
tell Mum that. When she asked did you see those books,
were they any good, do you want to talk, I just answered
yeah yeah no, I'm fine.

When Dad didn't phone for my birthday, I was
disappointed rather than worried. I hadn't got the
impression this trip was anything but a straightforward
domestic exercise, so I didn't have any reason to be afraid
for him. On other trips, though, he always managed to
get a radiophone hook-up to call me. He sounded like he
was beaming in from outer space. The first selection heat
for the state team was held at the Valley Baths, and I
swam the four hundred well enough without giving too
much away. I was in with a second to spare based on the
qualifying times for the year before, not as good as my
new PB, and still shy of Stephen Neilsen. Mum came
along to watch and offered to take me to dinner at Pizza
Hut to celebrate after, but I wanted to get home.

'He probably can't get to a phone, darling,' Mum
said. I'd hung around the kitchen all evening.

'You think he's all right?'

'Course he's all right.' But I knew from Dad that even
domestic exercises were dangerous. They planned for
casualties, he told me, because they knew in advance the
likely number of KIA — killed in action. 'You're mucking
round with equipment and explosives. Got to be collateral
damage. I've been lucky,' he said once. I asked him if they
took along the right number of coffins. He laughed really

loudly. 'They carry them in bags most of the way, and we always take one or two spares.'

Dad and I were restoring a car that year, a 1961 Jaguar Mark II he'd bought through a friend. Whenever he said Jaguar, Dad growled the word to make it sound like the big cat. It used to embarrass me. We'd done the motor and had started cutting the paintwork back to metal so it could be re-enamelled. Signal Red, which would look great, Dad said. The instrument panel was real walnut, and the handles were solid metal. None of this cheap plastic shit you get in modern cars, Dad said. He and I were going to get a special permit to take the Jag, unregistered, to the little town of Oakey where Dad's friend Kerry Vance had his workshop. At that stage it didn't even have a windscreen so we'd have to wear caps and goggles, just like in the old days. In Dad's absence, I'd finished the roof. It was a job that required gentle but constant rubbing, standing on the kickboard, reaching over, and Dad was much better at it than me. My thumb and index finger had blistered with the final effort. I remember noticing that Dad's tools had been taken down from the shed wall and his toolbox was gone. I figured they must be at the base in the boot of the Torana. He sometimes took his tools to work to help other guys with their cars.

Dad had had quite a few different hobbies before the Jaguar but when he dropped them, he dropped them completely, mostly selling everything or giving it away and throwing himself into the next thing. He was like that, all or none, never shades of grey. He was like that with people too. He either liked them or hated them from the start, and rarely changed his mind. He said grey was the appeaser's colour, and appeasers always lost. For a time before I was born, he owned motorbikes, four at one stage, and two helmets still sat on a high shelf in the shed, along with his leathers. According to Mum, he pulled his bikes apart and put them back together every weekend. When one of them broke down and he couldn't fix it, he sold the lot and took to cars, which he said were more reliable. They were more expensive too, and we owned fewer of them. The Jag was his biggest purchase so far.

For a while before he bought the Jag, he learned the trumpet. He did ballroom dancing too, although Mum wouldn't go with him, and eventually he gave that up. I don't know what happened to his dancing suits. The trumpet was given away to a mate in Melbourne. He collected stamps briefly, but he'd barely designed his letter-head and drawn up plans to open his own shop when he sold the entire collection one Saturday. He said it was because Mum wouldn't let him purchase the stamp he most wanted. The money would buy an education, Mum said. Once the stamps disappeared, the Jag had been taking all our spare time. Dad planned to do it up for sale and make a profit, although I didn't believe he'd ever sell it once he'd finished it.

I liked being on my own in Dad's shed. I have no interest in cars, but even now when I walk into a me-chanic's workshop and hear tools on metal and smell oil and grease, I go back there, to the sheds of my child-hood. Dad was quieter and there was more room between us, more space for me. It was the only place he ever really seemed at peace.

In the Brisbane house, Dad kept an Army trunk on the high shelf along the back wall of the shed. Once or twice he'd taken it down to show me. He had souvenirs from some of the places he'd travelled for work — a necklace of teeth from New Guinea where he'd done some jungle training before Vietnam, a beaten silver bowl from Vietnam, and little ancient soldiers made of clay from somewhere. He still had the prizes he'd won for swimming, and all his old Army stuff, from Portsea on.

Dad kept his father's service medals in the trunk, in a special ivory-inlaid wooden jewel box. Every so often he laid the medals out on a cloth on the dining room table and polished them. In our photos Dad's father is always in uniform. I only met him twice, once when Mum took me and Stella to see him at his house in St Kilda when we were in Melbourne, and later in an old people's home just out of the city. On the first visit, he made a big effort to be nice to Stella and me, with a treasure hunt for lollies he'd hidden around the house, as if we were still little kids, and proper tea in a pot for Mum, as if she never had teabags at home. He was old and shaky and it made him seem more gentle than maybe he'd been when Dad was a kid. Stella and I went along with the hidden lollies. Later I asked Dad if he'd had treasure hunts too. He just looked at Mum and laughed, loud and hard. When Stella and I were leaving, Dad's father gave me a model plane he and Dad had made, and he told me I was a wonderful kid. He asked Stella to ask Dad to visit him.

I went to Dad's father's funeral in Melbourne. So did Dad, although he said beforehand he wouldn't.

Afterwards he told me he wanted to make sure they put the bastard way down into the ground, but during the service he sat next to me and I could feel him shaking.

One Saturday not long after the funeral, Dad took the trunk down from its high shelf in the shed. 'Something I want to show you, kid,' he said. We'd been working all day on the car and it had got dark outside without me noticing. Dad lifted the lid of the trunk, took out a thick cardboard envelope, and sat up beside me at the workbench. He switched on the lamp and sat there for a moment more, running his fingers along the top edge of the envelope as if it was a car part he wanted to get the measure of before starting work. The lamp gave us both a warm glow and fizzed every time a moth touched it. Dad didn't look at me as he turned the envelope over, squeezed the metal clips apart and poured the contents onto the bench. These were Dad's service medals. I'd seen them before when he wore them for a parade. He didn't say anything, just stared straight ahead. Most of the medals were the size and shape of twenty-cent pieces. They had colourful striped ribbons and little gold pins. A couple were tarnished. Dad didn't look after his own medals like he looked after his father's.

Dad ran his fingers over the medals without touching them, as if he were a magician and now they'd disappear. Finally he picked up a leather case that had landed to one side of the little pile. He opened the case and swallowed and turned to me. His face wore a kind of scowl; he might as easily have cried as become angry. He picked up my hand and pressed it hard onto the cool metal inside the case; the embossing left the shape of a

Maltese cross on my palm when he let go. This was Dad's Victoria Cross, the highest honour bestowed on any soldier in the Commonwealth. Dad was one of only five Australians to be awarded the Cross out of Vietnam.

Dad did all this in silence, and I didn't say anything either. It wasn't that he didn't talk about his time in Vietnam. He did, very occasionally, but you had to wait for him to bring it up and he controlled the conversation. You didn't ask questions and you answered his questions as fast as you could so he didn't feel ignored. Not long after he'd come home, he pulled a gun on a couple of construction workers who'd yelled something suggestive at Mum. 'You want to repeat that?' he said. The construction worker who'd yelled out pissed his pants. Mum just pretended it wasn't happening, Stella said.

That's how we dealt with Vietnam in our family, as if it hadn't happened. Mum especially. She'd say, 'When I was pregnant with Scott,' if she wanted to refer to that time, as if my birth and not Vietnam had been the significant event. We were used to life being like that, like that one big thing in my father's life hadn't really happened. I think that was the case in most families. Ours was better off than heaps of others. Dad woke in the night and stuff, and he had a terrible temper if you contradicted him, but some families were blown apart by Vietnam. Lots of kids were worse off than Stella and me. We had it pretty easy in comparison.

Dr Bain, who was my doctor when I was in the psych hospital, says that families hide things when they become charged with emotion. He says you can walk into some houses and say there's an elephant sitting in

the lounge room and people can stare straight at the
elephant and tell you it's not there. I tried to explain to
him that it was different from that, that sometimes
Vietnam was so large in our lounge room that we all had
to pretend so he could keep himself from falling apart,
but Bain didn't understand that kind of stuff. He was all
for opening everything up. But I don't think it would
have helped anyone at our place.

Dad was a show-off when it came to some things, like
swimming and having good vision and hearing. But
Vietnam was something else. He never showed off about
it. I didn't even know he'd been awarded a Victoria Cross
until another veteran told me, a guy named Clive
Stephenson, who'd been stationed at the same base in
Vietnam as Dad for a few months. When we were in
Canberra, Captain Stephenson was posted there, and Dad
asked him along to one of our barbecues to meet some
other families. As was often the case with Army parties,
guys who hadn't been in the war were asking questions.
Usually Dad shrugged them off and changed the topic. If
he saw his Vietnam friends, which he only very rarely did,
they talked about anything but. At this party, the non-vet
guys from Dad's work who hadn't got a peep from Dad
were pumping Captain Stephenson for information.

Dad must have been inside the house when they
started and the first thing I heard was Captain
Stephenson saying that 'Clark' Goodwin was a legend in
the 'Nam. I moved closer. Stephenson only knew Clark
by reputation, he said, but the story was that Clark had
saved the entire US base at Bien Duh. 'He was a corp
with one of the special reconnaissance units. Our guys

were supposed to be helping the Yanks teach the Vietnam Army how to fight, but we ended up teaching the bloody Yanks as well. Our guys were fucken good, and the Yanks had no idea about jungle ops. On reconnaissance, they'd light themselves up like Christmas trees and play loud music to scare the VC off.' He rolled his eyes. 'Hopeless.

'Clark and his boys were real quiet. They'd get dropped out at night and sneak into Charlie's home turf to see what he was up to. They'd come out next morning quiet as church mice and meet the dust-offs, Charlie none the wiser, least not until the US guns and infantry were up his arse. That was the idea, anyway.

'The Yanks weren't supposed to put us Aussies in those high-risk situations. At top level they'd guaranteed minimum casualties, but our guys pissed all over them when it came to jungle work and they knew it. So we were helping out on the QT. We preferred to work without Yank involvement because the Yanks were so bloody hopeless.

'The way I heard it, this particular night Clark and an all-Aussie crew were supposed to be on a milk run. According to US Intel, the VC weren't that far south, and it should have been an easy op,' Stephenson said.

'The Yanks were wrong, as usual. There was an entire fucken VC battalion out there; underground. That's what Charlie did, built tunnels like a little mole.

'We're talking nine men against hundreds. Unbe-fucken-lievable.' Stephenson smoked fiercely. He wore a Hawaiian shirt that was tight over his gut. 'But the Gooks were unlucky. Clark was forward scout that night, and he managed to spot old Charlie before Charlie spotted him. That gave the Aussies a chance to radio a warning back to the Yanks at the base.

'From the Yanks' point of view, they had to get our boys out quick-smart to save face. They sent in big guns and air support, which meant big ta-tas for Charlie battalion.

'Apparently, Clark and the boys managed to hold off the VC until the Yanks got there. Way I hear it, Clark ended up running the whole show because the CO wasn't much chop. Clark rallied the men even after he was wounded. Thanks to him, they managed to defend their position and make holes in Charlie's strength.

'When the Yanks came in with gunships, Charlie turned and ran as usual.' Dad was awarded the Victoria Cross for his bravery, Stephenson said.

Stephenson paused, looking around the group for dramatic effect. 'We lost six good blokes. But it would have been worse if it hadn't have been for Clark. They reckon the battalion was planning to attack Bien Duh. The fact that Clark spotted them before they reached the base and managed to phone home saved the lot of us, pretty well.' Stephenson had a crewcut of thick yellow hair. He nodded slowly, looking more than a little drunk. 'This is despite the fact he'd been hit, for Chrissake.'

Dad had come outside and joined the group. I stood back so he couldn't see me. I noticed one or two of the others were glancing across at Dad too, looking away before he met their eyes. Dad had remained silent while Stephenson finished the story, and the look on his face was hard to read. Every now and then he'd almost smile, only it was like a twitch, the smile of a little kid who doesn't know whether to laugh or cry. 'You tell them,' Stephenson said when he noticed Dad. Dad just pointed his finger at Stephenson and shook his head and didn't say a word. Beware the quiet man. After the Stephensons left, Dad said Stephenson was a big poser who didn't know his arse from his elbow about Vietnam. 'See the gut on that guy?' he said. 'You wouldn't take him out on an op. Be like a target.' He laughed loudly at his joke.

Dad had been away for three weeks on that last exercise. I remember it was a Friday afternoon and I was home from training an hour early because we had another meet that weekend and I was supposed to rest. We still hadn't heard from Dad but I wasn't all that worried. I figured he must have been out of communication range. I just wanted him to come home, not only for the present I was sure to get for my birthday, but also to show off the Jaguar and tell him I'd made it through the first heat.

As I walked up the drive and around to the back door, I could see the lights were off in the kitchen and at first I thought Mum must have gone to meet Dad at the barracks. But the Torana wasn't back and Mum's 626 was still in the garage. I found Mum in the dark kitchen. The toilet light was on, and I could just make out the shape of her at the table. She was staring straight ahead. She didn't acknowledge me. The only sound was the tick of the clock on the wall behind her.

'What's wrong?' I said. She looked at me and started crying. She made an awful sound like she was sucking on the end of a milkshake. I had no idea what to do. I was scared to hear her cry like that. I turned on the light. She narrowed her eyes and looked away from me but said nothing. Tears ran down her cheeks and her nose was running like a little kid who doesn't know how to wipe. Her face was all stretched and loose. She didn't try to cover it either. I felt embarrassed. I asked again what the matter was. Then I looked round the kitchen but found nothing out of place. I started talking, said I'd make her a cup of tea. I thought I could smell soap, like someone had just had a shower, but there was no sign of Dad. It must have occurred to me that he'd had some sort of accident but I put that thought away.

As I made the tea I talked on, babbled really, for probably the only time in my whole life, to fill up space. I told her we found a toad in the change rooms that afternoon. It was gross, I said, and Jim Petrie stepped on it and it busted everywhere. I told her Mr Maitland said I should try out for the play, how I wanted to but I wasn't sure because some of the other kids said it was poofy, what did she think, what did she think Dad would think because she always hated me saying things like that were poofy but he always thought they were poofy and they'd joke about it. I wasn't used to having to do so much talking and I was running out of things to say. I made the tea, in a pot, with tea leaves. I think I put too much in, because it came out in the cup and floated, tons of it, and that made her cry even more. 'Sorry, Mum. I'm really sorry. I'll make another one.' She put her hand on my arm and shook her head, holding her lips together tight. 'Please tell me what's happened.' She opened her mouth as if she might talk but didn't. 'Where's Stella?' Stella would know what to do. She'd know how to make tea.

Finally I got up the courage and asked, 'Where's Dad?' Mum looked at me then and it was a look of disgust.

'Your father's left us,' she said in this throaty voice that wasn't hers, 'for that slut.'

chapter**seven**

Stella arrived then and took over, thank God. She put Mum to bed and ordered a pizza. After it arrived, she sat down with me at the kitchen table.

'He didn't even tell her to her face,' Stella said. 'He left a note.' She was working hard but unsuccessfully on talking quietly while she ate, spitting bits of pizza crust toward me. 'The bastard. He said they'd been growing apart for some time, and now she can stay close to her parents, since that's what she wants. As if it's her fault he's leaving. Grandad's sick. She just wanted to wait until he gets better.

'He's back from woop-woop. He came over here today with a tow truck while Mum was out shopping and he took the Jag and left the note. Growing apart? Can you believe it? All that fuckhead cares about are his fucking toys.

'Mum was furious. She called his CO who told her Dad was still on exercise in North Queensland. But get this. Dad's corporal answered Mum's call and let slip that Dad had requested the move to Melbourne. It's not a posting; it's a movement request. The corporal made some joke about how much Dad must love the cold. So Dad's planned the whole bloody thing, knowing Mum wouldn't want to go.

'At first Mum said it was her going back to study. He never liked her being better than him, and you know what he's like when it comes to anything academic. He can't stand all that ivory tower stuff. It makes him feel inadequate.

'But I'm pretty sure Mum knows he's on with someone else. Don't look as if you didn't know, Scott. I told you, last year, when he threw out his Y-fronts and bought jocks — first sign. And our old man in Levis? Come on. Didn't I tell you? He's a fuckhead.' Stella's whispering voice left no room for responses. Her energy washed over me. 'I mean, I know they had a crappy relationship but he's hung around this long. What's she going to do now? She's useless.'

I suppose they did have a crappy relationship. But to me, it always seemed like it was Mum who kept something back, not Dad. Dad talked to Mum about everything he did, but she just added appropriate yesses, agreeing with him but never telling him about herself. Even as a mother Mum was more like a favourite aunt — the little sister of our real mother — who was looking after us for a while. She wasn't confident about taking care of children, and she was vague, but she was lots of fun. Dad adored her, or at least I'd always believed he did. 'She's a goddess,' he told me once, 'and our job's to take care of her. You and me. Two sorts of women in the world, goddesses and good-timers. Do what you like with the good-timers, and find yourself a goddess to marry.'

Dad was older than Mum, only by two years, but sometimes he acted like she was a little girl. When he was away Mum was more in charge and less like a favourite aunt, but even then she wasn't like the commanding officer. I felt it, and Stella did too. Dad was more full of beans than Mum and yet, when he was away, everything in the house felt lighter. Maybe it was just that Mum relaxed a little and talked to us more. Maybe we all talked more to one another. It wasn't something I thought about until he'd gone, by which time no one was doing much talking to anyone.

'But he loves Mum,' I said that first night.

'Grow up, Scott. He's a complete sleaze.' I started to respond. Stella interrupted. 'Oh, for fuck's sake, he hit on Julie.' Julie Holt was one of Stella's friends from school.

'What do you mean?'

'Last year, at Coolangatta. He'd been hanging around us all afternoon like a bad smell. It was so embarrassing. I went back up to the unit for my togs, and he put his arm around Julie to tell her something and then put his hand on her breast. My best friend, my father. Why do you think I can't stand to be anywhere near him?'

I didn't believe Stella. She always dramatised everything, and she and Julie were mad together. 'Who told you he did that?' I said.

'Julie, of course. I've never seen her so upset. She said he put his arm around her and told her she was a great kid and then he felt her tit. She ignored him at first because she could hardly believe it. So he kept his hand there till she brushed it away. Then he pretended nothing had happened.'

'Did you ask him about it?'

'Oh yeah,' Stella said. 'Dad, by the way, were you trying to tit off my best friend? No, I didn't ask him about it. I just stay away from him. He's a bastard shithead sleazebag as far as I'm concerned.

'Mum will fall apart for sure,' Stella said. 'She's hopeless when it comes to Dad, just does whatever he wants. I think she's scared of him, to be honest. But I don't know who to call. I don't think she's got any friends here anymore who aren't Army wives, and she doesn't want them.' It occurred to me that the person we should call was Mr Rebo, which was ridiculous since I hardly knew him and Mum had only met him the once, but I thought he and Mum would most probably get on and his psychology could only help. I didn't know anyone to call from Mum's art class, or whether they'd help. The obvious people were Gran and Grandad, Mum's parents, but I didn't suggest them either. There'd be no way Dad would come back if he knew Gran and Grandad were involved.

'So, when will he be home?' It hadn't sunk in. I guess I was in shock. I wanted Dad back where he belonged.

Stella scowled at me. 'Have you been listening to a word I've been saying? He's left. He's not coming back. He doesn't want to see us. That's it. He's going to Melbourne and we're staying here.'

'What about the second heat? It's next week.' Stella was still wearing her white shirt and black skirt from work.

She'd pulled out the shirt and had kicked off her high shoes on the floor. Her hair was falling into her face. She looked scared. I was having trouble breathing. Not like asthma, but I had to keep reminding myself to put air in.

Stella stood to leave the room. 'You are so self-centred. I'll take you. And try to think of Mum for a change.'

Stella's approach to thinking of Mum for a change meant a furious cleaning of the kitchen in which all surfaces were scrubbed with something that left scratches, followed by cooked dinners every night for a week from Miss Schauer's cookbook. Veal pillows, steak à la something, chicken stuffed with mandarin rice then wrapped in bacon. Stella took down Mum and Dad's wedding photo and had a big fire out the back with any photos or other mementoes of Dad she found around the house. She said there were no recent photos of the two of them together and this was a sign. A few weeks later she dropped out of QIT and went nursing. She moved out into a share house because, she said, she simply couldn't cope with the load of me and Mum any longer.

Dad's corporal came over to pack Dad's things while I was at school. He had a typed list of everything Dad wanted which he left behind on the kitchen table, with all the items ticked off or crossed and initialled neatly, as if it were an inventory. Stella arrived before the soldier could finish his list and chased him out of the house. The list reminded me about Dad's original plan, that Mum and Stella were supposed to go to Melbourne while he and I stayed in Brisbane for the trials. I thought he might still be planning to take me with him. He might be coming back to get me. I might be on the list. I felt if I could just see him, he'd explain what was going on. I didn't believe Stella about Julie Holt. I didn't believe there was some other woman either. I just didn't. Dad would explain, I thought. He had an explanation for everything. Perhaps the corporal hadn't collected me because I'd been at school. When I checked, the list included clothes, papers, his trunk from the garage, but no Scott.

By the end of the month I think even I admitted he was gone, at least for a while. Stella was moving back and forth between home and her new house. I'd missed training every day. Mum had been in her room the whole time as far as I could tell. My saved pocket money had run out. 'Mum? You okay?' She didn't answer. 'Mum?' Still no response. I walked into the room slowly. 'Mum?'

'What?' A sleepy voice came from the bed. It was dark and smelled like ripe fruit.

'Were you asleep?' It was six pm.

'A little bit, yes, darling. What is it?'

Now that I had her attention, I wasn't sure what to say. 'I just wondered if you'd mind if I rang up for a pizza again.'

'No, that's fine.'

'Want some?'

'Might come out a bit later.'

'Has Dad phoned?' She croaked no and resumed those aching sobs that had frightened me the first day. 'Okay, well, I'll just phone for the pizza then.' She didn't respond. 'Second heats are next Friday. Supreme okay with you?' A sort of grunt. I left and closed the door.

Mr Rebo rang. I said Dad was away and I'd been waking up too late to ride my bike to training. The next

morning, and for the rest of the season, I got a lift to
training with him and Jennifer.

For my birthday I'd been given U2 concert tickets by
Mum. They were my favourite band, and Mum liked
that they had a song about Martin Luther King. The
concert was on a Saturday night at Festival Hall in the
city and I took Jennifer along. Not on a date, as such, but
as a friend. I caught the bus into town and met her
outside the hall. Before the show we bought Cornettos.

This was in the days before U2 were so famous they
only played stadiums. When I saw them later at QEII,
Bono looked like a fluorescent ant from where I sat. But
that night at Festival Hall, we had a good enough view
to see a string break on the Edge's guitar. He kept playing
until the end of the song. As they belted out 'Sunday
Bloody Sunday' I got the feeling I could do and be
anything in my life. Real exhilaration. They finished
with 'Pride (In the Name of Love)'.

Jennifer was one of those really good swimmers with
big shoulders, a skinny waist and green-blond hair. She
swam butterfly 'like a dolphin' according to Mr Rebo.
After the concert, we had a milkshake at Jo-Jo's and she
managed to get me talking about favourite bands. She
was into Adam and the Ants and Culture Club herself. I
sang the first few bars of 'Do You Really Want to Hurt
Me?' and she was pretty impressed. I told her I could
play the whole thing on guitar, which wasn't quite true.

After we'd exhausted bands, Jennifer talked about
swimming and how hard it was to be really good. I knew
she was more natural in the water than me. She talked a
lot, which made it easier. I'm a good listener, and I nodded

and smiled while she covered her best times and what she'd learned from Rebo. I didn't tell her about Dad.

Jennifer was wearing purple eyeshadow and thick mascara, which I hadn't noticed at first. It made her look different, pretty even. She told me she wanted to do hairdressing when she finished school. She had long bleached blond hair. Mostly when I saw her, it was tucked up under her cap or wet and straggly, but she wore it out that night which made her look less like a swimming champion and more like a girl. She asked me what I was going to do when I finished school. Surprising myself, I said I was going to join the Army. That wasn't what I was planning at all. I still wanted to do an arts degree and teach history like Mr Maitland. 'Following after your dad?' Jennifer said.

'I guess so,' I said, 'although he went to Portsea, which was much harder than Duntroon, where I'd go.' Dad didn't go on and on about me joining the Army or anything, but I knew it was what he wanted. He used to say a young bloke could do worse than officer training.

'My dad says your dad used to swim,' Jennifer said.

'Sure did. He made Olympic selection. They reckon he'd have gone on too, except he went to Vietnam. He was wounded. They nearly cut off his leg.'

She nodded. 'Do you get on all right with him?'

'Yeah, why?' She'd picked up the sugar dispenser and was pouring grains into the ashtray.

'Dunno. He comes to training, so I wondered, you know. Like, none of the other fathers come to training.' I wanted to grab the sugar dispenser from her and tell her to stop playing with it. 'He yells at you.'

'No he doesn't,' I said quickly. She looked at me incredulously. 'Sometimes he gets a bit excited, that's all.' Jennifer nodded but didn't say anything. 'We Goodwins are a little intense,' I said. I put on a voice and made a face as I said it. She giggled.

Soon after that Mr Rebo picked us up. Jennifer held my hand in the back seat on the way to my place. Mr Rebo left us pretty much to ourselves, checking in the rearview mirror now and then but saying nothing. Jennifer got out with me and smiled and thanked me for a great night before she got in the front with her dad. She dived in and kissed me quickly. I should have made more of an effort. I should have tried kissing her more, for the experience if nothing else. She went on to marry an Olympic champion. They've given Rebo seven grandchildren to train. I saw him not long ago. He still wears sandals.

On the Friday of the second heat for the state competition, I was sure Dad would be there. I was disappointed he hadn't arrived in time to wish me luck, but I knew he wouldn't miss it. I watched the entry gate. When my race was called, he hadn't arrived.

Mr Rebo always said that in those few minutes before a race we had to centre ourselves and think winning thoughts. Up on the blocks, in that moment before the gun, you had to bend down and visualise your body, your strong thighs pushing you up with everything they had, your long feet moving off the blocks and flipping straight back like a dolphin's tail, your sleek body taking off, flying through the air, flying above the water with no resistance, to the other end of the pool.

I watched the gates, but he didn't come through. I blew the start. We got back up on the blocks. The race restarted. I dived late this time; no second restart. I swam the first two laps badly, feeling Stephen Neilsen pulling away from me with each stroke.

I turned into the third lap, and I knew suddenly that Dad was there. It was so spooky. I figured he'd berate me on the way home. I should know by now, he'd say. 'This is not a rehearsal.' That was one of his sayings. He meant life generally, but he often said it about swimming. I'd know better than to point out he'd been late. I'd say I'd known he was there, when I was in the water, that I must have inherited his sixth sense after all. Or I'd just be thankful he was back.

Coming into the third turn I reckoned I was still a body behind Stephen Neilsen, who was always better over distance. We'd both shammed a little in the first heat, as you should (keep your powder dry), but I knew Neilsen would perform now. I still don't know how I did it. For the rest of the race I was as comfortable as I ever felt in the water. I passed Neilsen. I killed my brand new personal best by nearly six seconds. It was the finest swim I ever did. I got to the end of the pool and tore off my goggles. My pulse pounded in my head. I was taking huge gulps of air. I couldn't see him in the crowd.

Afterwards, I convinced myself he'd seen that swim. He'd been there the whole time. He'd stayed hidden somewhere in the stands. I even remembered seeing him as I dived. Before the race he'd wanted more than any-thing to come and tell me I had to focus better on my starts. He'd wanted to wish me well. He'd decided it would wreck my concentration. And then, after the race, Mr Rebo came up and hugged me, a great big burly hug, while I was looking for Dad, and I forgot to push him off. Dad would have seen that, and that would have been it. He'd have left without saying goodbye.

In the hospital I used to replay the race for the others. Three of us would have two matchsticks each for swimmers. We'd use a blue tea towel from the kitchen as our pool. And here comes Goodwin. Goodwin! Goodwin! Goodwin!, we'd scream, and I'd win over and over again. One guy would giggle the whole time and hold his dick like a little kid afraid he'd wet himself. On my own in bed afterwards, I'd be back there at training with Dad, hearing the roar of the water in my ears and a long cool buzz in my head that I always imagined was the sound of my brain. My racers slipping up my thighs like skin, my speed goggles, the smell of bleach for the rest of the day. Him yelling like crazy for me to get it right. 'For fuck's sake, Scott, this is not a fucking rehearsal!' To Dr Bain I'd do this Marlon Brando accent and say I could have been a contender, as if swimming didn't matter. Dr Bain loved to talk about Dad and swimming. Swimming had it all, as far as Bain was concerned.

Mr Maitland told my class that Australian soldiers were used as guinea pigs in nuclear tests in the sixties. 'Come on, Scott, surely you've something to add along patriotic lines.' I shook my head. Mr Maitland looked at me above his glasses for a moment, and then continued. He didn't address me again during class. After school he stopped me on the top verandah. 'Goodwin, you right for Saturday?'

'What's Saturday, sir?'

'Biol, the science camp with Miss Tyquin. We're going to Lamington National Park. You're one of the team leaders.'

'How come you're going on the biol camp, sir?'

'Just helping out a colleague,' he said. Mr Maitland had the hots for our biol teacher, at least that's what everyone said. He stood there for a moment without saying anything. 'You finished your essay yet?'

'No, sir, I've been too busy.' Maitland was helping me with an essay competition. "If I ruled the world" was the topic and I'd written about Aboriginal kids in Alice Springs.

'Everything okay?' Maitland studied his shoes.

'Yes, sir.'

'Sure?' I don't know why but suddenly I felt like crying. I nodded yes.

'Good,' Maitland said. 'Keep me posted on the essay then. It's due in two weeks. I want to see it.'

Although I'd given up on the idea that Dad might come and get me, I held on to the hope that he'd write and explain everything. I didn't think again about what Stella had said, that there was someone else, or that Dad had done something to Stella's friend. Knowing Dad, I thought, he'd be feeling guilty about leaving. He'd know Mum would be mad and he'd make himself scarce, but he'd write to me. I checked the letterbox ten times some days, even at night when the postman was long gone. Over time, this grew into a habit. Years later, I still checked my post office box daily and, while I didn't know why, I often felt the same disappointment I'd felt as a teenager. The only appeal of travel for me is that I don't need to worry about incoming mail and phone calls, not because they're a nuisance like they are for other people, but because they can only ever be disappointing in that they can never be from him.

I don't know why I still wanted to see him after what he'd done. I think I wanted him to explain; that's what I told Bain. We'd been his blood, that's what he called us, and then suddenly we weren't. Looking back, it was like I simply froze there, at just the point when I should have started seeing his flaws, when I was old enough to start believing all the stuff Stella said about him. But I was stuck. I think that's what started everything that followed.

One Saturday about a month after Dad had disappeared, Mum got out of bed. She looked pale and thin, her nightie was grubby and there were big dark bags under her eyes. When she said she needed a bath to feel human I nodded enthusiastically. I cooked mashed potatoes and sausages for dinner and we ate them together at the kitchen table. 'This is good, Scott,' she said. 'How come we never have this when I cook?'

'You have no imagination,' I said. 'I do peas too.'

She made a face. 'Not peas. I hate peas,' in a child's voice. She smiled. After dinner she insisted on washing up. Later she came into my room and sat on the bed. 'Thanks for being such a good boy.' I felt as if I'd been an adult all month and now suddenly I'd shrunk into a baby. She kissed my forehead, which I hadn't let her do since I was ten. She kept her hands on my shoulders for a moment and I didn't push her away. Still later, I heard her on the phone, and I guess she finally told her parents because they arrived at six the next morning, which was a Sunday, the only day I didn't have to get up for training and could sleep in, and they woke me. They must have left the farm in the middle of the night. All the same, I was happy to see them. They were so normal, my mother's parents, so much a part of the normal past I'd come out of, that I figured everything would be all right.

chapter**eight**

Grandad had joined the police force when the farm was doing poorly in the fifties. He was a reluctant policeman, Gran said, but he noticed things other people missed and was a good figurer-outer, so they moved him into homicide. Over time he grew to enjoy his work and kept it on even after the farm came good. For a while he travelled all over the state to work on murder cases. Under his house he'd kept all these crime files he'd put together. I loved reading them, not so much for the gruesome details, which is what Stella revelled in, as for the stories Grandad made out of people's lives. Grandad and I had that love of research in common, as well as our long legs and bad eyesight. I liked going up to the farm to stay with him. He answered your questions seriously, no matter how dumb they were, and he never laughed at you. I learned to trust him to tell me the truth. I knew I couldn't talk to Mum about Dad, so I asked Grandad. 'I thought your mother explained,' he said. We were sitting together on the back step. It was a hot afternoon that beat up at us off the concrete. Grandad's face was flushed.

I didn't say Mum hadn't talked at all for over a month. 'You think he'll come back?'

'I don't think so.'

'Can I talk to him?'

'I thought your mum had told you all this. He doesn't want to talk to us. He's written a letter. Did you read it?' I shook my head. Stella had read the letter, but Mum had never shown it to me. 'I can ask your mum for it, if you like, if that would be a help.' He went inside and returned a few minutes later. I read the letter while he sat quietly beside me. It was written in Dad's neat hand and signed with his full name.

Dear Anne
I am writing this down which is cowardly in a way but I'm not sure I could tell you face-to-face and I know this will make you angry.

For me, our marriage is over and has been for at least the last year. I did love you once, with all my heart and all my soul. But the gap between us now is so wide I hardly know where to begin. For the moment, I don't want to see you and the children. I'll contact you when I can face Scott and Stella.

I looked up at Grandad who was staring intently at me. 'It's like he feels guilty.'

'So he should feel bloody guilty,' Grandad said. He took a breath in as if to continue, looked at me and paused a moment. Then he said, 'I'm sure once things settle down, he'll be in touch. But you can't contact him. He doesn't want that. You'd only be making a fool of yourself if you go chasing him, now wouldn't you? I think it's better you keep away for now. He's got your number.' Grandad smiled at his little joke.

'But what if he feels so guilty he can't bring himself to call?'

'I don't think there's a snowflake's chance in hell that your dad would ever feel guilty enough about anything that it might stop him doing whatever he pleased.' I reread the letter. At least Dad would be in touch, once he settled down, even Grandad had said. A long time passed with me thinking that.

Grandad and Dad had never got on. Cars were about the only subject they had in common, and even then Dad said Grandad was a silly old fossil. Not to his face, of course. To get to Grandad's, we wound our way through the Toowoomba range and Dad generally took it pretty fast. 'Don't you kids tell your grandfather,' he'd say to me and Stella, winking in the rearview. But then he'd tell Grandad himself. 'That little Fiat of mine's a beauty. We hit the ton coming into Pittsworth this morning,' he'd say, when they hadn't even been talking about cars. Grandad would shake his head and glare at Mum.

'It's not you, it's the other bloody driver,' Grandad would say to Dad. 'You've got no buffer, man.'

Grandad's buffer was the buffer of a giant, with at least four car lengths in front. He drove the Ford he'd owned since he'd left the police. Everyone passed us, beeping or yelling something like, 'Get off the road, y'old bastard.' And every time they yelled, Gran used to turn to Grandad and say, 'Mad hound, I bet he's been on the bottle.' Grandad always nodded agreement, hunched his shoulders over and peered through the windscreen as if watching for more mad hounds.

When I was little, I loved Dad's fast driving. I felt the same awful thrill I felt when he'd toss me up in the air and catch me, never sure he'd be there to cushion my fall. He told people I was a smart kid. 'See,' he'd say to a nervous passenger. 'Scott's laughing his head off. He knows he's safe.' He'd build up speed and yell and squeal to entertain us. 'Faster, faster!' I'd say from the back seat. I loved the rush of wind in my face and the feeling of gravity holding me back when he accelerated, especially in the powerful cars. And then, just when you least expected it, he'd rip on the handbrake, screaming on top note. We'd spin round like a ride at the show, a hundred and eighty degrees, and then head back in the opposite direction. I screamed along with Dad, but I was never sure if I was excited or scared by the time the car finished spinning.

Dad fitted one of those police radar detectors onto his car after the second time he lost his licence. The police were the pigs as far as he was concerned. When I said, 'But Grandad used to be in the police,' Dad said, 'And he can be a bloody pig, your grandfather.' Sometimes Dad tried to be nice to Grandad. He took him some car magazines and once a bottle of special port. He even suggested the three of us go on a camping trip. Grandad was cool. 'Maybe,' he said. 'We're shearing, so I'm needed here presently.'

Dad got in a terrible temper on the way home that day. We came up behind a car with L plates. It was sitting

in the right overtaking lane. 'Selfish cunt,' Dad said. He
pulled in behind the other car and sat so close behind I
don't know how he didn't hit it. He drove like this for
what seemed like ages, even though the slow lane was
clear. I could see the side of his face, white with anger,
and I could imagine the vein down his forehead that
always stuck out blue when he was about to lose his
temper. He was talking softly to himself. I couldn't hear
what he said. Then he blasted the car in front with his
airhorns, which were so loud they gave me a fright, even
though I saw him reach for the switch. The car in front
pulled left. Dad took his pistol from under the driver's
seat and passed them slowly, waving the big gun their
way, laughing. He had to reach right across Mum,
keeping his right hand on the steering wheel. The people
in the other car, a young girl driving and what looked
like her father in the passenger seat, just stared at us.
Mum turned to me and Stella. 'How about we play I
Spy?' she said. It wasn't that she wasn't scared, because
you could hear in her voice that she was making herself
talk slowly.

Gran liked Dad even less than Grandad did, if that's
possible. Once I overheard a conversation where she said
to Mum she'd have preferred another baby than have
Mum feel she had to marry beneath herself. I already
knew Mum was pregnant with Stella before they got
married. It wasn't a big deal. When I asked Mum about
what Gran said, she said Gran was only talking, and of
course Gran loved Dad. But Gran gave Dad a frypan for
Father's Day one year, which was funny since the only
thing he could cook was toast.

Mum made plans to go back to university. Gran offered to stay and help look after the children if that would assist. The children was me and, as Mum pointed out, I was nearly an adult. I don't think Mum wanted them staying on. According to Stella, Gran blamed Mum after Dad left. She was ashamed Mum had been unable to keep Dad even if, in Gran's view, Dad wasn't worth having in the first place. Gran told Stella that men were like stallions, '... and if you don't service them regularly, they don't run for you.' I used to make a horse-snort at the dinner table if Stella was there. She'd giggle and have to excuse herself.

I really grew to hate swimming after Dad left. I kept up squad for a while after the state trials but it got so that even the smell of chlorine, which I'd always liked, was making me sick. Some mornings I had to eat cereal to settle my stomach before I got in the pool. My times were shithouse too. Eventually I dropped out of the squad. For a while I still went along to the afternoon session to watch Jennifer train. We hung around together a bit, although she'd started going out with a guy in the squad, Trent Burwood, the Queensland champion breaststroker, so it wasn't as much fun as before. Mr Rebo kept telling me I should come back to training, which made me feel bad. I soon stopped going to the pool altogether and didn't see Jennifer anymore.

After Christmas Mum and I moved out of our house and into a unit at Toowong which was cheaper. On the day we moved I said to Mum, 'How will Dad find us?'

'Oh, darling boy,' she said, and hugged me until I pulled away.

'Well, how will he find us?' It was the first time I'd persisted. 'He is my father.'

'I know that, Scott. But he doesn't want to see us.'

'He doesn't want to see you.'

'He hasn't tried to contact you and Stella,' she said carefully.

'How do I know that?'

She went to respond quickly but checked herself. 'You've had to grow up way too fast, haven't you? A crazed mother to look after, Stella and all her problems, and no help. Maybe you should try to ring him.'

'Would that worry you?' I felt I'd be being disloyal.

'No, of course not. You need to find out for yourself and maybe he'll talk to you. I'll get you a phone number.' I don't know if Mum had tried to contact Dad herself. Perhaps she had. But I knew she'd faced the fact he wasn't coming back in a way I hadn't. She seemed almost relieved, to be honest.

'I just can't believe he'd do this to me.'

Mum gave me a number, for Victoria Barracks in Melbourne, but every time I got to the switchboard I hung up as soon as I said his name and before I was put through.

I analysed Dad's leaving in every detail. A few weeks before he left, we'd had our last conversation about my future. I'd got a report card and I was doing well in history, science and drama as usual. For the first time I told Dad I wanted to go to university. He said that was all very well and I could do whatever I bloody well liked, but Duntroon offered a young bloke everything. I said I didn't think the Army was for me. 'You ashamed of me?' he said.

I said no, of course not. He looked at me for a long moment and left me in my room. He didn't mention the subject again.

I always knew I was not really the son he wanted, the one strong enough, fast enough, good enough, the one like him. And I was his only son. I suppose I've spent half my adult life failing graciously for him, and it's taken me a long time to learn to be someone else, someone who had nothing to do with why he did what he did, someone who could succeed and fail on his own terms. Perhaps I still haven't managed that.

chapter**nine**

It was two and a half years later that I got the call, early evening, the last Saturday in April of my first term at the Royal Military College, Duntroon. Yeah, Duntroon. I can't explain how I wound up there. I couldn't have been less suited. Mum and I had lived a pretty chaotic life since Dad left. She was studying full-time and working nights as a research assistant out at uni. We'd moved into the flat at Toowong. We ate nothing but takeaways, and we lived in a constant state of mess. I'd have to say it suited the two of us pretty well. It was only later at Duntroon that I became the neat freak. Stella used to look furious when she arrived at Mum's place and she'd clean up madly before she left. Stella was more like Dad on that score. Mum said she was obsessive. It was our private joke. Duntroon was the opposite of life with Mum and maybe that's what I felt I needed, a bit more order, a bit more organisation. At Duntroon everything had a place and a purpose, like in Dad's sheds. There was no mess anywhere.

I remember that Saturday the sky had been this gasping blue. Canberra was cold enough to induce a nosebleed and clouds had wandered past at lunchtime like sheep celebrating icy weather. We'd been out on a training exercise in which Blue Teams were supposed to find and capture Orange Teams and Orange Teams were supposed to evade capture. We were dressed up in combat fatigues and had painted faces, as if we were in the jungle, except we were on the grassy slopes around the college. I was an Orange Team, paired with Colin Rawlins, the only real friend I made at Duntroon.

I met Colin on my first night when we'd all assembled in the Great Hall for a briefing, two hundred or so new cadets and some of the First Class, whose job it was to supervise us, along with the staff. Most of the boys had had haircuts ahead of time, in the futile hope we might avoid the Army barber, but Colin Rawlins hadn't bothered, and his long brown hair was tied back in a ponytail, not quite balancing an overgrown fuzzy red beard. He was sitting next to me and we introduced ourselves. No one else seemed to be talking. Most guys, including me, wore the kind of smart casual gear listed in our briefing notes, slacks and collared shirts. Colin's version of smart casual was faded jeans with a missing back pocket and a T-shirt. I noticed he had really long nails on his right hand; those on his left were bitten.

Our staff sergeant yelled at us for ten minutes without switching on the microphone they'd set up for him. This would be the last time we'd see each other as civilians! he boomed, because in the morning we'd be Roy-yal Milla-terry caddettes. That's R! M! C! Our next three years would be the most difficult we'd ever experience, he could assure us. We'd be tested MENTALLY! PHYSICALLY! and EMOTIONALLY! to see if we had what it took. We'd be allowed restricted home leave for the first year, and after that our absences would be further restricted. A disciplined body and mind were the keys to success. DUNTROON! operated along the line of command, just like the Army, and we were juniors. JUNIORS! did as they were told. First Class is just that, FIRST! CLASS! We were Fourth Class behind One, Two and Three. Any QUESTIONS!? he yelled at the end, with the inflection on the last syllable like he was belting out a march.

Colin put up his hand. 'Yeah. Are you for real?' he said. Everyone laughed except the sergeant, who didn't say a word.

When I looked for Colin and didn't find him the next day, I figured he'd changed his mind about Duntroon, which didn't surprise me. Later that evening I heard his voice in the mess. I looked over, but the guy with his voice looked nothing like Colin. They'd sheared and shaved him, as they had the rest of us, but Colin's crewcut looked like dust on his scalp, as if they decided to cut more off because there was more to cut. I guess this was the staff sergeant's revenge. With no beard to hide them, Colin's red lips stood out. He had bright red cheeks too, and eyes that looked too soft for a place like Duntroon.

I must admit that my decision to apply to Duntroon had been helped by Mum and Mr Maitland, who'd told me they felt I wasn't suited to the Army. Maitland went on about my independent mind. Mum just said the Army wasn't for someone like me. I wanted to prove them wrong. I also wanted to pay Stella back. She'd been studying at QIT when I was in Year 10, and she'd left to do nursing. Her wages had helped to keep me at Marist Brothers when Mum was studying full-time. Duntroon paid you to do your degree. I was determined to stick it out.

The Duntroon day started at six-fifteen am with reveille, and we worked until lights out at ten-thirty pm, six days a week. It was organised around the notion of following standard operating procedures, or SOPs. The idea was that in difficulty, if you just followed SOPs, everything would be all right. Mr Maitland would have said it proved his point about the Army and independent thought. When the First Class ordered you to do stupid things, like clean their kit, you were expected to do them because the chain of command dictated that you should. Colin Rawlins was the only one who didn't go along with it. He was on a Defence Department scholarship and was the same age as most of First Class. He already had a degree. He told First Classers to bugger off. It won him few allies, especially among the staff who encouraged the hierarchy.

That Saturday in April, Colin and I had positioned ourselves in a bunker on Deadman's Hill, which was the most obvious hideout we could find. Initially I'd pointed out that we were supposed to avoid capture, not encourage it, but Colin said if we didn't give the Blue Team a fair chance we'd be out all night. The Blues were led by a fellow named Brett Anderson, who was tough but thick. They walked right past us, crashing through the brush, and Colin had to call them back. 'Surrender, Dorothy,' he said to Brett in falsetto. Brett didn't smile.

Brett and his Blue Team marched us back in front of them like we were trophies. The sun was behind us and the red and cream buildings of the college in front looked as though they were on fire, with yellow Mount Pleasant beyond. It was quite a sight. Colin seemed oblivious to how much he was annoying Brett, and teased him all the way back, despite several nudges from me. It made me nervous. I knew guys like Brett, boarders at Marist Brothers. You didn't push them.

When we got back Colin and I were bawled out for being captured too quickly, and given extra duties the following week. Anderson smiled smugly, as if he'd won a great victory.

It was seven-thirty that night, after dinner and just before study, our only free period in the six-day week. I was in my room. Another cadet pounded on my door. 'Phone, Goodwin. She says she's your sister.'

Although Mum rang me every week, Stella and I didn't talk much after I left home for Duntroon. In Year 12 I used to hang around her flat with her and her boyfriends if they'd let me. Most of the boyfriends were med students or junior residents, and they nicked stuff from hospital pharmacies to try at home. I drank rum with Stella, but I steered clear of the drugs at that stage.

As far as I knew, Stella was still sleeping with a visiting doctor from America who was the latest boyfriend. She'd keep dating him right up until he decided he couldn't live without her, then she'd drop him as quickly as she could.

Stella changed boyfriends like undies. She looked like Mum did as a young woman, only Stella was more charming — at least that's what Mum said. Mum was being kind. Stella wore that tough, bright makeup of the mid-eighties, and charming was not a word I'd have used to describe her. 'Were you a witch?' I asked Mum.

As for Dad, he hadn't contacted us, not once since he'd left. It was like we didn't exist. I hadn't contacted him either and when I think back now, I can't explain to myself how or why I let it go on so long. Pride, maybe, or fear of what I'd find. I drifted through my last two years of school, nearly failing most subjects, and before I knew it, there I was at Duntroon. Mum and Stella didn't mention Dad at all, and that made it easy for me to pretend everything was normal. I told myself I'd finish my first year at Duntroon and go to Melbourne and find him. I'd ask him why he'd done what he'd done. But other than that, I didn't think about him, not during the day anyway.

At night in bed it was a different story. It started soon after he left. I got into this habit of getting to sleep by making up stories about what had happened. It sounds stupid now but it was my way of getting by. Dad had gone on a mission he couldn't tell us about, not even Mum. That was why he hadn't contacted me. I used to picture the scene of him coming home. On an afternoon when the sun was at the right angle to slip under the back door, it would burst open, and he'd climb out of the bright light just as he always had, up the steps and through the door. He'd grip his hat, ease his bag down onto the linoleum, and reach out for Mum to run into his arms. He'd smile in that way he had, with his whole face, and we'd be back together as a family.

If anything, history fed my dreams. I learned about the CIA in Chile and nuclear tests at Maralinga. Anything seemed possible. In my favourite dream I found out where he was. I demanded the Army tell me what had happened to him. He was being held prisoner. I'd go in alone to bring him out. It was always the jungle, and he'd be barely alive when I captured the camp single-handedly. I'd have to feed him and give him water from my canteen for a day. We were in great danger, I'd tell him, but not to worry. He'd learn he could rely on me. He'd learn I was as good as him. I could kill for him. It seems pathetic now, but it kept me going.

Stella was different. Her response to his leaving had been to leave him back. 'If he walked through that door right now, I'd walk out,' she'd said. 'And I'd spit at him on the way.' Stella turned to hate in the way Dad might have. Years later, after she'd tried Chinese herbs and colonic irrigations and psychotherapy and God knows what else to try to purge him from her system, she concluded we were simply one of his hobbies, like his motorbikes or stamps or cars. When he was interested in us, we were everything. But once he'd given us up, he gave us up completely, like we'd never existed. That seemed enough for Stella. It was about him, not us.

'God, I'm glad I got you,' Stella said on the phone that night, her voice strangely gentle. 'It's Dad,' she said. I can remember that I wanted to tell her to shut up before she said the next words. Because I knew. I might even have said shut up, but she said them anyway. 'He's dead.'

I watched the black telephone cord move with my nods. I heard a car wipe the gravel drive outside. 'An asthma attack, while he was out walking. His puffer was in the car, but they were ten kilometres out.' My sister's voice, on the verge of tears, was high and strained. I didn't believe her.

'What happened?' I said. The words were like glue on my tongue.

'I just told you, asthma.' Stella was annoyed that I hadn't listened. Her anger gave her energy to speak. Her voice became easier and more even. 'He died in hospital last night, but they didn't ring until today, as if we're not even his family. Not only that, he's back in Brisbane, or on the Gold Coast at least. He's been there for six months. Six fucking months. I'm going over to Mum's now. Get home as soon as you can. Scott?' I don't know if I said anything. 'I know, it's terrible. We'll never get over it, ever.'

Stella hung up. I stood at the end of the corridor with the receiver at my ear and listened to the engaged signal. I closed my eyes.

chapter**ten**

It was mid-morning now and sunlight had come through the motel room window onto the top of Emily's hair. She lay on her belly with a pillow under her chest, her head resting on her hands. I asked if she wanted a break. 'No,' she said, 'go on. As long as you're willing.' She said it tenderly. I wanted to go over to her, tell her this was the end, there was no more story. But I'd started now and the only thing I could do was to keep going.

The Duntroon CO pulled some strings to get me home. I wound up on a troop carrier on its way to north Queensland. I arrived at Amberley just before dawn, after four hours rattling around the hold where the engine noise drowned out my thoughts.

Stella was waiting at the airbase gates. She walked towards the checkpoint, stopped a few paces away and looked as if she might fall over into my arms for a moment before she straightened. 'Jesus fucking Christ,' she said. 'You're never going to believe the story.' She drove me to Mum's unit at Toowong. The sky was pink by the time we arrived. I was still in uniform. Mum had been up all night. She was in jeans and a sweatshirt, drinking black coffee. Her hair was a grey frizz, her face drawn. 'My baby,' she started to cry as she pulled me down into a hug. 'I'm so sorry, darling.' She rubbed the back of my head.

At first I pulled away from her hug. She wiped the tears from her cheeks. 'God, what have they done to you? Your beautiful curls,' she said. 'And those clothes, they look wrong.' I was still in my greens.

'That's Duntroon for you,' I said, trying to sound cheery. But seeing Mum, it finally hit me that Dad was gone. 'Oh, Mum, what are we going to do?' I said, and I know I sounded like a little kid. 'Shoosh,' she said softly. 'We'll be all right.' I buried my head in her neck and smelled her coffee smell.

Later that morning, just before ten am, I sat down with Stella at a table in a small meeting room at the Gold Coast branch of Eternal Rest Funerals in Nerang. We'd crawled down the Pacific Highway where roadworks slowed traffic to a halt. Stella listened to Bruce Springsteen's *Born in the USA* on the way down. Bruce was loud, so there was no chance to talk. I'd felt edgy, and thought it was because the traffic jam might make us late.

We weren't late, in the event. We were early. We'd just sat down and were taking in the décor — soothing pink vertical drapes giving onto a concrete enclosure, pink walls too, to keep us calm, pink flowers in a vase — when we were joined by a young woman with three

children in tow. She introduced herself simply as
Marion. I knew Marion was the person who'd phoned
Stella to tell her Dad had died. Stella had asked Marion
how she'd known Dad. 'I'm his wife,' she'd said,
affronted, according to Stella. Dad married Marion the
week after he divorced Mum, a year to the day after he
left us. So Stella was right; there had been someone else.

Marion was a lecturer in environmental studies at
Griffith University in Brisbane but living in the Gold
Coast hinterland with Dad, who was stationed at the
Canungra Jungle Training Centre. She'd met Dad soon
after we moved to Brisbane, when Dad went to talk to
students about Army life as part of a recruitment drive.
They used to get veterans to do that in the universities.
I don't think it convinced anyone to join up, but the Army
was like that. According to Stella, Marion's specialist area
was peace studies and she'd gone to Dad's lecture to
heckle. 'Go figure,' Stella said to me. Mum hadn't seemed
to care about Marion. 'I told you she knew,' Stella said.
'Those two are fucking weird.' I didn't know which two
she meant, and I didn't ask.

Marion was long-limbed and thin with almost black
eyes and black hair tied back. 'I'm so sorry,' she said, as
if it was all her fault, then looked down and away. I was
horrified to think she might cry. Two little boys stood
either side of her like guards, holding an arm each. In her
lap was the baby, like a shield between us. I stared at the
baby. 'Didn't you know?' Marion said to Stella, who
must have been staring too.

'No, we didn't know,' Stella said. 'Dad...' she
trailed off.

Marion seemed about to respond but closed her mouth and looked past Stella and me to the concrete wall outside. No one said anything for several moments. Finally Marion swallowed hard and spoke. 'This is Michael, who's six,' she said as she put her arm around the taller boy, 'and Jason, who'll be five next week. Won't you?' Jason stared at Stella and me. 'And this is Candice.' She jiggled the baby on her knee. 'Who's one. Don't suck, darling.' She pulled Candice's hand from her face. Candice made as if to cry but stopped and grinned instead.

It only registered in stages that Candice was our sister, half our sister, our half-sister. She was dark with dark eyes like her mother, and chubby and featureless as babies often are. I couldn't get a sense of Dad from her. When I remarked to Stella later how weird it felt to be confronted with a half-sister I never knew I had, Stella said it didn't matter, and that Candice was about as much our sister as Dad was our father.

'And you,' Marion said as she released Candice to the care of her half-brothers on the floor. 'You're Scotty.' Marion smiled at me, and her smile had no malice or insincerity that I could see. Stella had told me Marion didn't want us there. Stella had to insist. I could feel Stella next to me, glaring across the table.

I realised I hadn't spoken. 'Yes,' I said. 'Scott. Hello.' I felt I had a big hole in the middle of myself and you could see straight through me to the chair back. I couldn't seem to react to anything quickly enough.

Like Mum, Marion was soft-spoken but where Mum was calm no matter which planet she was beaming in from, Marion was flighty and kept reporting back like a

little pecking bird. I couldn't picture her with Dad. He'd
think she was shy. She wore those peasant clothes that
were fashionable in the late seventies, even though we
were now passing the mid-eighties, and she smelled of
something sweet, like an Indian restaurant. She looked
not much older than Stella, who had just turned twenty-
one. Stella said Marion should have been dating me,
not Dad, we'd be closer in age, although I learned later
she was twenty-six. Occasionally Marion looked up at
me and quickly looked away when our eyes met. Once
she held my gaze and said, 'You're just like him, you
know, you could be brothers.'

We'd almost run out of conversation when we were
joined by a middle-aged woman who made a grand
entrance from double doors at the opposite end of the
room. Her name was Dulcie, she said, as she took her
place at the head of the table between us, and Dulcie was
a Grief Consultant. Dulcie the Grief Consultant opened
a vinyl binder full of plastic inserts and slid it Marion's
way. On the table in front of Dulcie there was a
clipboard with a form on one side and a notepad on the
other. She said there needn't be anything difficult
between mixed families, and smiled and nodded at each
of us in turn. She said Michael and Jason were bewt-ee-
full boys in-deed, and baby Candice was gorge-ee-ossal.

To me, Dulcie was the antithesis of Stella. Stella
appeared hard after what had happened, but only to cover
a softness that would kill her if she let you too near
it. Dulcie appeared soft. She had a blond beehive and
one of those big bosoms that looked like it could
provide succour. But Dulcie wasn't soft at all. She was a

shagpile carpet with a concrete underlay. If you fell on her, you'd surely bruise. She had no true sympathy in any part of her.

Michael and Jason were taking apart the pink floral arrangement on the coffee table in the corner and feeding the petals to Candice. One of them knocked the vase onto the floor. Marion and I jumped, Stella scowled, and Dulcie continued her introductory spiel without missing a beat. Moments later, an attendant came through the double doors and cleaned up the mess. I don't know how Dulcie managed to call for help. I kept feeling like I wasn't really in the room, I was floating on the ceiling in one of those near-death experiences, and I was watching the four of us have a meeting to talk about my father's death from up there on the ceiling, and it all seemed incredibly funny, like a situation comedy.

It was Stella who'd told me Marion was an academic, but Marion looked too young and timid to be responsible for anything like a classful of university students. I figured she must have something in reserve because Dad would have blown her away if she was as shy as she acted. She seemed nervous about the meeting, biting her fingernails while Dulcie lectured us, frowning whenever she was asked a direct question, as if this was some sort of exam and she wasn't sure she'd studied enough. Dulcie addressed Marion almost exclusively, seeking details ranging from Dad's family background, which Marion recited perfectly, to his funeral preferences, which she also knew by rote. Stella and I might as well not have been there. Dulcie wrote things on her form as she went.

Eternal Rest Funerals made a whole stack of different coffins, from tiny white models for dead babies to mahogany brass-handled specials with real silk lining. Stella said later it was a cacophony of coffins. I didn't laugh. Marion let Dulcie go through the merits and disadvantages of just about every adult model, her eyes darting round the room, then picked the basic box. It was selected by price, as everything turned out to be. She picked a plastic crucifix for the top of the coffin instead of a wreath. It was the cheapest ornamentation they did.

'If there are any outstanding accounts Dad didn't have time to pay, we'll look after them,' I said suddenly. Dulcie swung from the chest towards me, her beehive and bosom moving as one. She stared at me as if I was a dog that had talked.

I didn't make the offer out of generosity. I didn't have any money to give them anyway. It would have to come from Stella, whose glare I caught in my peripheral vision and did my best to ignore. To me, it was simply a way I might reclaim some part of Dad. While I had their attention, I kept going. 'And maybe we should have something different for his coffin. I think Dad would have liked a hardwood.' Marion's choice was wood-veneered chipboard with gold painted plastic handles. The Jag had solid walnut panels on the dash and leather upholstery. I knew Dad would want a good coffin, with real brass handles and silk lining. I was in a kind of fug, I realised later, not quite aware of what his death meant but wanting to hold on to some part of him. The trappings were all I could grasp for, and even they were being stolen from me.

'The estate will cover outstanding accounts.' Marion

frowned. Her eyes held mine until I looked away. 'I like what we've already selected.'

Dulcie took this as the final word. 'Religion?' she said to Marion.

'He's Roman Catholic,' Marion said. 'And our local priest will say the funeral mass.'

Dulcie said, 'Are we burying or cremating?'

'It's a burial,' Marion said. 'He has a plot at Yeronga.'

'Was he a serviceman?' Dulcie said. Marion nodded. 'You didn't mention that over the phone. Normally, someone from Army Liaison would be here.'

'He doesn't want a military funeral,' Marion said.

'Graveside service?' Dulcie asked. Marion shook her head.

'Excuse me,' I said. 'Dad also talked to me about his funeral.' He must have told me a dozen times how it would be. A lone piper plays 'Amazing Grace' on a distant hill ahead of a twenty-one gun salute. The bugle does 'The Last Post' and the Brigadier speaks. They bring Dad's coffin to the grave service in a gun carriage. Afterwards, they fold the flag and hand it to Mum. 'He always said he'd have a military funeral.'

'He was proud of his service,' Marion agreed. 'But he didn't want the Army involved in his funeral. He'd changed since you saw him.' I looked to Stella for support. She said nothing. I was relieved I'd thought to bring a notebook. I took a record of everything said. Marion stared at my notebook.

'When did he tell you this?' I said.

Marion looked surprised at the question. 'It's what he's always said.'

The attendant who'd cleaned up the vase came back and whispered something to Dulcie, who apologised and exited to take an urgent phone call. I had no idea what could be urgent about grief consultancy, but there you are.

Marion said to me, 'He so much wanted to see you.'

Stella exhaled loudly. I said, 'Did he say that?'

Marion nodded. 'Many, many times, Scott. He was devastated that you cut off from him after he and your mother split up.' I looked at Stella and she at me.

'Cut off from him?' Stella said. 'Given up for adoption more likely.'

'Yes,' Marion said, ignoring Stella. 'He'd have loved to have you stay with us.'

When Marion said that he wanted to see me, I felt panicky, as if I might lose control. I breathed in and held it. Dad told stories about me at Michael's age, Marion said, what a smart kid I was, how I was the best speller in my class, which amazed Dad because he couldn't spell to save himself, even as an adult, and yet I was brilliant at it. 'You're a swimmer, aren't you?' Marion said to me. Her eyes were so kind. I nodded. 'He said you were really something. He heard you were off to Duntroon too. That must be coming up soon, is it?' I told her I was in first year, and then had a terrible urge to show off about my school results, which were nothing to show off about anyway.

Dulcie came back into the room and apologised before she looked at each of us in turn and said, 'Now, where were we?' She turned a page back on her clipboard. 'Yes.' She frowned. 'Will anyone want to … view the body?' This was such a delicate matter, Dulcie said it almost inaudibly and made a little pink ring out of her mouth.

'No,' said Stella and Marion.

'Yes,' I said, at the same time. 'I want to.' I don't even know why I said it. We weren't the kind of family who examined our dead, and I certainly wasn't suspicious that things weren't as they should have been. It was just that everything seemed so unreal. I think I wanted to shock myself, to show myself he'd really gone.

'We can easily arrange —'

'That's not a good idea,' Marion interrupted Dulcie. She was frowning hard. 'It'll be a terrible shock to you, Scotty. You haven't seen him in a long time. He's been sick with asthma. He's lost weight.'

'Quite frankly, that's none of your business,' Stella said. 'If Scott wants to see our father, he will, thanks very much.'

Dulcie said we mustn't worry, and that for those family members who wanted a viewing, she'd arrange for him to be available, as if it were an appointment she'd be putting in his diary. When would suit us, she needed to know; the diary was already pretty packed. I made a time for the following afternoon, and the meeting was over.

'I really don't think it's a good idea, Stella,' Marion said. 'Scotty will hardly recognise him.'

'We'd hardly recognise him alive,' Stella said. 'But if Scott wants to see his father's body, that's none of your business, is it?'

'What's with the notebook?' Stella said in the car afterwards. We'd watched Marion pile her three kids and their stuff into an old Fiat 124 I was sure Dad must have picked for her; she didn't look like a Fiat driver at heart. Stella stared hate while I waved weakly. I felt almost sorry for Marion. She'd said to take care when she left us and wished me all the best with Duntroon. She told me we'd all move on eventually. There were tears in her eyes and she put her hand on my arm like a friend might.

'I wanted to make sure I didn't miss anything,' I said to Stella. We drove out of the funeral home gates and through the little town of Nerang, past Super-Chicken and Moreton Hire and back onto the Pacific Highway, which was now at a virtual standstill in the opposite direction from our trip down, just in time for the trip home. Almost immediately the scene inside became less real in my mind. When I tried to visualise it later, it was like one of those art films where they've changed the colour mix to brighten the picture. All pinks and oranges and greens, no brown or grey. Other than that, I felt perfectly normal. The last thing I was thinking was that Dad was gone forever.

'Miss what?' Stella said. I didn't know. 'God, I hated that. It was like we didn't have a role, even though he was our dad. I feel sick.' Stella wound down her window. She was moving through the gears, looking for a chance to change lanes.

'Watch out!' Stella had veered onto the shoulder. She shifted back into her lane too fast and nearly lost control. 'Marion said he wanted to see us. I always wondered, you know, if he felt guilty about leaving and if we'd just called him, it would have—'

'That is complete and utter bullshit. He left us. He couldn't have given less of a fuck. When I finished nursing, he didn't even come to my graduation.'

'Stella, he didn't know—'

'I know what I'm talking about, all right? He had every fucking chance, believe me. God, Scott, the bastard came back here and didn't even bother calling us.' Stella's voice wasn't steady. She looked at me. 'I mean, I don't care, I'm over it, but you're just a kid and he was your father.'

'What about the funeral?' I said. 'He wanted a military funeral. We ought to do something about that at least, Stella, call his CO.'

'Fuck him. I hope he goes straight to the Army's version of hell.' She laughed harshly. 'Which should be like normal hell except everyone stands up straight to burn.'

chaptereleven

When I asked Stella to drop me off, she said she wanted to come with me to the chapel after all, 'to look after you, Scotty.' She'd taken to using Marion's nickname for me. Stella and I had spent the night at Mum's, the three of us huddled around the small dining table not saying much. I was relieved Jim wasn't there. He was Mum's new boyfriend, a psychologist she'd met at uni. Jim was one of those touchy-feely guys who pretend to be good listeners but spend most of the time talking. He had a deep, believable voice and he used to try to be my buddy, for Mum's sake probably. I couldn't stand him, although Stella said Mum was happy and I wanted to be mature about it.

When Stella told Mum I was going to see Dad's body, Mum said she could understand I'd want to. She wasn't coming to the funeral, she said. It was as if Mum had cut out the part of herself that had been with Dad and had put it away somewhere. Stella told me Mum was relieved after Dad left. Mum had told her it was like walking on crutches and not knowing she didn't need them until they were knocked out from under her.

After Mum went to bed Stella and I sat up drinking rum and Coke for a while until Stella's boyfriend, Josh, a resident at the hospital, dropped over. Josh was about three on from the American doctor Stella had been dating when I left for Duntroon. Josh brought a pipe and some seeds and he and Stella went out onto Mum's verandah for a smoke. Stella said I could join them if I liked. I'd only smoked marijuana once at that stage, and on that occasion nothing happened except I felt sick and got a sore throat.

I went with Stella and Josh out onto the verandah which overlooked our quiet street. They were making jokes about Marion; I didn't join in. I took a long pull on the pipe when my turn came, hoping maybe for the oblivion that drug education classes promised. I held my breath in for what seemed like minutes. I felt the drug go from my lungs to my heart and from there to my brain where it fizzled out. I figured nothing was going to happen again. Then all of a sudden my brain caught fire and everything started connecting into this enormous web: Dad's dying, his leaving, Marion turning up, him being nothing like she said he was. Join the dots, finish the sentence, find Wally. It was on the tip of my tongue, the solution to the whole puzzle, when Stella hit on it. She said Marion was tricking us. 'How do we know she knows Dad?' Stella said. She seemed to be talking slowly, like a cassette running out of battery power. 'She could have found him dying in a hospital and made up the story about being his new wife. Maybe she didn't know anything about him.'

'Which is why she wouldn't know he'd want a military funeral,' I said, amazed at how right this all seemed. Why didn't I think of it before, I thought.

'Yeah,' said Josh. 'And I bet she got him to change his will so she gets a big fat inheritance as well.'

When I fell into bed a long time later, I lay awake and listened to the night. Before dawn a bush curlew cried and I got the shakes. I pulled a sheet around me and formed myself into a tight ball. I didn't get up until the bush curlew was long gone and the sun was high in the sky outside the window.

'That was another thing,' I said in the car on the way to the chapel. Stella and I had been listing all the differences between Dad and the man described by Marion. 'Dad never called me Scotty. He hated nicknames.' I noticed my knee had started jiggling of its own accord and I couldn't keep my hands still. When we stopped at traffic lights, I willed them to turn green. I felt all on edge and anxious.

Stella had taken the next step. Marion had moved from being a cruiser of wards in search of a likely case to a murderess. 'I've got it,' Stella was saying. 'She's been feeding him sugar pills instead of his steroids, which would be impossible to detect. She knows this will bring on an asthma attack. She waits. Every time they go somewhere, she hides the puffer. Finally, it pays off. Bingo, she snaffles him.'

'Dad's asthma was never bad enough for that,' I said.

'Bullshit. They don't put you on steroids for nothing.'

'But what's the motive, Watson?'

'I don't know. Maybe he gave her all his money.'

'He didn't have any.'

'Okay then, she insured him for millions, like in *Double Indemnity*, and then did the steroid thing. It wouldn't take much. Just hold back the puffer long enough so he overdoes it.'

'Do you really think she'd do something like that?'

'Of course not, but we don't know, that's the point, Scott. We don't know her from a bar of soap. All we know is Dad's dead. She can tell us whatever she likes about him now and we have to swallow it. I don't trust her, I know that much.' But Stella didn't trust anyone, so I didn't think twice about that.

We arrived back at the funeral home gates, veering left this time, away from the office where we'd met Dulcie, towards a smaller cream brick building that looked nothing like a chapel, except that it sported a neon cross and a sign that said 'Chapel — Non-Denominational'. Behind the chapel squatted a larger concrete structure, with high fume chimneys and stacked air conditioning plant covering its roof. We were greeted at the door of the chapel by a burly attendant. When I asked him what the building behind was for, he said it was the mortuary, where they could store fifty bodies, apparently. 'Plus our treatment rooms,' he added after some thought. I didn't know what treatment bodies needed but I wasn't about to ask. The attendant wore a dark suit with a white shirt like a bouncer at a nightclub. 'Loves his job,' Stella whispered to me.

As we walked into the vestibule from the bright carpark, I thought I was blacking out until my eyes adjusted. The attendant remained at the entrance watching us like a store detective. As we walked up the centre aisle I saw a door to the left which I figured connected the chapel with the mortuary building. I thought about the bodies in the mortuary. I even said to Stella, 'Imagine if they brought out the wrong guy, and we farewelled someone else's dad.'

'Like Husband Number One,' Stella said. 'You know he died in weird circumstances too?' We'd reached halfway and had stopped. We could see the plain brown coffin Marion had selected at the head of the aisle. Neither of us moved forward.

'Who told you that?'

'Remember Dad's friend Kerry Vance, the car guy? He asked me out a couple of times. I never went, but I rang him after Marion first called. I wanted to find out who she is. He knows her, he said. Apparently her first husband was killed in a car accident on the Sunshine Coast. One of those single car accidents where he ran off the road and rolled.' Stella sighed and looked at me. 'Well, here goes nothing,' she said, and took off up the aisle, with me following several steps behind.

The chapel had no altar, just a glass-tiled wall that looked out to a garden of plastic plants. Birds chirped over a small PA system. I had this bizarre picture of a duo of little birds standing at a mike singing away like the Everly Brothers. We walked slowly, stopping again a few metres back from the open coffin. I kept forgetting to breathe in. I was slightly dizzy. Stella turned and looked at me. She swallowed and plunged forward, so she saw him before I did. She let out a little sigh as she grabbed me and pulled me forward. I took one long look and laughed out loud.

I said, 'It's not him.'

'I know, they look so different, don't they?' Stella said.

'No, I mean, it's not our father.'

'What are you talking about?' Stella's voice was loud as a stage whisper.

The man in the coffin had dark brown hair like Dad's, only straighter and more receded at the front. His complexion was sallow where Dad's was blueish. I suppose, looking back, receding hair was natural and a sallow complexion would be the least you'd expect of death. But I was sure the body wasn't my father.

The man wore a pink polo-neck sweater and a navy blue pinstripe suitcoat, neither of which Dad had ever owned. Dad hated polo-necks, he found them irritating, and at any rate he'd have been in uniform. I knew the clothes could have been organised by Marion, but when I looked at the man's face, especially his chin, I was sure they'd made a mistake. He was not my father. 'They've brought the wrong body,' I said to Stella. Before she could respond, I was heading towards the back of the chapel. 'Excuse me!' I called out. 'This is the wrong person.' I was talking too loudly in the small space, I knew, but I didn't seem able to talk more softly. 'We want to see our father!' I yelled. I had the most ridiculous notion that the body we'd been shown was that of Marion's other husband, probably because Stella had mentioned him.

The attendant came towards me and we met in the middle of the chapel. He kept a hand on my shoulder as he took a yellow slip of paper from his pocket. 'Settle down. Let's just check what we got here.' I could see I'd rattled him. He stared at the sheet of paper in his left hand, his right hand flat on my chest to keep me where I was. 'Allan Goodwin, that's who you've got. Number twenty-seven, see? Allan Goodwin. Is that who you want?'

Stella was behind me. 'Yes, it is him,' she said. 'Scott, it's Dad.'

'No it's not, Stella,' I said. 'They've brought the wrong guy.'

'You want me to check?' he said to Stella.

'No, that won't be necessary,' Stella said. She looked at me. 'Yeah, okay, if you can, that'd be good.' He asked us to wait outside. I imagined cadavers had toe tags like they did in the movies and he'd have to remove the guy's shoes to confirm it was the wrong person. That's how convinced I was.

Stella led me out of the chapel into the hot sun. She said, 'What the fuck's with you?' I could see she was feeling the pressure.

'It's not him,' I said calmly. 'You wait.'

I was head and shoulders taller than Stella, but she'd been bigger than me for most of our childhoods, easily able to beat me up, and we acted as if this was still the case. She grabbed my arm and yanked it hard and looked up at me. 'I know you're upset. You were probably closer to him than any of us. But it is Dad. I'd know that bastard anywhere.'

'I'm telling you, it's not, Stella. It's just a guy.' I was amazingly calm.

'Fuck, as if this isn't hard enough. He's dead, Scott. We're alone, and you better face that. He left us for that bitchface bitch and then his dirty little life ended on a trail out bush. He's a shithead and that's the shithead in that coffin.'

'No, Stella,' I persisted.

She slapped my face. 'Get a hold of yourself!' she yelled. 'We're here to see our father's body!'

I could taste blood in my mouth where my top lip had hit a tooth. I wondered if Stella was right. Surely they couldn't mix the bodies up. I hadn't had a good look, just glanced before I'd moved away. Stella was frowning, close to tears. I felt calm. Maybe too calm, I thought. Maybe this was denial. Maybe I should listen to Stella. 'Are you sure?' I said.

'Yes, I'm sure. I've seen a lot more dead bodies than you have.' She took a big breath in and blew it out. 'Sorry I hit you,' she said.

The attendant came out of the chapel. I noticed he didn't have a neck; his head went straight into his shoulders. I kept noticing small details like that, and remembering them. Later, the scene was nothing but those details. 'It's Allan Goodwin is who it is,' the attendant said. 'I got my supervisor and we checked. You're here to see Allan Goodwin?'

'Yes,' Stella said, 'it'll be all right now.' She took my arm and held on to me on the way back into the chapel and I let her. The attendant waited in the rear with his hands joined respectfully over his groin.

Stella and I remained in an embrace of sorts as we walked up the aisle for the second time. We reached the coffin, her hand gripping my right arm, my left arm around her waist. I'm not sure who was comforting whom but I kept my arm around her. We stood over the coffin for a long moment. I took him in properly. Stella must have thought I was coming to grips with reality. At some stage she broke away from me and went to some private place with the man in the coffin, steadying herself on the front pew and sighing softly.

I wasn't coming to grips with reality, not with Stella's reality anyway. I was looking at the guy's chin, or lack of a chin. Dad's jaw is like a rock carved onto the bottom of his face. He had this chin you noticed. I could accept that Marion dressed him to suit herself. But the chin in the coffin was not Dad's chin, or at least I didn't think it was. When I looked more carefully I could see that the guy was a little like Dad, lean, maybe handsome in life. He wasn't chinless either, but his chin wasn't a prominent feature like on Dad. He was younger than Dad would have been by then, I thought. It was hard to tell what he'd have looked like alive. I'd have known him on the street if I saw him, I think. I was sure he wasn't my father.

I'd brought my camera which Stella had made me leave in the car. 'I really want a photo,' I said.

She was relieved I wasn't going to keep going with the 'bring me my real father' routine. 'If you must.'

On the way out to the car I beckoned the guy at the door and walked him outside with me. He kept looking back at Stella in the chapel as if she might steal something. 'How did you know the one we wanted is the one you had?' I said.

He smiled sheepishly. 'To be honest, I've never had anything like this happen before,' he said. 'I didn't know what to do. We give them an identification bracelet and write their name on the thigh as soon as we pick them up from the hospital so we don't get them mixed up. But apparently our mortuary attendants take photos as well. We checked the fridge to make sure you had twenty-seven. Then I checked the ID, and the boss went and got his photo.'

'Thanks,' I said. So this was no simple mistake. I took my camera bag from the car. Stella was sitting in the front pew with her arms folded. She told me to hurry up. I took two shots of the face, leaning into the coffin to try to get as much profile as I could. I didn't use a flash as that would have attracted the attention of the guy at the door. I hoped my hands were steady enough for the shutter speed. Stella told me again to be quick. I didn't think she'd be willing to sit the dead man up for me so I could get a proper profile. By now I was so convinced it wasn't Dad I was casual around this body. He was a stranger to me. I took another shot using the coffin side to steady the camera, and a final shot of the hands before Stella stood up and said it was enough. She came over to the coffin, took a last look, scowled, and turned and walked out, assuming I'd follow.

After we left she said, 'You know what I felt seeing him there? I felt powerful. When he was alive he wouldn't let us have anything to do with him. Now he's dead, he can't stop me.' In the chapel Stella had put her hand flat on his forehead. 'God, he's cold,' she'd said.

'I went to see him in Melbourne,' Stella said in the car on the way back to Mum's. 'I wrote to him at the end of the year he left. Kerry Vance gave me the address. I was driving to Adelaide with a group of girls from work. We stopped in Melbourne. He hadn't replied to the letter, but I called him anyway, at Vic Barracks.'

'Why didn't you tell me?'

'We met for lunch at a pub in town. He paid. He said he was glad to see me, it had been difficult for all of us, he and Mum had grown apart, and that was no reason to hate him. He said he'd met someone else, someone we'd like. We had wine with our lunch, like we were hoity-toity.'

'Did he want to see me too?'

'It was bullshit, Scott. He was bullshit. He said he couldn't stay long. He had to get back to work, but he'd call.' Stella smiled. 'He never did.' She took a breath and held it for a few moments. 'The girls and I stopped in Sydney on the way home. We got really pissed on OP rum and threw each other into the fountain in Hyde Park. I met this guy. We had so much fun, we …' She bit her bottom lip. It was the closest I ever saw her to tears over Dad.

chapter**twelve**

'The story gets difficult from here,' I said to Emily. 'This is where you regret you met me.' I said it as a joke, but I meant it too.

'You're in for a surprise then, because I don't do regrets.' Emily could make fun of just about anything, but she never made fun of me. 'I'll always be glad I met you.'

I sighed heavily. The morning after the chapel, I told Emily, I went into the city and hung around the photo shop while they processed the film. There were a few shots of Mum and Grandad from a weekend we had at the farm before I left home, and then some Duntroon photos — me in camouflage gear, looking like someone I didn't know, sunset on the hills, a pinky dawn, and Colin Rawlins at morning roll call, small and skinny compared to the burly boys either side of him, his rifle askew and shirt sleeves unevenly rolled. Then came the three photographs of the dead man's face. They were so blurred I couldn't make anything from them. 'Can you get them any clearer than this?' I said to the guy at the counter, pointing to the last and best of them, knowing that it was camera movement not processing that had caused the problem. When I looked up, the guy was staring at me. 'What?' I said.

'Nothing,' the guy said. 'No, we can't get them any clearer.' He told me the price. The other two staff had stopped what they were doing to watch me. I guess they'd all seen the photographs, including the ones of the dead guy. There was probably something vaguely weird about photographing the dead. I paid and left.

At Mum's place I found a few photographs of Dad in an album that Stella's purges hadn't destroyed. The first was taken when Dad was about ten, at his father's house in Melbourne. Dad's in a school shirt and serge shorts, sleeves tortured up past his elbows, tie pulled down but not quite off, socks at his ankles. He's standing in front of an old Austin A40 holding what looks like a dead snake that's as long as he is. He seems proud of himself.

The other two shots were more recent, taken at the Gold Coast a year or two before he left us. In one, he and Stella are side by side, facing the camera, both of them sucking hard on banana Paddlepops, their favourites. Dad and Stella stand the same way, hips forward, legs apart, arms out from their bodies, Dad at attention, Stella managing to make it look like a slouch. In the second shot, closer up, Stella's looking past Dad at someone out of the frame. Dad's looking at Stella as if they're having a Paddlepop-eating competition. His Paddlepop is a few inches from his mouth. He's either just taken or is about to take a bite. His hair, long in the fringe, is blown back off his face in a breeze. It was a good profile, which I figured was just what I needed.

The photographs were taken on a holiday. We used to stay in these Army units that were right near the airport at Coolangatta. Dad would swim all morning while Stella and I played volleyball with other Army kids. I remember one day we watched Dad swim right out past the waves to where the water was still. He became smaller and smaller and then I couldn't see him anymore. After Stella had gone up to the unit and all the other kids had left, I stayed there on the beach, pretending to muck around, but every now and then peering at the sea to find him, getting more and more worried as time went by. After two hours the current carried him to shore, a long way from where I waited. He came marching along the beach towards me. I was so relieved I couldn't keep from crying. He smiled, and put his hand on my head and said, 'I'd never drown without asking you first, kid.' It took me a week to get over the sunburn.

The beach photographs could have been taken on the holiday Julie Holt came along on, the last holiday we'd had. Stella said Dad had touched Julie's breast. I stared at the photographs of Dad and Stella but found no clues either way.

I put the second beach shot next to the clearest of the shots I'd taken at the chapel. The man's head was three-quarter profiled against the cream sateen, at almost the same angle as the Gold Coast shot of Dad. Dad's forehead was higher and more prominent than that of the man in the coffin and his hair was thicker and more wavy. The dead man had a smaller chin, as far as I was concerned. Dad's chin jutted out, just as I'd remembered. They were not the same person, I was positive.

Stella came over that night and after Mum had gone to bed I took the two photographs from my pocket and put them side by side on the table. 'Is this supposed to be the old man?' Stella picked up the coffin shot. At first I thought she'd finally seen what I'd seen. I was about to say so when she said, 'Gross!' She held the photograph a few inches from her eyes, as if her eyes were in the wrong and not the camera. 'God, it's blurry. I thought you were a photographer.' She put the coffin shot on the table and picked up the other one. 'Was this one taken at Bribie?'

'You think they're both Dad?' I said.

Stella looked at me. 'Of course they're both Dad. You took that yesterday, right?' I didn't say anything. 'And this is from Bribie, isn't it? Or the Gold Coast. Who else could they be?'

'Look at their chins, Stella. They're different.'

'You can't even seen his chin in the coffin, Scott.' She put the photo on the table. 'Is that the reason you took pictures yesterday?' She eyed me carefully. 'Scott, he's dead. I know it's hard for you. I'm sorry I overreacted. But you can't keep talking like this. You're scaring me.'

'I just wanted to be sure,' I lied. 'You're the one who said we shouldn't trust Marion.'

Stella slipped the photographs back into the envelope. 'Yeah, but I was mucking around. Weren't you?' I nodded yes. 'Are you really okay now?' I assured her I was fine. She handed the envelope over and left soon after.

But I wasn't okay. To me, it was as if all my night-time fantasies of what might have happened were becoming real. I didn't have proof, just my own conviction. Marion's description didn't match what I knew of Dad, but that didn't prove anything. I hadn't seen him for three years. And Stella, who was ten times as sharp as me normally, couldn't see what I saw in the photographs. If the body we saw and Dad were alike enough to fool Stella, those photographs would certainly fool someone who hadn't even met Dad. I needed something more. I lay awake in bed, thinking about what to do next.

At nine am, I called the funeral home and said I'd like to see my father's body once more. I could tell Dulcie was put out. This wasn't included in the price. I made my voice choke up and said, 'I want to say goodbye alone.' Still unmoved, Dulcie conceded. She said she could arrange for him to be on view that afternoon at three.

Having finished my grieving before it started, I ignored as much as I could of the funeral arrangements that seemed to have gripped Stella. She was using them as an opportunity to fight Marion. I felt it was important to keep moving forward. At first I said I wouldn't go to the funeral, but Stella told me I had to. 'To show her, if nothing else,' Stella said, meaning Marion. While I made my plans, Stella argued on the telephone with 'her' about whose children would be listed first in the death notice, what we'd say by way of remembrance. Stella must have called me twenty times. 'Separate funeral notices, I've decided,' she said in one of these calls.

'Marion wants to say he was a loving father. He wasn't a loving father. I'm not having that in the notice. What do you think?'

'Surely we don't need two notices,' I said.

'Marion's going to put partner instead of husband. It sounds like a business relationship. She's weird, Scott. She doesn't want his Army friends there either.'

'What do you mean?'

'She told Dulcie to put in the death notice that it's a private service.'

'In that case, I'm with you. Let's have a separate funeral notice with details of where and when. He'd want his mates there.'

I found Kerry Vance in the phone book. 'Scott Goodwin.' He said it as a statement and loudly, as if he had to shout the entire distance from the Darling Downs' exchange.

I told him we hadn't seen Dad. 'He'd remarried,' I said, 'and we lost touch, but not by choice, sir.'

Dad always reckoned he was a man of many acquaintances and few friends, and those friends were lifelong and blood-loyal. Kerry Vance had been Dad's CO in Vietnam. Dad still called him sir to his face, even though Kerry had left the Army and Dad outranked him now in any case. I knew Kerry would want to help me, provided he thought I was on Dad's side.

'Understand completely,' Kerry Vance said. 'Your Dad and Marion stayed here a couple of times, when your dad was … in Brisbane, as a matter of fact.' He let out a quick laugh. 'Nothing's easy where your mother's concerned, is it?'

I didn't respond. 'The funeral's tomorrow, and I'd like to talk to you about a couple of things,' I said.

'Sure, no worries. Stella going?'

'Of course.'

'See you there.'

For my three o'clock meeting with the man in the coffin, I caught two buses and then walked nearly a kilometre from the highway exit, and for half of it I could smell something dead.

The attendant who'd looked after Stella and me came out of the chapel, in the same bouncer suit and possibly the same white shirt. It was a warm dry day. 'Back again?' he said, squinting in the sun.

'I won't be long,' I said. 'I came to say my last goodbye.' He nodded.

The bouncer stood at the door as he had the first time, which made what I wanted to do difficult. I walked up the aisle and stood at the coffin with my back to him. The dead man's hands were crossed over his chest like the hands of Dracula in the movies. I turned around and smiled. 'Hard to get used to him like this,' I yelled above the bird orchestra.

'I bet,' the attendant yelled back, thoughtfully.

I stood side-on, in line with the dead man's hips, as if taking a long last look. Only I didn't look at the dead man's face. I knew if I did I'd lose my nerve. I looked at the glass wall in front of me. My right hand was by my side. With my left hand, I reached into the coffin slowly, as if I might be going to rest my hand on his. The material of his coat felt cool to the touch. I unbuttoned the coat and found a belt. I undid the icy buckle and top button of the pants. I tugged at the zipper, trying not to move my upper arm too much. I got the zipper down and peeled back the pants on both sides. There was a gauze pad that went down between the man's legs. I peeled that back too, and used it to wedge the fly apart. The man wasn't even wearing jocks. They probably didn't bother; birth and death are without dignity. The guy had a lot of pubic hair, which I thought was a lighter brown than the hair on his head. It was dim in the chapel and hard to make out details. I could smell disinfectant and sweat; the sweat was probably mine. The bird orchestra continued its eternal loop.

I swallowed hard, took a breath in and grabbed the man's dick and balls and pulled them aside gently. His body had no give in it like living flesh does. I pushed the pants further down and tried to make out the man's right thigh. I bent down to get a closer look when I heard footsteps behind me in the short aisle. 'You right?' the attendant was calling out.

'Yes,' I turned and straightened. 'Just give me another moment, would you mind?'

The attendant was a third of the way up the aisle and still coming. I was exposing a dead guy, and I knew this was a pretty strange thing to be doing, if not a criminal offence. I moved my hand away from the body and looked at the attendant. He stopped where he was, halfway up the aisle now, and smiled helpfully. I was trembling with fear. When I was sure the attendant was stopping where he was, I turned back to the dead man. Instinctively, my eyes drifted to his face. I felt shame then, under my fear, as if I was trespassing. The man's dick and balls had flopped into their natural home between the legs. They looked so sad.

The attendant was still halfway up the aisle. I shoved the gauze back and started to rezip the fly, coughing to cover any noise. But the zip caught on something, gauze or hairs, I don't know. I gave a good pull then and something ripped. I heard footsteps behind me again. I didn't worry about the pants button and belt. I redid the coat button and pulled it down over the zip.

'Bye, Dad,' I said loudly and sobbed.

'Take all the time you need, mate.' The attendant was standing beside me. 'He's not going anywhere.'

chapter thirteen

The next day dawned a lie, hot and sunny when all the while it was planning to storm. I hadn't slept, and from the verandah of Mum's unit I watched a silver horizon bloom pink then orange before an edge of sun made me look away.

The funeral was at Our Lady of the Blessed Assumption where, according to Marion, she and Dad had worshipped. On one side of a carpark was a tiny wooden chapel built in the late nineteenth century when families first settled the Canungra valley, before the Army took over and created its jungle training centre. On the other side was one of those huge seventies barns with a soaring, sloping ceiling in praise of God, and room for hundreds of Catholics. This is where the funeral service was held. There were around twenty mourners other than us, bearded middle-aged men and skinny women in jeans who looked like Marion's friends from the university;

no one we knew. Marion had refused Stella's request for
a funeral notice, and the newspaper wouldn't let Stella
do anything without the permission of Dad's next-of-kin.
His next-of-kin was Marion, they told Stella. So there was
a death notice from Marion, and it said the funeral was for
close family and friends only.

The priest looked like a bearded, born-again version
of the ABC 'Countdown' host Molly Meldrum. He didn't
know Allan Goodwin well, he said. But tragedies were
made more tragic when one was struck down early in life
with something like asthma, which could be prevented.
'Sounds like an ad for Ventolin,' Stella whispered. We
were off to one side of the church. Marion was sitting in
the front row looking across at us. 'At these times,' the
priest said, 'we wonder what we must have done to deserve
such bitter loss.'

Stella got the giggles in the final hymn, which was
'Be Not Afraid' and not really funny. But Stella stood
beside me red-faced, biting her lip and snorting quietly.
I felt tense enough to laugh too, but managed to hold it
in. I didn't look towards Marion, but I could feel her eyes
on us.

Mum's little brother sat behind me and Stella. Uncle
Ben and I were born on the same day fifteen years apart,
and every year we'd had birthday parties together until he
went to live in New Zealand when he got married. He
and his wife Jacqui were staying with Gran and Grandad
for a few months. He was over to help with the farm.
I think Mum asked them to come to the funeral to look
out for Stella and me because Mum wouldn't be there
herself. Or perhaps Ben thought that's what you did with

family. He was that sort of guy. After the service he gave
Stella a big hug she didn't want. 'Hey, Scotto,' he said to
me, shaking my hand and pulling me into a loose
embrace. He kept his hand on my shoulder. 'Look at
you. Big lad now, eh?' He laughed. 'Why don't you come
up home with us tonight? Me and your Grandad are
shooting tomorrow.' I said I had too much to do before
I went back to Duntroon. 'Well, I wish you'd bloody visit
now and again. I could use the help.' I'd stayed with Ben
and Jacqui for holidays after Dad left. They had a little
organic dairy farm on the South Island. I promised him
I'd be over first chance I had.

Kerry Vance got up when the service was finished and
said that a few of the boys were putting on a wake at the
Advancetown Tavern. Marion told us she wouldn't come,
pointing to the kids. Outside I noticed her talking to
Kerry. Her arms were folded and she was shaking her
head. She looked frail and tired and as if she might cry at
any moment. Kerry had his hands on his hips. Occasionally he pointed his finger at her as if telling her off.
Stella said we should go to the wake, but I wasn't to offer
to pay for anything. Michael and Jason ran around the
mourners like maniacs. Candice bawled. The hearse took
off slowly, unaccompanied. No one but me even noticed.

The Advancetown Tavern was a chocolate brick affair
with plush pink-orange décor. The Canungra Hotel,
which was older, more atmospheric and had been the
watering hole of Dad and his mates when they were in
Canungra prior to Vietnam, had banned Army groups a
few months before after a brawl that had cost thousands
in repairs. So, Advancetown it was. When we arrived a

dozen soldiers and ex-soldiers were already drinking in the bar. I hadn't seen any of them at the service. They must have found out about the wake from Kerry via the veterans' grapevine. Dad's Vietnam mates formed a tight-knit group wherever we lived. It was something that set them apart from other soldiers, Dad said. We arrived just after eleven am. I'd never seen people drink so early in the day but if they were unaccustomed, it didn't show.

I noticed a small group from S-12 — Corporal Peter White, who'd worked for Dad, a captain I vaguely knew, and two or three others I didn't know. Like me, they were in their dress blacks. They stood around a table not drinking and looked as if they weren't planning to stay long. I was on my way over to talk to them when Kerry called me from the side of the bar. Light came through brown glass doors and spilled over the stacks of glasses in front of us. Kerry was in a light blue suit. The smell of Old Spice drifted off him.

'Now, before you start,' he said, 'I got something I have to tell you. Your dad contacted me before he died.' Kerry took a long pull from his beer that left a froth moustache he took a moment to lick off. He'd retired from the Army after Vietnam and had opened a vintage car restoration workshop. Dad always said a man could do worse. 'He knew what he was doing, sound mind and that, if you know what I mean.'

'Sir, I'm pretty sure Dad's not dead,' I said. 'That's what I wanted to tell you.'

He stared blankly at me. 'What are you talking about? We've just been to the funeral.'

'I went to see the body, and it wasn't Dad.'

'Of course it was him. Don't be bloody daft.'

'No, sir, it was someone else.'

'Listen, Scott, I saw your dad not two months ago. That's what I'm trying to tell you. He was sick. His asthma was real bad, he told me, worst he'd ever had. That's why they sent him back here from Melbourne, to recuperate. He'd lost a stack of weight, and he was a skinny bastard to start with. You should have seen him. Well, you did, obviously. I don't know why you did but you did.' He ordered another round from the bar and offered me one, forgetting or not caring that I was underaged. I asked for a rum and Coke. 'And I certainly wouldn't-a let a young girl like Stella near him. Must have nearly killed her.'

'But it wasn't him. I couldn't find the scar.'

'What?'

'The scar on his leg, from the operation, it wasn't there. Not only that, Dad wasn't circumcised and I think the man in the coffin was.'

'What the fuck are you talking about?'

'The body, I went to see the body and it was circumcised. Dad had a thing about it.' Dad reckoned men who hadn't been circumcised got infections unless they looked after themselves. Sex was better though, he told me once.

'How do you know the guy in the coffin was nicked?'

'I checked.'

'Jesus.' He looked at me. 'What, you pulled his pants down?'

'Sort of. I was looking for the scar on his leg.' Dad had been wounded in Vietnam. He had a long

scar from the top of his thigh where they'd removed a
piece of a mine.

'In front of Stella?'

'No, I went back on my own.'

'Did you?' He pulled his chin in and made a face.
'They got a name for that sort of thing.' He smiled.
I didn't join him. 'You sure that body was nicked?
Because if it was, your dad was, because the body was
your dad's. It fucken well had to be.'

'How can you be sure? I know it's incredible, but
something's wrong. I just know it.'

Kerry looked blankly at me. 'Give me a sec to take
this in,' he said. 'This wasn't what I was expecting.' He
ordered himself another beer. 'Dicks change when a man
carks. I've seen enough dead dicks to know what I'm
talking about.' He placed his beer on the bar and cupped
his hands, one on top of the other, as if they were still
holding a glass. 'They shrivel.' He squeezed his hands
into two fists. 'First thing to go. Did you actually see the
sheath?' When the dick had caught in the zip I'd felt
something, but I hadn't seen it clearly and then I'd had
to get out quickly. And it was the same with the scar. It
was so dim in the chapel, I could easily have missed it.
'He'd been dead a few days. He wouldn't have been stiff
anymore or anything.'

'No,' I said more confidently than I felt. 'This man
was circumcised and Dad wasn't.' Kerry went in the
chopper with Dad when Dad was injured. When they
got to the hospital, the doctor said they had to amputate
Dad's leg, but Kerry made them airlift Dad to Saigon for
a second opinion. Dad had been unconscious. He always

said he had Kerry to thank for the fact he could walk. Even after the operation, though, they'd said he'd never get full use back. But Dad had worked on it, and didn't even have a limp.

'You sure your dad wasn't circumcised, son? I just reckon you're wrong about that. Matter of fact, now I think of it, he and I used to have a laugh about it. He always said he'd get his kids done so they'd be the same as him.'

'I should know if my own father was circumcised.'

'But you're not sure, are you? You're not sure about that body, I can tell, and you're probably not even a hundred per cent sure about your dad either. If the body in the coffin was circumcised, then your dad was circumcised. If it wasn't circumcised, then your dad wasn't. Because that fucken body is your fucken dad, like or no. And the scar, well, maybe you weren't looking in the right place.' Kerry had been watching me as we spoke, even while he ordered drinks. He was right; it was dark. I wasn't sure enough.

'Listen, kid,' he said, 'you're the man of the house now, you gotta look after the girls. You can't be running off about this sort of shit.' I tried to interrupt. He put his hand up to stop me. 'I got something to say and it's not easy as it is, even without you going on with all this body stuff. Jee-suss. Way I see it, you thought you saw something and you didn't. You're upset, and people do stupid things when they're upset. Fuck, there's no way that body's anyone else's. You gotta stop talking like that or they'll put you away.' He smiled weakly and took a long pull on his beer, his hand held out in front to stop me talking.

'Your father left your mother and he was with someone else, and I happen to know he loved Marion and they were happy, whatever your mother and sister and you might feel personally. And whatever he did, and I don't know what he did exactly, but I do know he knew what he was doing. If you know what I mean.

'Marion was good for your dad. She's one of those rare birds, just takes people as she finds them, and that's exactly what old Clark needed. Whereas your mum … she was different is all I'll say. Nothing was ever good enough, if you know what I mean.' Kerry put his hand up as if I might argue this point. I didn't respond. 'Anyway, you gotta tell Stella and your mother they gotta respect a man's last wishes, which will be the wishes he put in his last will. That's what he asked me to tell you.'

'He asked you to tell me that? Me, specifically?'

'Sure, when I saw him, he said, tell Scott I know what I'm doing and tell him to make sure Stella and Anne don't do anything silly if something happens to me. He said you'd know what to do. Now, I know your dad had some insurance. And I reckon he'll make sure Mum's all right. So she should just sit tight and mind her own business, if you know what I mean.'

I didn't pay much attention to what he was saying. I was still thinking about the body. 'Look, Kerry, I know it sounds ridiculous, but I need your help. I know it wasn't Dad in that coffin. I'm absolutely sure. Even if I didn't hold his dick up and take a picture, I know what I know.' I took the two photographs from my coat pocket and placed them on the bar mat. 'I did get these.'

'What's that?' He was pointing to the shot of the man in the coffin.

'That's the dead guy,' I said. 'I know it's not a great shot.' I hadn't looked at the photograph of the dead man since I'd shown Stella. Already the image in my memory had started to fade. The blurred photograph looked pathetic.

Kerry picked it up and held it close to his eyes and squinted. He left the shot of Dad on the bar. 'This is your dad, Scott. I'm sorry, mate, but it's him. See, I saw him not long before he died, and this is what he looked like.'

My eyes moved to the other photo of Dad, the one taken at the beach. His grin jumped out at me and I felt this stab of pain that made me grab my middle and slump back onto a stool. I swallowed hard. 'I was think-ing about the missions he used to go on,' I managed to say. Kerry was still holding the shot of the dead guy but he was looking at me. His eyes softened. I tried to concentrate on what I was saying. 'Things Dad couldn't talk about. I wondered if the Army involved him in something and it went wrong and they can't say.' As I talked, the awful feeling abated. I didn't look at the shot of Dad at the beach again.

'What missions are you talking about?'

'I know S-12 is supposed to be anti-terrorist but he did other things as well, I'm sure he did. When I saw the body and it wasn't him, I wondered if he was in on some covert operation. I suppose it sounds stupid now.' Kerry looked at me as if the penny had finally dropped. 'I'm worried something happened to Dad and they've covered it up.'

'You mean the stuff he was doing in Asia?' I nodded. I didn't know what I meant. Kerry drained his glass and banged it on the bar to signal for another. 'Scott, I'm going to tell you something in total confidence, but before I do, you have to promise me it won't go anywhere else, and you'll leave this business with your dad alone after today.' I quickly nodded assent. Kerry ordered us both another round. We leaned into one another. 'You're right.' He looked around to check no one was listening. 'Your father worked on top secret stuff. We discussed some of it, but some he wouldn't even tell me about. That's how top bloody secret it was. Army Intelligence, contradiction in terms if you ask me, but he did stuff he couldn't tell anyone about. It wouldn't surprise me if he has been somewhere that's embarrassing, and he's been killed in the line of duty. The Army's covering it up because our guys weren't meant to be there.

'When I was in Korea, some of my boys got sent on reconnaissance into communist bloody China. They were killed by Chinese soldiers, but we had to say it had happened in the line of duty in Korea. I had to write to these boys' mums and lie. That's the fucken Army.'

'So, it isn't Dad's body.'

He picked up the photograph and looked at it again. 'That's pretty far-fetched, son. Looking at this, it's imposs-ible to tell. Maybe if there were bullet wounds. That's all I can think of. In that situation, they'd have to get a differ-ent body. Or maybe if he was blown away, like completely. That happens, you know. Boom!' He made an explosion with his hands. 'Gone. And you can get bodies easy. On the black market, I can get you anything you want.

'Course, that would explain the dick, wouldn't it? Like, the body's a guy who was nicked, your dad wasn't nicked, and they didn't figure on you checking.' Kerry was nodding as if to convince himself.

When we were kids, Kerry Vance showed us a copy of an amateur film of John F Kennedy's assassination, the famous one where a man in the crowd near the cavalcade opens an umbrella seconds after the first shot is fired. Kerry said the umbrella was the command to open fire. As JFK's head lurched forward then back, then slumped forward again, Kerry said there were too many angles of fire for a lone gunman. Kerry blamed the communists. Mr Maitland would have agreed about the umbrella being a signal, and about the conspiracy, but he would have blamed the CIA. Afterwards I asked Dad if he believed Kerry. Dad said he did, although Stella, who was sitting in the back seat with me, circled her ear with her finger, which meant cuckoo-land.

Kerry Vance was the one friend Dad trusted absolutely, and I didn't have anyone else to confide in. Stella hadn't believed me. I hardly knew Marion and she might have been involved in whatever had happened. It never occurred to me to go to the police. I thought Kerry could help me discover the truth. I thought that was all I needed to do.

'What I can't figure out,' I said to Kerry, 'is that Marion is supposed to have been with him when he was supposed to have had an asthma attack and died.'

Kerry nodded slowly, thinking this through, then shrugged. 'Who knows? Maybe Marion's got some reason to do what the Army tells her. They get things on people. Maybe the whole bloody thing was staged.'

'So, he could still be alive?'

He took a pull of beer. 'Nah. Why the hell would you fake a death for someone who wasn't dead? I reckon they musta decided they didn't want to admit he was KIA because of where they'd sent him. Like the boys in China I told you about. Maybe they couldn't afford the risk of people finding out. Matter of fact, now I think of it, he said something to me about a mission when he spoke to me. That's right, it's coming back to me. He was worried about it, and maybe that's why he said the stuff about his will, like he knew it was coming. That would make sense, wouldn't it? He knew he was in danger.'

'What was the mission?'

'Dunno, but it was in Cambodia, I think. Yeah, that's right, Cambodia was what he said. Makes sense, doesn't it? Some covert bloody op to get rid of someone. Instead, your dad gets killed and the bastards move the whole bloody thing into civvie street to cover it up. They wouldn't do that unless he really was dead. What's the point? I'm sorry, kid, but he's left us for good. He would have contacted me if he was still alive, I'll guarantee.' He smiled weakly.

'The other photo,' I said suddenly.

'What other photo?' Kerry said quickly.

'The funeral home photographed the body. It would have to be better than this. And if we had a clear photo of the body, we'd be able to tell them apart. Then we can go to the police and get them to dig up the body and check.'

'What photograph you talking about?'

'The funeral home takes pictures of all their bodies to

make sure they don't muddle them up,' I said. 'I'm sure they'll give me a copy.' I started thinking up a story for Dulcie. 'And they must have records at the hospital too.'

'Naked, you mean? They photograph them naked?'

'I assume so. It's for their records. I'm sure they'd let me have a copy.'

'Whoa there,' Kerry said. 'One step at a time. You let me find out what happened first. This is dangerous stuff, Scott. Then we'll see about police and digging up bodies. If the Army did this, chances are the police already know. Leave it to the experts.'

Kerry put a hand on my shoulder. He'd stood up. I was still sitting on a stool. 'Whatever you do, don't start telling other people, especially not Stella and your mum. It'll only upset them. If he's really dead, and frankly he must be, the Army's never going to tell us what happened, not if they've gone to all this trouble. And if you start snooping round where you're not welcome, they might arrange a little accident for you. They're not frightened to do stuff like that, believe me.' He made a cut-throat gesture with his finger across his neck. 'Leave it with me to find out what I can. I've still got contacts, and if something happened, I'll get to know about it. Wait to hear from me, okay?' I didn't respond. He repeated the question.

'Sure,' I said.

'You just keep your mum and Stella in line, and tell them to behave about the will.' He looked past me to the entry. 'Chooky. Marky. Bate-see,' he called out. He slapped me on the back and said, by way of farewell, 'You're a good bloody kid. Just remember what I told you. And mum's the word on the top secret stuff.' He

winked and walked over to welcome Chooky, Marky and
Bate-see.

On the way home in the car, Stella told me she'd
engaged a solicitor. 'What for?' I said. I felt a little dizzy
from the rum.

'He's getting us a copy of the will. We might need
representation.'

'Marion told you Dad was bushwalking when he
died, didn't she?'

'Something like that. He had a turn while they were
out walking, but she managed to get him home.'

'Why didn't she take him to hospital instead?'

'She said he left his puffer in the car and at first it
didn't seem all that serious. Once he had his drugs, he
was okay. He said he didn't need to go see the doctor.
You know what he was like about hospitals. But later
that night, he had another attack and the puffer was
useless. Marion did take him to the hospital then, but it
was too late.'

'Which hospital?'

'Some little place in the hinterland, Alloysius or
something.'

'Where were they walking?'

'O'Reilly's.'

'Originally she told you he'd died out walking
though, didn't she?'

'No, I don't think so.'

'That's what you told me, Stella.'

'Did I? I don't remember. But I'm sure she probably
told me the full story and I got it wrong. He definitely
died in hospital. He arrested because of the asthma.'

'So, did Marion tell you the whole story or not?'

'I just said, I don't know. I was upset. Why, what's the problem?'

'Have you got her address?'

'The solicitor would have. Why?'

'No reason,' I said. 'I just want to know where he was living.'

'You okay, Scott, about all this?'

'I'm fine,' I said.

In the evening Mum came into my room. 'When are you supposed to go back to college?' she said. I'd been in the middle of running out of the enemy camp supporting Dad on one arm and it took me a moment to adjust to my bedroom walls and her concerned look. She was sitting on the end of the bed. I had no idea how long she'd been there.

'They gave me three days' compassionate leave,' I said. 'I think I can extend it.'

'You know you don't have to go back, don't you?' she said. Mum had fussed over me since I'd been home, cooking food I had no appetite for. She said I was thin and there were dark patches under my eyes. She kept asking me if I was worried about anything. It wasn't like her to notice. I felt hemmed in by the attention. 'We don't need the money.'

'Don't be stupid, Mum.' My anger surprised me. 'Why wouldn't I go back?'

'I just think you could be miserable and try to stick it out for no reason except pride, which is no reason at all.'

'I love Duntroon.'

'You don't have to be like him, Scott.'

'What do you mean?'

'He wasn't so great, that's all, or if he was, it wasn't for the things he thought were great. He used to push you too hard. Now you do it to yourself.'

'I'm all right, Mum.'

She looked at me. 'You've got his good points, love, don't worry about that,' she said. 'But the Army's not for you. It probably wasn't for him either, to be honest.'

'Why have you always hated it so much?'

She sighed. 'All those bloody men, I don't know. They seem to get worse when you put them together. I don't want that to happen to you.' She looked as if she might cry. She took a big breath to stop herself. 'Anyway, I promised myself I wouldn't keep telling you what to do with your life, so I won't. I just came in to ask you how it went today.'

'It was okay,' I said. 'Better than I thought.'

'I'm glad you and Stella had each other,' she said. 'I would have ...' she trailed off. 'What's Marion like?'

'Like you,' I said. She frowned. 'But dumb,' I lied. Mum didn't say anything. 'Did you know about her?'

Mum's face hardened and she didn't answer for a long moment. 'I knew he'd changed, that he wasn't as interested in us as before. I think I guessed, yes.'

'Had he had other affairs?' I was thinking about what Stella had said.

'Who knows?' Mum said. 'But once you've betrayed someone's trust once, I imagine it's easier to do again. That was what he was like.' Her face was tight, like she was describing some rare, unpleasant virus she'd found under a microscope.

'Was Dad's asthma really bad, Mum?'

'He had an awful run when we were in Melbourne the first time. You were too young to remember, but they gave him adrenalin once. And he was on steroids to stop him getting another attack. Why?' She was looking hard at me.

'I know this sounds really stupid, but I don't think he's dead, or I don't think it was his body we saw.' Mum nodded but didn't say anything. 'It didn't look anything like him.'

'Stella mentioned you'd been unsure.'

'What did she say?' I didn't like the idea that Mum and Stella were discussing me behind my back.

'Just that you were a bit confused. It's pretty understandable, if you think about it.' She was choosing her words carefully. 'Your dad left. You hadn't seen him for a long time. He was so fit, wasn't he? And it's not like he was old. Even I was shocked. I can imagine how it must have been for you. You looked up to him so much …'

'Why did he leave, Mum?'

She took a long time to answer, pulling at the quilt. 'Sometimes I think I wasn't the person he thought I was. Maybe we both weren't the people we thought we were. Maybe Marion was better for him.'

'Do you still miss him?'

'No,' she said quickly. 'You and Stella were always the best thing about us.'

'He never even called us. He never called me.'

'You know what he was like. He didn't even see his own father. I think he was a coward when it came to facing what he did to people.' Neither of us spoke for a few moments. Mum said, 'Jim has a friend you could talk to, if you wanted.'

'A psychologist?' She nodded. 'You think I'm crazy?'

'No, I think you've had to deal with a lot.'

'What if I'm right, and Stella's wrong? And the body wasn't Dad's. Dad wasn't circumcised, was he?'

'What's that got to do with it?'

'He wasn't, was he?'

'No, but —'

'What if Marion killed Dad, if she shot him and swapped the body with someone else's?' I knew this sounded ridiculous. 'Or what if Dad was on a mission and something happened? Don't you think we should find out?' Mum didn't say anything. 'Well, don't you?' Mum was shaking her head. 'You do think I'm crazy.'

'No, I think you're mixed up. It might help to talk to someone.'

'Okay,' I said. 'Get me the number.' I had no intention of making the call, but I thought it might get Mum off my back. After she left the room I curled up in bed with the covers over my head. None of them believed me. They all thought I was crazy. And worst of all, I was starting to think they might be right.

chapter fourteen

The next night I went to Stella's and drank and smoked marijuana with her and Josh. I thought the drugs calmed me down. I slept soundly on the couch and dreamed a dream I used to have as a child. Dad always owned guns, including a big Magnum he bought went he got home from Vietnam. He kept the Magnum in the car, under the driver's seat. Apparently, when I was three, I locked myself in with the gun. Mum had gone back inside for something and had left her keys in the ignition. By the time the NRMA man arrived, just before Dad, I was playing with the loaded gun in the locked car. Dad cried after they got me out, and hugged me so tightly it hurt. Mum and Dad were furious at each other, according to Stella, Mum because of Dad's guns, and Dad because Mum had left me alone in a drivable car. More of a weapon than any gun, he always said later. For years, I dreamed that after I'd found the gun, Dad shot at me with it, but it didn't hurt.

In the version of the dream I had at Stella's place I'm grown up and Dad is holding the gun to the side of my head. He has my arm twisted behind me and every time I try to speak he applies pressure. His eyes are wild. Then he puts the gun to my forehead and pulls the trigger. I hear my skull crack. I feel my nerves weaving pain through my body. Then I'm safe in a hospital. I've managed to live but I'm badly injured. A nurse is changing the wound dressings. 'We're awake,' she says. The nurse is Marion, smiling like she means it.

When I finally did wake up the next morning I felt changed in that way that dreams can change you. I had a memory of fear that was enough to send a shiver through me every time I thought of the dream. After breakfast Stella told me she'd made an appointment with our new solicitor. I said I'd go with her, more because I didn't want to be left alone than anything else.

'Call me Tony.' Tony Matthews was in his fifties, with wavy white hair and a red nose. He had an office big enough for a first-fifteen of solicitors, and he looked small behind a big oak desk. He leaned over the desk to shake my hand. He could only just reach. His hand was warm and soft. He didn't move to shake Stella's hand until he saw hers hanging over the desk waiting. He didn't introduce us to the other person in the office, a boy about my age in a three-piece suit who sat in the corner and made a note whenever Mr Matthews looked his way.

Mr Matthews outlined our options if we wanted to contest the will. 'As dependants, your chances are pretty good, especially on Scott's behalf. Despite his Duntroon allowance, he has no real means of supporting himself properly, and he's suffered obvious hardship as a result of the death. I think we're in good shape.

'When we get all the documents, we'll know who's getting what, and your father may well have provided for you. What I can tell you is that our preliminary research suggests the estate could be substantial. Your father had over twenty years' Army service, so there's his pension, plus whatever he'd arranged in terms of life insurance.'

Stella asked a couple of questions, but the talk of money and a will was irrelevant to me. I told Mr Matthews I wanted him to ask for Dad's personal belongings. 'When he left us, he didn't leave much behind. I don't want his money, I just want whatever he left of his own stuff, if possible. Papers, photographs. He had a trunk of mementoes I'd like.'

'That's properly a matter for the executors. We can ask.' The executors were Marion and a solicitor Dad had engaged, Mr Matthews said.

'I'd also like his banking statements for the last year, and any other records,' I said. 'Phone, electricity, gas.' Mr Matthews asked why. 'Anything that might help me know about the last years of his life.'

'Okay,' he said, 'although they might refuse to give us banking details. What about your father's ashes?'

'He was buried at Yeronga,' I said.

Mr Matthews looked at the piece of paper in front of him. 'Not according to the advice we have from the funeral home. They claim to have his ashes and are awaiting disposal instructions.'

I shook my head. 'He was buried in the Yeronga

cemetery,' I said, flicking back through my notebook to find the page. 'Here it is, burial but no graveside service.'

'Scott's right,' Stella said. 'He was buried.'

'It could be a simple error,' Mr Matthews said. 'Let me check.' He went out of the office. His clerk followed. They came back a few minutes later and resumed their seats. 'I've just been on the telephone to the funeral home, and they've confirmed that your father's body was cremated,' he said carefully. 'They said they were acting under instructions.'

'That can't be right,' I said. 'We were at the meeting and Marion said burial. Look, here, I've written it down. There's Marion's name.' I reached across the desk and gave Mr Matthews my notebook, pointing to the item. He read for a few moments, flicked back through the other pages and gave the notebook back to me quickly, as if he might catch something from it.

'Well, Marion Goodwin's the executor, so she's the final authority,' he said.

'What about his will?' I was sure Dad wanted to be buried.

'It doesn't matter,' he said. 'Executors decide about remains.' He thought for a moment. 'Let's not get ahead of ourselves. Let me check the funeral home records more thoroughly. Over the phone they assured me everything was in order, so let's wait and see what they send us. If they've got the authority of an executor, I can only surmise that Mrs Goodwin changed her mind. If not, and it's a mistake, we can take action.

'With cremation, there is a provision for lodging an objection, but in this case, of course, no objection was lodged because, as you say, you weren't aware cremation was to take place. Did you feel strongly about burial?'

'Couldn't give a fuck,' Stella said. If Mr Matthews was shocked by her language, he didn't show it.

'I care about it,' I said. Stella stared at me. 'I think Marion did it purposely. She knew we might object, so she gave the impression she'd decided on burial and changed the instructions when we weren't there. We're his children and we didn't even have a say.'

'The law is very clear on this point,' Mr Matthews said. 'Disposal is at the sole discretion of the executor, who happens to be Mrs Goodwin. Do you have reason to believe she's failing to act in accordance with your late father's instructions?' Stella cackled. I didn't reply. 'Let's wait to see what the funeral home has to say,' he said. 'When there's a choice between conspiracy and cock-up, I'm a great believer in cock-up.'

'Couldn't give a fuck what they did to him,' Stella said again, to make sure Mr Matthews heard.

'Quite,' he said. He looked at his watch. 'Let's wrap up. Between now and when we next meet, I'll check this burial mix-up. And I'd like you two to think carefully about whether you want to make a claim on the estate if it comes to that. There's your mother to think of. She's not a young woman. She might be glad of a bit of help.'

'I don't want anything to do with his money,' Stella said. 'But I want to make sure Mum's okay.'

'But don't tell the executors that just yet,' I said. 'Until we get the personal effects I'm asking for.'

Mr Matthews nodded and smiled. 'You ever thought of a career in law?' I didn't return his smile.

On the way out I asked Mr Matthews for Marion's address. Initially he looked as if he might say no, until I added, 'I wanted to have a look at the place he last lived in.'

'Of course,' he said. 'I'll get the girls to look it up for you.'

In the car Stella said to me, 'What's all that bullshit about someone changing instructions purposely?'

'Think about it, Stella. What if Marion's got something to hide? She'd want to burn the evidence, wouldn't she?'

'Don't tell me you're still thinking the body wasn't Dad's.'

'You were there when she gave the instructions, Stella. She said burial. Why the hell would she change her mind?'

'How would I know?'

'You didn't tell her, did you, about me being unsure?'

'Of course not.'

Stella dropped me off in Boundary Street at Spring Hill. I told her I needed to get some film. Before she pulled away she asked me was I okay. When I said I was, she said, 'Really okay?'

'Of course.'

She looked at me a moment more before she drove off.

I rang the Eternal Rest office at Nerang from the McCafferty's bus depot in Fortitude Valley. 'What can I do for you, Mr Goodwin?' Dulcie said matter-of-factly.

'I've just found out you cremated my father's body,' I said.

'Yes?' she said. 'And?'

'When we came to see you, you ticked burial on your form, I saw it, and now your office is saying he was cremated.' She told me to hold the line please. The Gold Coast bus arrived.

I watched the bus leave without me. When Dulcie came back she said, 'I've got the original form here, and it looks to me like the arrangement was changed. I've got burial ticked, just as you say, but it's been crossed out and cremation's been ticked. Oh, here we are, there's a note on the file. Apparently we had contact from the executor after our meeting. It appears your father's will left no instructions about disposal, and the executor ... Let me see —'

I interrupted her: '— was Marion Goodwin, but she's the one who said on the form he was to be buried.'

'Well, she changed her mind, because this instruction about cremation has come straight from her. I've got her signature on this note.'

'I bet you have,' I said. I told Dulcie I wanted to come and see her about the cremation and another matter but she told me I'd need to talk to the manager. I made a time, got off the phone and waited fifty minutes for the next bus to the Gold Coast.

chapterfifteen

Marion lived in a low-set sixties weatherboard house in the hinterland, a long way from the sea, overlooking the Canungra Jungle Training Centre. For the rest of the day I sat across the road from Marion's, in a little park that housed a First World War memorial of a soldier with a slouch hat on his bowed head. If Marion came out, I figured I could hide behind the low hedge surrounding the memorial and still have a good view of the house. I remained there at the memorial until the sun was low in the sky and then caught the last bus back to Brisbane and the train back to Mum's from Fortitude Valley.

The next day I caught the first bus back to Marion's. I'd noticed the day before that the house next door to Marion's, a highset Queenslander, was vacant. For the next three days I stood underneath the Queenslander watching Marion's house through black slats.

I don't know what I was looking for. Marion came and went with the boys a couple of times, making jokes with them as they got in and out of the car with their chattels. She gave no sign she was overcome by grief. I started to feel a weird familiarity with her, as if, because she knew Dad, she knew me. I was tempted to go over and talk to her. In my dreamy mind, Dad would show up and we'd be together like a family. I'd be a big brother for Michael and Jason and Candice, and my old family, Mum and Stella, who'd sent Dad away from us, would disappear.

The next day I extended my leave from Duntroon. After lunch I took a sleeping bag with me on the bus to Marion's. I climbed over the back verandah of the vacant house and in through the open French windows. It was unfurnished so I presumed its owners weren't coming back any time soon. I cleared dust and possum droppings from the floor near the window and settled in to watch.

Marion came home at four-thirty pm as she had the other days. Just before nine a woman I didn't know arrived. Marion left soon after, alone, returning just before dawn, and looking as if she'd slept in her clothes. I don't think I slept at all. I watched this routine for a second night before I decided to follow Marion. The next night I told a taxi driver to pull up round the corner from the house. 'I'm just waiting for a car,' I said, 'and then I want you to follow it.'

'Why?' the driver said flatly.

'I'll give you ten dollars.' I knew from the movies that I should offer a driver money to get what I wanted, but I was surprised it actually worked. Within minutes Marion's little Fiat trundled round the corner and we glided in behind. 'Not too close, I don't want her to know.'

'Who's this, your girlfriend?'

'Yeah, that's right.'

We followed Marion down the hill and towards the Gold Coast proper, past treeless estates filled with banks of townhouses that all looked the same. The driver, who'd eyed me in the rearview from time to time, said, 'You think she might be on with someone else?'

'We're engaged,' I said, unnecessarily. 'And I think she's on with my best man. I want to make sure before I break it off.'

The driver chuckled. 'Well, let's hope she's visiting her sick mum.' We'd stopped outside Alloysius Private Hospital, the hospital where Dad was supposed to have died.

'Damn,' I said. 'My best man's a doctor here.'

When I tried to give the driver the ten dollars he said not to worry. 'Jesus, mate, you'll need that to get drunk. Good luck.' He drove off into the night.

I watched Marion go into the foyer and get into a lift. I hurried after her to check what floor she'd get off. The lift doors reopened.

'What are you doing here?' she said, moving towards me, forcing me backwards.

'Is he here?'

'What are you talking about? What do you want? Why are you hanging round my house?' She was backing me against a wall.

'Where's Dad?'

'Your father's dead.'

'Why'd you do it?'

'Do what? What are you talking about?'

Marion's kind face was hard now. 'Is he sick? Is that

what they're covering up? Did he get some disease in Cambodia?' She looked shocked. I was sure I'd hit a nerve. 'Can't I see him, please?'

'Listen, you can't follow me round. It's not normal.'

I grabbed her arm and held it pretty tightly. 'Please,' I said.

She looked at my hand on her wrist. 'You refused to see him for all those years. Can't you just leave us alone now?'

I kind of shook her. 'He refused to see me, you mean.' My voice was loud and Marion was trying to back away from me. 'He refused to see me. Look, just tell me what happened,' I said, 'and I'll leave you alone. Where is he?' I still had a hold of her arm.

She took a breath in as if to speak and then held it. Finally she said, in a low voice, 'Don't threaten me.' I held on. 'Your father is dead, that's where he is. Dead. Now get your hands off me right now or I'll call the police. I said now.' I let go. 'Go home.' She walked over to the desk and talked to the clerk. Within a minute two security guards arrived and escorted me out to a waiting taxi. As one of them pushed my head down into the taxi, I could see Marion waiting for the lift again. The security guard said, 'You ought to be ashamed of yourself, after what she's been through.'

The next morning I went back to the hospital. In those days it was surrounded by farms and bushland. Now it's dwarfed by industry and housing estates with locked gates, lantern-shaped street lights and security cameras. The entry Marion had taken led to a general surgical ward and a small kids' ward. It was nowhere near

Emergency, where Dad was supposedly taken the day he supposedly collapsed. I decided to go to Emergency first. It was quiet. I introduced myself at the front desk. 'I hadn't seen my father for some time before his death,' I said. 'He'd left us. And I was wondering if there's anyone I could speak to who cared for him here.'

A short maternal-looking nurse checked something in a card file then went into the room behind the reception area. I leaned over. Dad's name was on the card, which had also been stamped in red: 'Deceased'. The date of birth matched Dad's. The nurse came back with a manilla folder that held several sheets of paper. She confirmed Marion's story, that Dad arrived in a coma and died. 'There was nothing we could do, I'm sorry.' I wanted people to stop being kind to me. I wasn't experiencing the kind of grief that would warrant such kindness. It made me feel dishonest.

'Can I see the file?'

'Don't see why not.' I got out my notebook, copied down the names of everyone involved, the admitting nurse, the charge sister of the ward, the doctor who declared Dad dead. 'This doctor,' I said, 'Johnson. Can I speak to him?'

She said of course I could. 'I'll see if he's on now, if you like.'

About half an hour later I was joined by a fat little middle-aged man in a white coat. He had a row of pens in his top pocket, all different colours, and a stethoscope slung around his neck. He took me into an empty treatment room and sat me down. He looked at me with beady green eyes. 'I'm sorry,' he said. 'We did everything we could to save your father. But we lost him.' Johnson had a deep, rich voice, like a radio personality. I wondered how many times a day he had to say he'd lost someone, because it didn't sound sincere.

'How did he die?'

'Don't you know?'

'They said it was an asthma attack.'

He nodded. 'Yes, his heart stopped as a result.'

'Was there an autopsy?'

'No, we'd only do an autopsy if there was a query about the cause of death. Your father was an asthmatic who had an asthma attack.' Dr Johnson had put down his stethoscope.

'So how did you know it was him?'

'I'm not sure what you mean.'

'Was he conscious when he came into the hospital?'

Johnson looked at the file. 'No.'

'So, how did you know it was him?'

'He was admitted to hospital. His is the name on the chart.'

'But he came in unconscious.'

'With ID.' He stopped and read from the file he'd picked up at the desk. 'And next-of-kin.' He was still reading. 'Not only that, he'd been to Southport Hospital for treatment the week before. We'd have made sure he matched their records.'

'But you'd never actually met him.'

'No. Sometimes that happens. We try to make sure the doctor who cares for a patient is present to declare the death, but in your father's case, his doctor was a private GP, Dr Robertson, in Brisbane, and he'd always gone to

Southport Hospital before, not here. But there was no
question about ID. I signed off on extinction of life, and
your dad's private GP signed off on cause of death. It's all
in order.'

'But his GP wasn't here to see him.'

'No.'

'So, how did he know he was declaring the right
person dead?'

Johnson sat up straighter and rubbed his red nose.
'I'm not quite sure what you're getting at. Do you think
we could have made a mistake?' I didn't answer. 'We're a
hospital. We don't make mistakes. Dr Robertson can't
sign off on cause of death unless it's straightforward. He
must have seen your father recently.' Johnson tilted his
head as if it might help him understand me. 'Have you
some reason to believe it wasn't your father?'

'But Dr Robertson didn't actually see the body, did
he? No one who knew Dad saw the body. So it could have
been someone else.' I was thinking of babies being swapped and how that sometimes happened, only to be
discovered years later. They never swapped back. At first I
thought it was as simple as that, an accident at the hospital
in which my father's body had been swapped with some
other guy. Maybe Dad really was dead and they'd just
given us the wrong body from the hospital. But that
wouldn't explain Marion's silence, assuming she'd seen the
body. And surely she'd seen the body, in the hospital at the
very least. I left Dr Johnson with a promise that he hadn't
heard the last of me. I felt mature saying that.

I went back to the wing where I'd seen Marion heading the night before. I took the lift to each floor and walked

through the general surgical wards. I checked each patient, even the private rooms, with an apology — wrong room. They had a psych ward, and I checked that too. No sign of Dad. I sat in the foyer watching people come and go. Nothing.

I went to the ward where they said Dad died and found the charge nurse who'd been on duty that night. I gave her my speech about wanting to find out as much as I could about my father's death. 'Dad had a pointy chin,' I said. She smiled and nodded but didn't agree or disagree about her patient's chin. I couldn't really ask if he was circumcised. 'Do you know if his leg gave him trouble in his last hours?' I said finally.

'What was wrong with it?' She was looking at his chart.

'An injury. He had a plate in his leg.'

'There's nothing here.'

'It wasn't recent,' I said. 'It was a war injury that used to play up. I just wondered, you know, if he was comfortable in those last hours.'

'He would have been as comfortable as could be. We always make sure of that.' I asked another question about his injury. 'We weren't treating his leg,' she said gently. 'He was dead.'

From a public phone outside I called Dad's Brisbane GP, Dr Robertson, who wanted to help. 'I know it's rare we lose people to asthma these days, but …' He sighed. 'Anyway, I'm sorry for your loss.'

'Had you seen Dad recently, Dr Robertson?'

'As a matter of fact, he came in just a couple of weeks ago.'

'Was he ill?'

'He'd had a serious attack, he told me. I think it rattled him. I booked him in for some tests, but we never got to them. I did give him a thorough physical examination, of course. Let's see now. Nothing out of the ordinary. But that's the thing with asthma. One doesn't know.'

'Had he lost weight?'

'Not that I remember.'

'Did he look different?'

'No, not that I recall. Why?'

'No reason. Was his leg still giving him trouble, Dr Robertson?'

'Sometimes, yes. Amazing recovery, that, I must say. He was an extraordinary man, Scott. As I say, I'm so sorry for your loss.'

'Yeah, me too. Thanks, Dr Robertson, for your time. It's meant a lot to me.'

When I arrived home Mum was waiting in the kitchen. 'What did you do today?'

'Not much.' I walked past her towards my room. She followed.

'Where were you last night?'

'Stella's.'

'She said she hasn't see you for a few days.' I didn't say anything. 'Marion phoned me. Have you been at her house? Scott? What's going on?'

'Nothing.'

'Please tell me. Maybe I can help.'

'I said nothing! Now fuck off!' It came out louder than I'd intended and she turned and walked away without saying more. I slammed the door, which I wouldn't normally do, but I felt like it.

chaptersixteen

That night Kerry Vance called to say he had news. The next morning I caught the first bus up to Toowoomba and another from there to the small town of Oakey. I walked to Kerry's workshop, a timber shed with high windows in front of a small house in the centre of town.

Kerry lifted his mask when he saw me. 'God, you're a big lad,' he said, pulling off a glove to almost shake off my arm. 'Your Dad woulda been so proud of you.'

He was working on a red Austin Healy. 'Beautiful, isn't she?' he said when he saw me looking. There was a clean paint smell and the sun-filled air was fuzzy with pink spray. 'I got this one, and a silver, same model. Cost a packet.'

Kerry threw his mask and gloves onto the bench and led me through to the small windowless office which was really just a corner of the workshop, separated from the rest by shelving. From the desk he took a

report. It had a maroon cover and the 'In confidence —
AUSTEYESONLY S-12 Tactical' stamp I'd seen on
reports Dad brought home. On the inside cover was a list
of names, with the Minister for Defence at the top.

'Remember that hostage situation in New Guinea
about six months ago?' I didn't. 'Three guys kidnapped by
guerillas on some island. One of them was an Australian
journalist. New Guinea government supposedly nego-
tiating, more like fucking it up, standard procedure with
the fuzzy-wuzzies.' He handed across the report. 'Whole
thing went quiet a few weeks ago, usual standoff tactics.
I always follow stuff like that, and I remember when it
went quiet, I wondered. Like, that was two weeks before
your dad died, right?' I nodded. 'Well, get a load of
this.' He handed across the report. 'I still got mates on
the inner.'

I looked down the list of names on the cover. As well
as the Minister there was the Secretary of Defence, the
Chief of the Army and a short list of senior officers,
including Dad's CO.

'You can't ever tell anyone you've seen this, Scott, or
we'll both be dead.' I looked at him. 'I mean it, son.
They don't fuck around. Believe me, I know.'

The report was two pages, compiled by a Major Len
Barrington, whose name I didn't know, from Tactical
Support in S-12, Dad's section. It recommended
resolution of the hostage situation as a matter of urgency.
The situation was sensitive, the report said, and the New
Guinea government had failed to arrive at a negotiated
solution. The rebels had food and water but few weapons.
Barrington estimated a raid would require a ground team

of no more than eight with standby air support. Because of concerns about the integrity of domestic defence, it was recommended the New Guinea government not be appraised pending the outcome of the mission.

'They didn't even tell New Guinea what they were doing,' I said. I thought of my history teacher, Mr Maitland. 'How sure are you Dad was involved? At the funeral, you said he was in Cambodia.'

'Yeah, that's right, he went to Cambodia but that was before this. The guy who gave me the report couldn't get any more but he reckons your dad was with them, and look here, the dates match.' The report was dated a fortnight before Dad's death. 'They were planning the raid as soon as possible.'

'But there wasn't anything in the news.'

'Except this,' Kerry said. It was a clipping from *The Courier-Mail*, reporting the deaths of the three hostages. It said their bodies had been found by Australian/New Guinea joint forces in the area. Kerry had written the date of the article above the headline. It was the day after Dad's funeral.

Kerry took the report back. 'See, I understand crazies. We had a million of them in the 'Nam, and they were the ones on our side. If you were these rebels, you might kill one of your hostages to show you meant business, but you wouldn't kill them all and lose your bargaining position, would you? You certainly wouldn't kill the Aussie who's your big chip. I figure what happened was a botched rescue, but our Minister doesn't want to admit that, so, he decides to cover the whole thing up. S-12's the unit that does that kind of stuff.'

I looked at the report again. My father had gone into a hostile situation to save another Australian. 'So he might not be dead?'

'What?' Kerry said.

'Well, this fits with the body not being his, doesn't it?'

'No, that's just not possible. Why would they say he's dead if he's still alive? And if he's not dead, where the fuck is he?'

'Maybe he was injured or he's being held hostage and they can't admit it because they failed at the rescue. Or maybe he's sick.'

'If he was a hostage, they'd say so. He'd have to be dead, Scott. But I'll tell you one thing. He never died bushwalking. It's just like you thought. He died serving his bloody country, and Marion's gone along with them. From what I hear, she's not quite who you think she is.'

'What do you mean?'

'Let's just say she might be involved. That's what I reckon, anyway.'

'Marion?' Kerry nodded. 'But she's his wife.'

'So? Could be part of the act. I'm not saying Army, but a related security force. Can't say more, if you get my drift.'

'But they were married. You said they even stayed here.'

'Course they did. These guys are bloody thorough, Scott, they always set everything up nicely. They'd have planned for this. I'm not saying they weren't really together or anything, but I reckon she knows more than she's letting on.'

'But if I'm right and it wasn't his body, how can we be sure he's dead?'

'Course he's bloody dead.'

'So, what do we do?' I said.

'What can we do? Nothing. We keep this secret, between you and me, and we get on with life, like he'd want us to. You gotta promise me that's what you'll do. You can't take on these boys, Scott. They'll kill you, believe me.' Kerry looked genuinely frightened and that, more than anything else, frightened me.

Dad had told me that when he first arrived in Vietnam, fresh out of jungle training back in Australia, he and the other new blokes were spooked by artillery fire. Kerry sat outside in a folding chair reading a paper. 'Guns, what guns?' he screamed above the fire. Dad said Kerry did stuff like that to reassure the young blokes. They felt safe when Kerry was there.

'What about the other soldiers who were on the raid?' I said.

'They're S-12, Scott. What do you think? They're just going to breach every protocol to talk to us? They'll stick with the story, the ones who are still alive. We have to forget all this, and get on with life now.'

I stood to leave. On the way back through the workshop I noticed, next to the Austin Healy, an open red toolbox with expandable shelves. I walked closer. All the tools were neatly in their slots, open-ended spanners one side, closed the other, the timing light, the feeler gauges, the old red rag he used to wipe his hands, the jars labelled 'useless screws' and 'useful screws'. I turned round to face Kerry. 'How'd this get here?'

'Your dad gave it to me.' Dad told me once he looked after his tools because one day they'd be mine.

I lowered the shelves and closed the lid. I found the dent on the bottom corner where I'd dropped the box on cement as a kid. Dad had asked me to get it from the shed. It was too heavy for me, even using two hands. I was terrified when it crashed. But he just looked over and smiled and told me not to worry about it. Later, he sanded and repainted the dent with touch-up paint and said there were very few things broken in life that couldn't be fixed. I ran my fingers over the place.

chapterseventeen

After I left Kerry I called the cadet supervisor at
Duntroon and extended my leave again. He told me
I needed special permission for any further extension of
compassionate leave.

I was early for my appointment with the Eternal Rest
manager, so I sat in the soft pink foyer of the building
where we'd met with Dulcie the first day. There were no
other visitors. I felt like laughing for no reason I
understood. Adam Taylor came out and shook my hand
and led me through to the small back room he used as an
office. He wore a plain white shirt and dark company tie.
I told him I hadn't seen my father for some years after he
left my mother. I wanted a recent photograph. It wasn't
a lie. Mr Taylor said he was sorry to hear of my loss.
I couldn't stand people saying things like that. It was like
they made him dead when I was investing everything in
him being alive.

Taylor had big dark eyes and a thick moustache that made him look like a ventriloquist doing still-lipped talk. 'How long ago did he pass away?' he said.

'Just over a week,' I said, and swallowed. 'I was wondering if I could get a copy of the photograph of Dad you have in your records.'

He nodded slowly. 'We do take photographs, but they're not for relatives. It's not a good way to remember a loved one,' he said. 'Didn't you come here to see your father?' I nodded. 'I remember.' He must have heard about me.

'A bad photo would be better than nothing,' I said and smiled weakly.

He looked hard at me. I hoped he wasn't going to check with Marion. 'What was your father's full name and date of death?' I told him. 'And you came to this office originally?' I told him yes. 'There may be a problem,' he said. 'Excuse me for a moment.'

He returned a few minutes later. 'I'm afraid we won't be able to help you after all,' he said. 'We had a break-in last night. Unfortunately, some of our paper records, including your father's, were destroyed. All I can suggest is that you contact the executors, who might have a photograph from your father's personal effects.' He closed the file as if to end the meeting.

'Did they find out who did it?' I said.

At first he looked as if he didn't understand what I meant. Then he said, 'You mean the break-in?' I nodded. 'We've had trouble before, a gang of local kids who think people's grief is some kind of joke. But this time, the laugh's on them. The police got some good fingerprints and one boy looks like being charged. I just hope they get the rest of them. They smashed a coffin and painted obscenities on the chapel wall.'

In addition to the photograph, the destroyed files included the only other documentation that would have helped me — the mortuary attendant's report on the man's body.

'I don't suppose I can talk to the mortuary attendant who looked after Dad?' I said.

'The mortuary attendant,' Adam Taylor repeated carefully. He looked at the wall behind me before continuing. 'That would have been Shirley Stapleton. I can ask her something for you.'

'I'd prefer to talk to her myself.'

Adam Taylor was nodding obligingly. 'I'd like to be able to help you, Scott, but it's not normally what our mortuary attendants do. They're not used to talking to clients. I'd prefer you to give me a list of questions and I'll talk to Shirley.'

'Don't worry about it,' I said. 'It isn't that important.' I thanked Adam Taylor, said goodbye, and walked out as if heading for the front gate. Instead, I walked around the side of the office block and past the chapel to the mortuary building.

Entry to the building was via large garage doors which were fully open. There was a refrigerator along one wall. It was more like a shed than a mortuary, although I'd never seen a mortuary and had no idea what to expect. I found two undertakers loading a coffin into a hearse. I asked for Shirley Stapleton. Without speaking, one of them pointed to a door to the left of the garage.

I went through the door and found myself in a narrow corridor with doors on either side. It was cold enough to cause a shiver and although there were no windows, white fluorescent light bounced off the walls and gave the concrete floor a polished look.

After a few minutes of knocking on and opening the wrong doors (a tiny kitchen, an even smaller office with a bespectacled and surprised Dulcie etc.), I found Shirley Stapleton in a clean little cell furnished with a body-length bench and a large steel sink. Shelves along one wall were stacked with bottles and what looked like bandages. Shirley was on the phone when I arrived. She finished the call, stood up and came over to the door. She wore a white coat over what looked like a uniform. She was younger than I expected, although I had about as much experience of mortuary attendants as I had of mortuaries. I told her I wanted to talk about someone she'd worked on. She looked uncomfortable, and I guessed she didn't have many visitors. 'Not in here,' she said, as if the dead could hear us. She took me back to the big garage where three more hearses were backed up awaiting drivers and coffins. I thought of that scene in *Monty Python and the Holy Grail* where the soldiers are chanting, 'Bring out your dead,' and a guy tries to load his still-living father on the cart.

Shirley and I stood at the back of the garage. On a high shelf behind us I noticed three tiny coffins with names of hospitals on them. There were hundreds of sadder stories than mine out there. In one corner was a cupboard-sized room with glass walls that looked like a despatch office. Except for the cold room and hearses, the whole thing looked just like a mail despatch centre, posting bodies off to eternal rest.

Shirley lit up a cigarette and looked around nervously, as if she wasn't supposed to be smoking. 'What did you want to know?' she said.

'My father disappeared some years ago and may or may not have died,' I lied. 'You looked after someone last week and it may have been my father. For reasons I can't go into, I'm not able to ask this man's present family if he was once my father.' Shirley looked understandably confused. I thought I'd better shut up. I was getting too complicated. 'I'm pretty sure this guy was my father, but I have doubts. Does that make sense?' Shirley was nodding. I felt she wanted it to make sense. She wanted to help me. She was a nice person. 'I just have some doubts,' I said.

'Doubts,' she said.

'I know this sounds ridiculous, but I have to be sure. His name was Allan Goodwin, not when I knew him, but when he died,' I lied. 'I don't suppose you remember him at all?'

'Sure,' she said. 'Goodwin. He was the guy who changed his instructions from burial to cremation, wasn't he?' I nodded eagerly. 'Yeah, I remember. It's a different preparation, see, so I had to redo him. It's a pain in the neck, once you've cleaned them, because for burial you fill the cavities, but for cremation you leave them empty and you flush out the cleaner, else they can explode. I'd never had to do it before, and it took ages. Anyways, I never forget a face,' she said, and smiled, showing dimples.

'Right,' I said. 'Different preparation. Do you

remember anything distinguishing about his body, any marks or scars?'

She didn't answer straight away. Then she said, 'Like what?'

'Did he have a scar on the top of his leg?'

'Oh yeah,' she said, taking a huge pull on her cigarette and looking down at the ground before she blew out. 'A scar.'

'Are you sure?'

'Absolutely. We fill out a form, and I remember something about it. An op scar, wasn't it?'

'Yeah,' I said, too eagerly. 'He'd been injured. They had to reconstruct his upper leg.'

'Yeah, that's right, op scar, leg. Knee to groin. See, I remember my clients. Passes the time. I like to imagine their lives, you know, what they did.' I thanked her for her help. 'No trouble,' she said. 'So now you can rest easy. It really was him.' I looked at her and for a brief moment I thought she hadn't been truthful. Maybe Adam Taylor had spoken to her before I got there. Maybe he'd been the one she was talking to on the phone. If he turns up, just tell him whatever he wants to know.

'By the way, what life did you imagine for Dad?' I said. But despite my pleading, she wouldn't tell me. As I was leaving I said, 'Which leg had the scar?'

'Right,' she said, but to me it looked more like a lucky guess.

chaptereighteen

When my flight left for Canberra the next day, I felt weighed down in my seat much more powerfully than by the gravity that wanted to keep our jet on the ground in Brisbane. Mum had dropped me at the airport and I must have said goodbye without noticing we were parting. I couldn't remember our conversation. I'd been going over and over in my mind what Kerry Vance had said. It didn't add up, however much I wanted it to.

At the wake Kerry told me that Dad had been preparing to go to Cambodia and was worried. Then he'd said Dad had gone to both Cambodia and New Guinea. Dad couldn't have gone to both places, not in two weeks. The way Kerry told it, Dad would have deplaned from one mission and taken off almost immediately on another, no debriefing or briefing at all. Even Kerry would know that was impossible. I needed to see Dad's staff records and find out where he'd been in those last few weeks, to confirm or disprove what Kerry claimed. Kerry also said Marion was involved, implied she was some kind of spy, but I couldn't see this either. And covering up a major stuff-up like that, a botched rescue, surely they couldn't do it?

Dad was like a boy with a big brother when he and Kerry Vance were together. What happened to blokes in Vietnam was almost as strong as blood, Dad said. Mum reckoned Dad had some strange friendships. Stella felt creepy round Kerry Vance. I knew what they meant, although it was hard to put your finger on. Dad trusted him completely. I wanted to believe Kerry Vance, but there were holes in his story. And the thing that kept coming back to me was that whatever else Kerry Vance had told me, he was the only person other than me who knew the funeral home kept a photograph of the man's body. He knew because I told him, and then the photograph, the only evidence that would prove the body wasn't Dad's, was destroyed.

Stella and Mum believed Dad was dead, or at least they acted like that's what they believed. All I had was a photograph and no one else saw what I saw in it. Then I had my memory of the man in the coffin and an older memory, a boy's memory, of Dad. I had no way of knowing what I'd do to find out the truth. What if I was wrong after all, and the rest of them were right? I know I started to doubt myself around this time, but the alternative, that Dad was dead and I'd never see him, I didn't consider.

As the jet pulled higher I started feeling anxious. I looked out the little window to the sprawl of Brisbane split by its snake of a river. Dad's toolbox at Kerry's place, that was the worst thing. As we climbed higher, the houses and swimming pools and roads shrunk to nothing but patchwork on the world. I felt old suddenly, and my mouth tasted sour. I saw myself shrinking with that world below, a little life stretching down one of those roads, lived in one of those houses, doing lap after bloody lap in one of those pools, a life in which I wouldn't see him, not even once, a life with no chance to ask him what the fuck happened to him and why he went away. My breath quickened and my heart was bouncing round my chest. I told myself that it wasn't Dad's fault, none of it. It was the Army, or Kerry Vance, or Marion, or all of them. Or he was dead, as Mum and Stella believed, from asthma. And gone.

A flight attendant leaned over my neighbour, who was staring at me. 'Are you okay?' the attendant said. Maybe I'd called out. I couldn't be sure. I said I was fine. For the rest of the flight I counted the little diamonds in the fabric of the back of the seat in front of me and then rivet holes along my section of the ceiling. There were fifty-four rivets and too many diamonds to keep count.

Stella gave me this book about human endurance a few Christmases ago, written by a priest who reckoned that when you get a thorn in the ball of your foot, deep enough that it hurts like crazy to stand on, it's human nature that you don't pick it out because that will hurt too, and we're understandably scared of pain. Instead, you walk on your heel and adjust to accommodate the thorn. Before you know it, your calf starts to ache with the effort of keeping the ball of your foot off the ground, then your thigh muscle, hips, arms, neck and head. Finally, your whole body's tense and in pain, all for want of pulling a thorn. This book said we're scared to suffer and everything in us can go awry because of that. Whereas if we just dug out the bloody thorn, we'd have a short, sharp pain and be over it.

When I arrived at Duntroon around dusk, there was a message in my dorm that the Commandant wanted to see me. Although it was late when I called, Colonel Jakeman's corp said the Commandant would meet with me immediately. I went to his office in the main building, which during the day looked like one of those desert outposts, red brick with wide verandahs onto dry grass. At night it was still as death.

Colonel Jakeman had piercing blue eyes and black hair that stood up like a cock's comb. He'd been injured in a boating accident, not service-related, and he couldn't move his head without his whole torso moving too. He told me to take off my hat and sit down. 'Trip home all right?' he said. I said it was. 'Good to have you back.' I nodded. 'How's the family taking things?'

'Pretty good, sir,' I said, not knowing which family he meant, mine or Marion's.

'Good to have you back,' he said again, nodding from his chest. 'Although I never met him, I'm sure your father was a fine officer.'

'Yes, sir, he was, sir,' I said. 'And thank you for arranging the flight home for me, sir.'

He waved my thanks away and shifted in his chair uncomfortably. He looked hard at me. 'One of the things I love about the Army is that it's a great equaliser.

It doesn't matter who you are when you come to us. You can be the son of a great officer, or the son of a drunk like I am, and you're all the same. In the end, Scott, you'll be judged entirely on your own performance. You know that, don't you?'

'Yes, sir.' It occurred to me that perhaps he knew more than he was saying, perhaps he knew what happened to Dad. Maybe Kerry was right after all, and there had been a botched rescue.

'You're your own man here, Cadet. Don't forget it.' He stood and came around his desk. I stood too, replaced my hat and went to salute him, but I didn't get it finished by the time he reached me so I bumped into him. I apologised. He said not to worry and put his arm around my shoulder as he walked me to the door. 'You'll be fine,' he said. Momentarily, I felt the same panicky feeling I felt in the plane. I broke into a sweat and my stomach growled. I nodded and left quickly without saying sir, but he didn't pull me up.

While I'd been back in Brisbane a boy was injured in the dorm on the other side of mine. Brett Anderson or one of his crew was writing something on the boy's buttocks with a sword and slipped and tore into the muscle. The boy never said who did it and then left the Army. The general view was that he didn't have what it took. The press got hold of the fact that no one was charged. Mum saw the story in the paper when I was back in Brisbane and said she worried about me. I told her I knew how to look after myself. I saw Brett Anderson outside the main building.

'Hey, Goodwin, sorry about your old man,' he said.

I mumbled my thanks for his sympathy. I wanted to move off, but he stood in my way. I said thanks again. He said, 'You swim, don't you?' I told him I hadn't swum competitively in three years. He nodded. 'We thought you might want to be an Argonaut.' When I didn't respond straight away, he said, 'Think about it,' and walked off. The Argonauts was the name of Brett's group. Becoming an Argonaut involved having your bum written on with a sword. Refusing might be worse.

On my way back to my dorm I saw Colin Rawlins and walked with him from the study hall. 'You done your extra parade?' I asked him.

'I was excused because of work.' Colin managed to remain in his own little world with Duntroon all around him. His uniform was never quite at standard, he missed classes and drills, and he eluded most punishments. He was also allowed to go into town to work for the Defence Department, even though the Duntroon hierarchy hated it. He never put up a fight about anything, just folded as soon as someone pulled him up, but he did whatever he liked.

Colin asked me where I'd been. I said home and he nodded without saying more. I assumed he hadn't heard about Dad. I was glad. I wanted someone I could be normal with.

'I'm after some records,' I said. Colin had access to Army computer systems, which in those days were less secure than they are now. I thought he might be able to help me. 'It's about my father, actually. I want to see his service history.'

Often Colin closed his eyes tight to blink and then

opened them wide as if he had something in them. It was almost a facial tic. He said, 'I've seen the Commandant's entire staff file. Only the computer part though. They have the paper files with all the juicy bits locked away in the staff section bunker. Did you know Herr Commandant's appointment was nearly blocked?' I didn't. 'Yeah, he's liberal, if you can believe it. The guy the Army wanted was right of Genghis Khan. But the university weighed in and said they had to get someone with academic credentials. Stop the bastardisation.' Colin giggled nervously, a habit that, along with the facial tic, had gone when we met up later in life. He shifted from one foot to the other as he talked.

We'd stopped outside the dorm and blokes were filing past. I lowered my voice. 'I want to see where my father went in the last year,' I said, 'and the Army won't let me.'

Colin winked and whispered, 'The snows are heavy in Moscow this year, Boris,' in a thick Russian accent, which he thought was really funny, only it wasn't.

Brett Anderson and one of his friends passed us then and said, 'Hey, girls.' Colin didn't respond to them.

The next night I snuck out of Duntroon in the boot of Colin's HQ Holden, moving to the front with him just outside the gates. We drove through the flat, wet streets of Canberra, past groomed gardens and Frank Lloyd Wright style houses, and into the city centre. Colin said that in Canberra even the graffiti was part of the town plan.

I told Colin about Anderson wanting me to join his group. 'Do you want to?' he said.

'Course not,' I said. 'They're a bunch of wankers.'

'Just tell him that, then.'

'I'm not sure he's the sort of guy who'd understand a polite refusal.'

'So tell him you think he's a wanker.'

'Oh yeah,' I said. 'That would be so easy.'

'I don't see why you can't,' Colin said.

'Well, you don't see most things,' I said.

'God, Duntroon's a stupid place,' Colin sighed. I didn't respond. 'For instance, if you get caught tonight, you're AWOL and you'll be expelled, just for coming into town with me to play on the computer.'

'Don't remind me.'

'On the other hand, everyone in college knows Anderson nearly killed Michael Shannahan. But nothing's happened to Anderson. In fact, Michael Shannahan's the one who left.'

'What's that got to do with joining their group or not?'

'Everything. If you say no, it could be the start of something.'

'Why don't you say no, then?'

'They haven't asked me to join.'

Colin had a card to clear him into the carpark and the computer centre. Later, I learned he worked on Australia's first satellite defence system, but at the time I had no idea what he did. I wasn't questioned at the gate, although we agreed he'd say I was a new programmer if anyone asked. We were both in civvies.

Colin didn't have legitimate access to the files we needed. The department's computers were secured on a need-to-know basis and the only user with access to everything was the system manager. All we needed, Colin said, was the system manager's password.

'You going to guess it?' I said.

Colin was smiling. 'I don't guess.'

I looked over at the skinny girl sitting at the desk in the glass machine room that was at the centre of the large open-plan office where we were working. 'Torture?'

'You can take the boy out of Duntroon ... No, I'm not going to torture her, Scott. Wouldn't do any good anyway. She doesn't know it. But the system manager has already written down his password and dropped it right in our laps.' I was confused. Colin smiled and blinked hard. He'd written a little program, he said, that emulated the central computer's operating system. He left the program running on the system manager's computer terminal. When the system manager came to log in, the program did all the things the operating system normally did, including prompting for password. But when the system manager typed the password, it told him it was incorrect and to start again, which was what the operating system itself would do if the password was in fact wrong. Then Colin's program ended and took the user back to the real operating system. The system manager logged on as normal. 'Meantime, the program has stored the first password he typed, correctly we hope, in my file,' Colin said. 'It's brilliant, even if I do say so myself.'

While Colin worked I watched the operator and the flashing lights and spinning tapes of the computer behind her. This wasn't the central computer, Colin told me, just a connected minicomputer that could access the Army's databanks. The central computer was two floors down from us.

'Hey, was your old man discharged?' Colin said. Flashing in green at the top of the screen was my father's name: Goodwin, Maj Allan George. It took me a moment to catch up.

'No, he wasn't discharged,' I said. The information Colin scrolled through — Dad's full name, date of birth, date of joining — was correct as far as I knew. 'Why?'

'They've closed his file. That usually means discharge.'

We passed the list of Dad's decorations. 'He had a lot of tin bits,' Colin said, pointing with a long elegant finger. He was a guitarist, I learned, which was why his nails were long on one hand. 'Bugger. They won't let me in to his PERSII file, which is the active service file. It says PERSII has been archived. This is as far as it goes.'

We scrolled further down the PERSI screen. I saw Dad's postings since he'd joined the Army: Melbourne, Toowoomba, Albury, Toowoomba, Vietnam, Too-woomba, Canberra, Townsville, Melbourne, Brisbane, Melbourne, Canungra. 'With the other guys I've looked up, I got into work history and stuff which is in PERSII,' Colin said. 'Look here.' We'd come to the end of the list of postings, after which the record ended with 'FILE TERMINATED' and a date, just over a month earlier. 'That's what makes me think he must have been discharged.'

'He died a month after that,' I said. 'Would that explain it?'

'No, unless when you die they take out your service records like they do when you're discharged. And I suppose they might do that, but I don't know why. You'd think they'd mark you as dead because the pension's different.' Colin blinked hard. 'What did he die of, by the way?'

'Asthma.' Colin nodded. There was a pause. 'I want to know where he went in those last few months. I hadn't seen him for a while.'

'Right. Well, it says here he was last posted to Canungra, and that was six months ago, so I assume that's where he was.'

'You said they recorded movements. I reckon he went somewhere overseas in the last couple of months. I want to know where.'

'Now you're getting tricky.' In all the time I've known him, Colin's never mentioned that night again, why I wanted the information, or anything to do with my father. He didn't offer sympathy then or subsequently, even though he must have worked out how recent Dad's death had been. I was glad he didn't. It made the job easier.

'You didn't tell me he was Intelligence Corps,' Colin said. 'They're good at secrets. Maybe that's why I can't get into the other files.' He typed in commands for a few minutes more and said, 'Bingo. Movements over the last year. It's not everything, but it's a start.' I looked at the screen. The posting to Canungra, a trip to Canberra for an interview of some sort, and at the bottom, before the crosshatch symbol indicating the end of the record, was Dad's final move with the Army. He'd been airlifted to

Darwin six weeks before he died, two weeks before the file was terminated. From Darwin he could have gone to Cambodia or New Guinea. The records could have been altered to delete the mission. Kerry might have been right, after all. The dates were a fit.

'Could he have gone somewhere from Darwin,' I said, 'but not have it in the records?'

'I don't know. I suppose S-12's like the Secret Service. They do what they like.'

'Can you get me any more details?' I said, pointing to the Darwin entry.

'Holy shit,' Colin said suddenly. 'We're in trouble.' On the screen was a flashing message: 'User #62839, please identify'. 'I think we've been sprung. That's from central office. They're a bit quick tonight. We better get out of here.' Just as Colin logged off, a second warning message asked him to identify himself. I looked over at the machine room. The operator was on the phone but it didn't look like a work call. 'Won't be her,' Colin said. 'They've discovered a system manager logon to the mainframe and they're wondering who I am.'

The next day, Colin was questioned by two Defence Department investigators about why he'd logged on to the system and how he'd obtained the password. They knew it was him because he was the only programmer who clocked on that night. He told them he'd guessed the password. They didn't believe him. The password was changed every week according to a secret formula. Did he know the formula? No, he said, it was a lucky guess. When he told me about it, he didn't seem worried. 'What are they going to do,' he said, 'sack me?' They knew he'd cracked something, though. They told him they weren't going to take it further, this time. They changed the formula.

'Let's just forget about it,' I said. 'I don't want to get you into trouble.'

'Who cares?' he said. 'I wouldn't mind if they fired me, to be honest. But I think the guy in the carpark told them about you, so we might wait a few days before we try again.'

I left Colin at study time. He was going back to work and I had to catch up on the night before's study. You couldn't afford to get behind at Duntroon, and I'd already missed a lot of classes while I was back in Brisbane. I sat there for hours in a carrel in the library, but I couldn't concentrate. I read the same page over and over but nothing went in. Finally I gave up and went to bed. It was after lights-out when I reached my room. I went in quietly, undressed, putting everything away as I went, and prepared my kit for the morning. I soon fell into a deep dreamless sleep. Some time later, I was woken by a cry at the end of the corridor. It was such a desperate sound that I was sure I'd dreamed it. By the time I started to relax back into sleep, another cry was breaking the still Duntroon night. I sat up in bed. 'Please. No,' someone moaned after the second cry.

I got out of bed, opened my door and looked down the corridor. The bathroom doors had been closed but the lights were on. I figured Brett Anderson and his buddies were initiating some guy who'd changed his mind about being an Argonaut. I was just glad it wasn't me. I hadn't given Anderson an answer to his invitation yet and was hoping he might forget. I heard another moan. The poor bastard was making it worse for himself showing his fear. Never show fear, Dad always said. I got out of bed and walked quietly down the hall past the other rooms to the bathroom door. I opened it a crack and peered in. It was Anderson and his group, all right, half a dozen surrounding a little guy on the floor. Anderson was facing me and I think he saw me. I went back to bed.

I was never much good at fighting. Any time Dad tried to teach me, I was never fast enough. He said I didn't have the right spirit. En garde, he'd say, but he'd get through my defence in a second. Dad would have been able to help a guy who was calling out in the night. I lay in bed for a few moments more. I heard another little moan. I got up and walked towards the bathroom, slowly and purposefully. 'Beware the quiet man,' I whispered. When I opened the door this time, Anderson and his boys were crouched down around the guy, who was now still and silent on the terrazzo floor. They had a pillowcase over his head and his pyjama pants halfway down. His legs were really white. He'd gone so quiet and limp that in my dreamy state I wondered for a moment if they'd killed him.

I walked up behind Anderson, who now had his back to me. The other boys stood back. I tapped Anderson on the shoulder. 'What the fuck are you doing?' I said, trying not to sound scared.

'What's your problem?' He was holding a toilet brush in his right hand. It looked so surreal. I didn't imagine you could write on someone's bum with a toilet brush.

'I don't have a problem,' I said, 'but this guy doesn't want to be in your club.' The guy on the floor still hadn't moved.

'Is-at right?' Anderson said. He had a big face with dull grey eyes. I nodded and said yep, emphasising the p in a tough way. 'Well, I reckon you ought to mind your own business.' I was looking around, planning an exit with the guy on the floor. Anderson's boys had gathered at the dorm end behind me. In front were the fire stairs; we might go that way. I knew none of my colleagues would lift a finger to help me against Brett Anderson. I moved towards the boy on the floor. Anderson dropped the toilet brush and moved between me and the boy. I stood up to face him.

'You don't want this,' I said.

I blinked slowly and looked at us in the mirror, two boys facing off. Anderson wasn't quite as tall as me at six three, but he was solid where I'd got skinny. I relaxed my body and watched his eyes, like Dad had shown me. When they narrowed just slightly, I bent down and headbutted him in the chest as hard as I could. It took the wind out of him and his swing missed me by a mile.

While he was off balance I started punching, anything I could make contact with. When you punch, punch mean, Dad said, punch whatever you can. Don't ever let anyone tell you to fight fair. If it's a fight, you're there to win, not to be fair. I shoved Anderson towards the basins, clearing a way to the exit. 'Run!' I screamed at the guy on the floor as I felt my knuckle hit tooth. He was getting up, pulling up his pants and at the pillowcase over his head. And then I saw. It was Colin Rawlins. 'Jesus,' I screamed, 'you bastards.'

By the time help arrived, Anderson's boys had worked me over well enough to send me to the infirmary. Two of them pulled me off Anderson and held me by the arms while he punched me in the stomach. I vomited my dinner on him and passed out. They kicked me until they broke a couple of ribs, and left me just before the dorm officer came in to break it up.

I felt great when I was hitting Anderson. He seemed so small. I felt I could kill him and it would feel like the best thing in the world. Early the next morning, stoned on painkillers, I was back on a summer evening in the shed with Dad, cicadas singing the evening in, the Jag under a light globe, perfectly sanded shiny grey metal. He shows me how to guard my face against a blow, like I did with Anderson, how to use one arm for protection, one arm to strike. He moves my hips and legs in a dance to show me how to avoid being punched. His heroes were Cassius Clay and Elvis Presley, both dancers, he said. Elvis gave a woman a Cadillac once because he could. That's the generosity of the man, he said. En garde, he used to say. En garde. No matter how good I got, I could never manage to hit him.

I didn't have the courage to blow the whistle, but Colin did. He stood up in the investigating committee, in front of them all, and said what they'd done to him. No one at Duntroon had dared do that before. He named them. They were going to fuck Colin with the toilet brush, not to initiate him, they said, but because he was a poofter and would enjoy it. I admired that Colin could stand up and say what those cowards did. I don't think I could have managed it. He came to see me the night after it happened. He thanked me. 'I hate it here,' he said. There were big dark patches under his eyes. He was almost in tears.

The Army's respect for discipline was cursory when it came to some activities. We were all suspended, but almost as a joke. 'A week's suspension, and then it's your first term holidays,' our dormy told us. He winked. 'Just like an extended vacation.'

Colin left Duntroon for good that day. So did I, although I didn't know it at the time.

chapternineteen

Mum let out a little cry when she saw the bruises on my face. By then they were deep grey and green and looked worse than they felt. My ribs still ached but I was mending. Mum said she knew this would happen and she wished I'd never gone back. She'd cooked me this banana cake that looked like you could kill someone with it. She said it was my favourite, but I don't remember ever eating anything quite like it in my life. I had three pieces and they sat in my stomach for a week. I left a message for Stella that I wanted to come and stay at her place. I didn't think I could cope with Mum fussing over me.

A letter for me from Dad's CO provided a copy of Dad's movement sheet, which I'd requested before I went back to Duntroon. It showed where he'd been posted to, and when, from the computer records Colin had found for me. They also included records of his war service and commendations, including the citation for his Victoria Cross. It said he'd been forward scout for a small group intercepted by a superior Viet Cong force. Dad was severely wounded in the leg, the citation said, and he and the other six men were separated by fire from their CO, Sergeant Kerry Vance and the other survivor, Corporal Dick Jarratt. Dad had managed, despite injury, to rally the group to form a defensive position. By personal example and inspiring leadership, the citation said, Dad had held off repeated assaults by the Viet Cong force until, with ammunition exhausted and himself weak from loss of blood, the group was reunited with their CO. Only then did Dad permit himself to collapse.

The letter also provided a report on Dad's performance at the US academy where he'd been trained for S-12. It had been a computer technicians' course, which surprised me. His most recent moves, from Brisbane to Melbourne and then to Canungra, corresponded with what we knew. They'd included the airlift to Darwin with the explanation: 'on exercise'.

I called Dad's office from a public phone and spoke to Corporal Peter White. I said I wanted more information. 'I sent you everything I could, I'm afraid. You'd have to write to Canberra to get access to anything else. And I don't like your chances. We deal with a lot of classified information, as you can appreciate.'

'I'm Duntroon,' I said. 'Does that give me privileges?'

'Doubt it. There's the thirty-year rule, and personnel stuff is never released. It's confidential between the individual soldier, his unit CO and the Staff Officer.

You're not worried about anything in particular, are you? I don't know what rumours you might have heard. Maybe if you tell me what you're looking for, I might be able to sort you out over the phone.'

'I was after information on what he actually did.'

'I can send you his duty statement which tells you about his job, who he reported to and so forth.'

'It's more than that,' I said. 'I want details of the missions he went on. We didn't always know where he was. I believe he was in New Guinea just before he died, but that's not marked here.'

Corporal White was cool. 'We can't release that kind of information, Scott. As you know, S-12's work is sensitive. We're not where you think we are, kind of thing. But your dad wasn't a field officer, so he didn't go on our missions.'

'What do you mean?'

'Our Signals staff work in-house. Your dad only went away when there was a technical problem. He used to stay at the base here a bit when they were trying to meet a deadline. But he didn't go on missions.'

'What?'

'He was one of our techos. Signals.'

'Thank you,' I said and hung up. I didn't believe him. Kerry Vance had told me to be careful about snooping round the Army. He'd said I could be in danger.

I asked Mum, 'What was Dad's job?'

'He was in Intelligence. You know that.' Mum looked at me differently when we talked now, as if she was wary about where conversations might go. I'd noticed her and Jim whispering in the kitchen, stopping and smiling too keenly when I walked in. At times I felt like I had a bomb inside me.

'And he had to go on missions.'

'He went away with work.'

'What was he doing?'

'He worked on computers.'

'But he didn't work on computers when he went on missions, did he?'

'I'm pretty sure that's all he ever did. They weren't exactly missions, I don't think.'

'But he was out in the field all the time, on secret missions.' Mum didn't say anything. 'Dad wasn't a liar.'

'No, and he did travel for work, but he worked on computers. You know that. He went to the States to retrain.'

'But he said his work was top secret.'

'Of course, darling, and it probably was. But he wasn't involved in active service. I think sometimes he exaggerated when he talked to you kids. You know what he was like.' Mum was smiling nervously, as if we were sharing an intimacy about someone's small flaws, not a lie about my father and what his life had been made up of.

'Then why did you lie to us about where he was going?'

'I didn't lie. He went on exercises in Australia. I don't remember any real missions, though. He couldn't do active service after Vietnam because of his leg. I think he just liked you to think well of him.'

'You used to worry about him.'

'Well, of course I did. He was away from home and I was a lot more nervy when you kids were little.'

'But why didn't you tell me what he did?'

'I always thought you knew. I didn't think you or Stella believed his stories.'

My father hated lies. The truth will set you free, he'd say after he'd locked you in your room for a lie he knew you were telling. Lies were worse than selfishness and liars were the lowest form of human life. Eventually their lies caught up with them. According to the Army and Mum, Dad had lied to me about his work, if not with an out-and-out lie, then with a lie by omission. He'd been in Army Intelligence since Vietnam. When I'd asked if something was dangerous or if there was gunfire or did he kill anyone, he'd nod his head and say beware the quiet man. He'd tell me young people on their overseas trips didn't know what they were seeing compared with the overseas he'd seen, the real thing. And all the while, according to my mother and Peter White, he'd been at home, or in an office somewhere, listening to messages or working on computers.

The next morning I caught the six am bus back to Marion's. I stood on the front step. There was a brass bell. I knocked on the door loudly. Marion opened it a crack. There was a chain lock. 'You have to tell me where he is,' I said to the chain.

'You can't come in,' she said. She was wearing men's pyjamas, his pyjamas.

'Is he here? Is that it? You have to tell me. I'm his fucking son.' I realised I was crying.

'I don't have to do anything. You can't come here, Scott. You must know that. Your father's gone. There's nothing you can do now.' There was pity in her voice.

I could only see one of her eyes. There was pity there too. I looked away.

'Please,' I said. 'I just want to know what they did to him.' My voice was unsteady. I was shaking.

'No one did anything to him. He's just gone, that's all. He can't come back.'

I left Marion's and wandered the streets of Canungra by myself. I don't remember what I did. I couldn't focus. An episode, the doctors called it when they talked to Mum and Stella. Eventually I found the bus stop and waited for an hour for the last bus home. Marion must have phoned again, because by the time I got to Mum's, Jim and Stella had arrived and we were in family conference mode.

I was put on the couch by myself and they faced me on hard-backed dining chairs, like an interrogation committee. Mum was talking. 'She said she can understand you're upset, Scott. I can too. But you can't go to her place. It's not normal.'

'What was she doing at the hospital all night?'

'Her daughter has asthma. She spends nights there.'

'Jim has this colleague I told you about,' Mum said. 'Someone outside the family you could talk to. You've had to deal with more than a boy should at your age. Maybe you could tell her about these problems you've been having with Dad's death and she could help.' Mum went to take my hand across the coffee table. I pulled away. 'I want you to go visit this psychologist Jim suggested. And you're not to go back to Duntroon until you're well.'

'You can't stop me,' I said.

'Hey, Scott,' Jim said. He had a quiet voice and fat on his hips and gut. He was nice. He was weak.

'Anyway,' I said to Mum, ignoring Jim, 'if it weren't for you ... You made him leave us,' I said, and at that moment I truly believed it. 'I couldn't go and see him.'

'I didn't stop you, Scott.'

'Yes you did. You fell apart and I had to look after you. I couldn't leave you, could I?' Stella tried to interrupt. 'And you, Stella! Fuck you! You cleared out, left me to manage by myself. It was fine for me to be the grown-up then. You all let me do that. Now, when I really do know something the rest of you don't, I'm just some mixed-up kid. Dad was involved in a mission to New Guinea. He might be sick or injured. But you wouldn't care, would you? As far as I'm concerned you can all go fuck yourselves.'

I'd stood up, and Jim came over to grab me. I suppose I was pretty worked up, and I swung a bit of a punch his way, and it connected with his cheek. My fist hurt, as I remember, and his cheek blushed straight away. That ended the family conference.

'You're going to turn out just like him, aren't you?' Mum said. She left the room followed by Jim, who was nursing his cheek and telling her not to worry.

Stella glared at me. 'You can't possibly believe Mum's done anything wrong, Scott. She's looked after you, we paid for a good school, and made sure you had whatever you wanted. You're a bastard sometimes. You're getting more and more like Dad every day, and I like you less and less.' Stella had said it as an insult, and Mum had too. I nursed my fist and felt proud of myself. I was just like Dad.

chapter**twenty**

I'm embarrassed now to think of some of the things I did, I told Emily, and all I can say by way of excuse is that I was stretched. She said she could understand, and looked as if she meant it. She was being careful with me, I could see, but not out of fear.

Looking back, I wish I'd acted differently, that I'd been a better person, but I was seventeen and inexperienced about the world even for my age. He'd kept us from people outside the family unless they were his friends. Mr Rebo, Mr Maitland, the father of one of the guys at school — Dad wouldn't let me spend a Christmas on their property out west. Even Grandad. Dad didn't like me being close to anyone he didn't approve of. As a result, I didn't know what was safe or who to trust. Dad always knew if people were good or bad. I never had to suss that out for myself because he did it for me.

That night I went home with Stella. While at first

she wouldn't speak to me, by the time we got onto the freeway, she'd forgiven me my outburst. Stella couldn't hold a grudge against me if she tried. Back at her place we smoked a few joints and she told me I had to get my shit together and stop being horrible to Mum. The next morning I caught a taxi back to Mum's to pick up some clothes. I thought it would be best if I stayed at Stella's for a while. I left it until eight, knowing Mum would have gone to work. In the lounge, the little answering machine light blinked. There was a message.

'Hey, kiddo, that you? Heard you got roughed up at Duntroon. Hate to see the other guy. Ha ha. Bet you can't guess who this is? See you real soon.'

I called Stella at work. 'Get over here. Dad's phoned.'

She arrived twenty minutes later. 'Are you okay, Scott?' I took her in and played the recording. She looked at me. 'Did you make this?'

'What are you talking about?'

'Is it your voice?'

'Don't be fucking stupid. It's Dad. I told you, he's not gone.'

I played the tape again.

Stella said: 'It's someone we know, Scott, but it's not Dad. It doesn't sound anything like him. The accent's not broad enough. It sounds … like you.' Stella was talking gently. I didn't like this. Stella wasn't gentle. It made me feel crazy.

'Look, Stella, I went to see Kerry Vance. He reckons Dad was part of a mission to New Guinea to save some hostages. Dad could be hurt or sick somewhere and trying to contact us.'

'What are you talking about? What mission?'

'Kerry showed me a report that proves S-12 was in New Guinea around the time of Dad's supposed death.'

'Jesus, Scott. Kerry Vance believes little people from Mars are mining the moon. The guy's a lunatic.'

'I've seen the report, Stella. It recommends they attack the rebel camp.'

'So?' Stella said. 'There must be a million reports like that. The Army's full of guys who want to attack other guys.'

'Dad was airlifted to Darwin just before the mission.'

'I know. He was on an exercise. Marion told me she thought the climate change had something to do with the asthma attack. It doesn't mean anything, you idiot. I left work for this. I have to get back.' She leaned forward and pressed erase on the answering machine. I lunged too late.

'No!' I screamed. 'Fuck, Stella, fuck fuck fuck! What will I do now for proof?' I ran out of the house with Stella following me to the door. Up the street I caught a bus to the city.

I took another bus from the city to Marion's place, accompanied by a group of tourists from Japan, on their way to the Gold Coast and its glitz. From across the street in the soldier park I watched as Marion piled the kids in the car. After she pulled away, I crossed the street. The sun was hot on the nape of my neck. I walked around the house to the back and climbed up onto a low deck which had French doors into the house. I broke the glass on one of the doors with a rock. The noise startled me. I reached in and unlocked the door with my

T-shirt wrapped around my fist, like I'd seen on television. I went inside.

The house looked vaguely eastern, grass mats on the floors and cane furniture. Off the entry was the small kitchen, finished in seventies green laminate and quarry tile.

I found Marion's room, simply furnished with an Indian spread over the bed and shelves of books I'd never heard of. I went through the dressing table. The bottom drawer held T-shirts and sweaters. The middle was underwear. In the top drawer I found a mess of papers, bills, notes, pencils, pens, makeup and jewellery. There were a few dozen of the standard-issue envelopes the Army used. I picked one up. He'd written to her. I took out the letter. He'd put the date and location coordinates in the top right hand corner, just like in his letters to me. He was in western Queensland. 'My darling Marion' at the top, in his neat script.

I miss you madly and I can hardly believe it's only a few days to go. We've had a great month. They gave out the awards yesterday ahead of demob. My section was the neatest, not bad for the motley crew they started as. I never thought they'd pull into line. They're good young blokes, just didn't have the right leadership. They sent the first CO home and the new bloke's much better. I don't know what will happen or if they'll charge the first guy. I don't think they can, really.

I was with some Yanks last night. They're here for the last two weeks. We sat around the mess drinking and talking until late. Turns out we'd all seen some action one way or another, which is pretty rare these days. One Captain who'd done three tours of Vietnam had been at Long Tan as a medic. He joined regular after the war and now he's a doctor. A lot of blokes make jokes about what happened in-country, or they fume, but this Captain just stared it all in the face, everything all of us ever did, almost like he understood. It gave him such power. He was in tears as he spoke. You'd have liked him, I think. He had true courage.

Some of the other blokes wanted him to stop talking but he kept right on until he finished. He was there when they found the ten guys who died sitting up. He said they looked as if they were having a beer together. There were wounded everywhere he looked, he said. He didn't know what to do to help anyone, there were too many and he was scared shitless. He went and hid under a truck. I really understood that.

After he left, one of the other blokes, a Yank, said that while he hated being in combat, he also loved its memory. A few of them agreed. You're going to be upset to read this, Marion, but I realised that I couldn't be anywhere else but in the Army. Will you forgive me for that, do you think, my darling?

Before I forget. The school thing. I don't want Michael forced to do anything, and I don't want him punished. It's supposed to be a state school and we're supposed to have a choice. Did the principal say why he has to go to one of the classes? Why can't he go to the library or something? That's what kids used to do. I'm right behind you on this one, sweetheart. If you don't want him to go to their religion, tell them he doesn't need it shoved down his throat. He's only five. Tell them about our Sundays, enough religion to take us all to Heaven (just kidding). They make me sick, the sanctimonious do-gooders.

Give Jason a kiss on the knee for Daddy and tell him we can fix the bike soon as I get back. And a big hug for Blossom. Hope she's over the vomiting thing.

Love to you too. I'll get this off now to catch the mail (16:00 H).

PS One of the guys here said his kids were given exemptions from religion and they let them do sport instead. And his kids didn't even go to another church. Tell that to the principal. The school was in Shepparton. I can get the name if he needs it.

PPS I just found out they're sending my section on tomorrow as part of the advance. I can't stand the idea of being fired on, even if it's only a make-believe enemy. You never get used to it, not as long as you live. I saw the Kangaroo team, my enemy, huddled round their tents this evening. Don't worry, the humour of a situation where you go to bed with your 'enemy' didn't escape me. You'd have been proud of my self-reflection, I think.

I miss you and the kids so much.

I didn't want to read any more. It was making me feel sick. I left the envelope on the dresser. In Marion's walk-in closet I found his clothes, his Army uniforms, his white singlets hanging there as if he'd put one on that morning. I stood in the closet and looked out into the room. Then I saw a photograph of him on the bedside table. He was standing out the front of Marion's house, in shorts and a T-shirt, washing the Fiat. His hair was messy, and he was grinning at the camera, squinting in the sun. It was Dad as I remembered him, and not the man in the coffin. To me, it looked different enough to convince someone else. I walked out of the closet, pulled the frame apart and took out the photo.

I sat down on the bed. Dad hadn't lost weight. If anything, he'd filled out. He smiled like someone who'd just found out they'd won the lottery, like the photograph of him dancing with Mum. He looked happy and well. In front of him was a kid's pool. He'd said 'My darling Marion' in his letters. He'd said 'our kids'. He was going to fix their bikes. He'd objected to religion classes for Michael. He'd done the same with me.

I heard a noise outside, a car pulling into the drive. I got back into the closet. I heard Marion's voice, talking loudly. When I heard sirens, I wondered where they were going.

I fought the police. I know that it was the wrong thing to do, it made me look crazy, but I'd started to think that everyone knew something they weren't telling me, even Mum and Stella. It was the older of the two officers who found me. 'Well well,' he said. 'Where did you come from?' I took a dive, somewhere in his middle. He collapsed backwards with me on top. His partner was in the doorway, legs apart, yelling, 'Down on the floor, hands in front! Down on the floor, hands in front!' like Ricardo or Sonny on 'Miami Vice'. The older officer was up on his knees, outside the closet, and I was facing him, breathing heavily. The one in the doorway had a gun pointed at me. I figured I could probably push past him while the older one was recovering.

I heard Marion's voice behind them. 'Wait!' she yelled. 'Please, he's just a kid and he hasn't done anything. God, Scott,' she called to me. 'Why didn't you tell me you

were here?' as if we were friends. She was peering through
the door from the hallway. She looked scared and upset.
Everyone looked scared and upset. 'Scott,' she said, 'just
do what they tell you. Please, he's mixed up, not a robber,'
she said to the young officer.

'Down on the floor!' the young officer screamed.

'Hang on, Mike,' the older officer panted, still
rubbing his ribs. 'Did she say Scott? His name's Scott?'
The older officer was looking at me, his hand giving a
stop signal to his partner behind him. His eyes were light
blue. 'Hey, Scott. I'm Brian,' he said with a big calming
breath. 'You have to come with us, son.' His voice was
soft too. I felt like crying. I slipped the photograph of
Dad into my jeans pocket and let him take my arms.

In the car he said I sure packed a wallop.

It could have been worse. I could have been charged
with break and enter, assaulting a police officer and God
knows what else. I could have a criminal record. Mum
called Stella and Stella called Tony Matthews, who
arranged for a partner in their criminal division to
represent me. Marion didn't press charges.

I tried to tell the officers who interviewed me what I
knew, that Dad wasn't really dead, or if he was, he wasn't
in the coffin, that Marion said he hated the Army now
and he didn't as the letter he'd written to her proved, that
I could get my photo, compare it with a photo of Dad
and prove to them it wasn't Dad in the coffin, that he
was cremated instead of buried to destroy evidence, that
he was on a mission to save Australian lives and the Army
faked his death, that he might still be alive and we might
be able to find him, that I could show them if they only

gave me a chance. I talked fast, to get it all out. They listened patiently. I was raving.

The police agreed with the lawyer to section me, which meant I had to go to a hospital to be assessed by psychiatrists. Mr Maitland could have dined out for a month on the story of this infringement of my civil rights. The doctors reckoned I was in a drug-induced psychosis. They said it in such calming, assured voices. I was delusional. Schizophrenia. Late adolescent onset. Common. When they heard all that, Stella and Mum were more than happy to sign me in. Maybe they even thought it would fix me. I was committed until further notice. I wasn't scared, which shows how crazy I really was by then.

In the hospital Mum's brother visited and said he'd made the call on our answering machine. My young uncle and aunt looked uncomfortable in the whiteness of the psych ward. Mum had phoned him to tell him she was worried about me. 'We're coming back to Australia to live, and I just thought it would be fun to tell you. I'm real sorry, kiddo.' I didn't believe him.

Marion had phoned the police station and the police came to the hospital to collect the missing photograph. What I wondered, of course, was why on earth Marion would want that photograph back, unless she was worried it might prove the dead man wasn't Dad.

chapter twenty-one

Dad used to say that the trick with swimming in the sea is not to fight. In the hospital I had the bed near the window because I was the only one who didn't mind the outside. It was one of those old-fashioned pull-up windows, with ropes to hold the sashes in place, only they'd taken out the ropes and had sealed the window shut. It still whined and rattled whenever there was a breeze, which spooked the guy in the bed next to me, who thought it was a dog. A dog cried the night his wife died, apparently. The frames had been painted sloppily, leaving a crooked line of white on the glass down one side.

Mum withdrew me from Duntroon. 'How will Dad know where to find me?' I said the first time she visited.

'Please come back to us,' she said, as if I was the one who'd left.

Only one of the half a dozen doctors who examined me took my story seriously. His name was Dr Manko, but he wasn't a psychiatrist yet like the rest. His job was to take a history, he said. Over several days I told him everything, even my doubts. Manko had big ears and a big nose and sad, gentle eyes like a clown. He put me at my ease.

At first Manko asked the standard questions they all asked about me — Dad, the family etc. — but slowly he got interested in the story itself. He asked me about Marion and I told him she'd organised the funeral for someone who was nothing like Dad, and that a couple of times I'd thought she was on the verge of telling me something. Manko was interested in Kerry Vance and his story of the mission in New Guinea too. Manko asked questions that suggested he accepted my suspicions, although in the back of my mind I knew he probably didn't believe a word I said. He said we should do 'an appreciation of events'. On a clean page of a sketchblock Manko requisitioned for the purpose, I wrote down all the things I thought I knew. Then we had to distinguish between evidence, deduction and assertion, Manko said, and sometimes this was difficult.

I told Manko I'd come to believe Mum and the Army and Stella were lying about what had happened. Manko chuckled at that and said that just because I was paranoid didn't mean they weren't all out to get me. I didn't understand the joke. 'They said he worked in Signals,' I said. 'That he worked on computers in an office.'

'Maybe he did. So what?'

'He went on missions, and they're saying he worked on technical stuff and that what he did wasn't dangerous.'

'Well, maybe he did work on technical stuff. They shoot technicians too, I bet.'

'That would mean he lied to me.'

'Yes, it would. Maybe being a big guy was more important to him than the strict truth of a matter. He wouldn't be the first person to feel that, would he?' I started to protest but Manko stopped me. 'And maybe your sister truly believed the body was your father's. That's understandable too, isn't it? You're the only one who thought otherwise.

'And maybe your father's friend, Kerry Vance, is just plain stupid. Then again, maybe he's involved in something, like you've asserted. I've been thinking about all this, Scott, and I reckon it's possible you've been blind to the obvious. When you list down all the evidence like we have, and separate it from your assertions, there's a pretty logical deduction we could make that you've missed. If you accept you haven't been seeing too clearly lately, you'd be left with an interesting possibility.'

'What?' I said. I thought Manko was using his logic in a bid to convince me I was wrong. I was shaking my head.

'Let's start by crossing out the bit about the Army and Stella and your mother.' I didn't want to. 'Indulge me for a moment.' When Manko smiled, as he did then, his ears moved. He looked like a little elf. It was disarming. I ruled a soft neat line through three points on my sheet of paper. 'Look at that bit of paper, Scott.' I didn't see. 'Turn it round. Read it upside down.' I did. I still didn't see anything. 'Who's missing?' he said. I didn't know. 'Look again.' Nothing. 'Where's your father, Scott?' he said, gently.

I saw where I thought he might be headed. Marion could have murdered Dad. 'Stella's idea,' I said. 'But then the body would still be Dad. Why bother with a second body? Unless she'd shot him or something.' I thought about that.

Manko smiled. 'Bastard's got you blind.' I didn't know what Manko meant, and he was starting to annoy me. He turned the page over so I was looking at the blank side. 'You've said it yourself. If Marion killed your father, you'd still have his body. And the only thing you absolutely don't have is that bloody body. So, who's missing?' he said. 'We've got one dead body who isn't your father. Who don't we have?'

'Dad.' The penny dropped and everything clicked right into place as if it had always been there. Of course. 'You're saying my father did this.'

'Exactly.'

'But why?' I said. I stood and walked to the window and pulled at the sealed sash roughly.

'Was he paying your mother maintenance?'

'Yeah, so?'

'Maybe he needed money for something. A habit of some sort. But if it really wasn't his body, and bear in mind that's still an assertion, then maybe the bastard's alive somewhere, just as you've always believed. That's one theory.

'You're not a fool, Scott, just loyal. One thing about people who die, they always leave behind a body. Trust me. It's death's calling card. And the one thing you've assured me you don't have is your father's body. If you're right, you're not crazy. You're just like the rest of us.

You've been had.' He said this last sentence so tenderly, I could have cried.

'There's a flip side,' Manko said, resuming his deductive tone. 'If the body isn't your father, then who is it? That's the other thing about dead bodies. They're always attached to former living people. If I was on your investigation, and I believed your story about the body not being the body, I'd start by finding out who the dead guy was. Follow the body you've got, that's my tip.'

The one person I'd never considered to be part of the deception was Dad. But as soon as Manko said it, I saw it was obvious, even as I wanted to hit Manko for saying it. I noticed a smokestack blowing white smoke or steam from another part of the hospital. In the Vatican, the white smoke would mean the Cardinals had managed to elect the new Pontiff.

It all fell together neatly. Marion was no kind of spy, and the Army would never use a civilian situation. If they wanted to lie about how he died, they'd simply pretend he'd been killed in an accident somewhere other than New Guinea. Kerry Vance had to be involved. The convenient New Guinea mission, the way he led me to it by the nose. I'd been stupid to trust him. I imagined him telling Dad how clever he'd been, how he'd thrown me off the track, how naïve I was. They probably wrote the report I saw and had a few laughs. Dad's toolbox in his workshop. The newspaper report could have been months old. Kerry had handwritten the date. I hadn't even checked.

Marion wasn't confident like Kerry, but she knew too, I was sure. She might have been scared at the funeral home, scared every time she saw me, but she went through and stuck to her story. She changed the instructions about disposal of the body to get rid of the only evidence that could prove he wasn't dead. Stella and Mum and me had been had, all right, but not by the Army. It was Dad himself, and Marion, and Kerry Vance, and they must have had a reason. And I was in a psychiatric hospital because of what they'd all done, with no chance of getting out in a hurry. I looked up to ask Manko what I should do now, but Manko had already left.

The next morning he came into my room and said the hardest thing anyone's ever said to me, but by then I trusted him well enough to hear it. 'If we're right, Scott, and I'm not saying we are, but if we're right, and the body wasn't your father's body, and he's not dead, and he knows you've been looking for him and he hasn't come to see you, he's making one thing clear. He watched you go mad, son. He doesn't want to see you. He doesn't care.

'And if you're wrong about the body, and you still could be, if he is dead, he didn't want to see you when he was alive. Either way, he doesn't care.

'And your challenge is to accept that and get on with your life, and be happy, for God's sake. It's enough.' He walked out of my room without saying goodbye.

Later that day I lost my temper with a nurse who wouldn't let me go to the toilet alone in case I did myself an injury. I told her to fuck off and I punched a wall. That afternoon I was assessed by another doctor who disagreed with Manko. He found me psychotic, tending to violence. He started me on a drug regime that stopped me thinking anything at all. Over the next several days

I didn't see Manko, only this other doctor. The more tenacious I became about Dad, the more drugs I needed, apparently. It was like swimming, a battle of wills. The more he tried to convince me he was right, the more I was convinced he was wrong.

Mum visited and accepted what the doctor told her. I was sedated because I'd been violent. It would pass, this phase of mine, the doctor said. But weeks wore on, and then months, and the doctor started saying it might pass and I might be well again, then that perhaps we should consider more long-term care. I only found all this out later. Mum said she started to believe she'd lost me for-ever. She'd visit and cry and I'd hear her but she was too far away to reach. Knowing what I knew about Dad, I was seething underneath, so every time I popped into consciousness, I had to be restrained. I thought I'd die there too.

I hated feeling so out of control, but if I surfaced to consciousness, however briefly, unpleasantness gave way to rage and terror. The only thing worse than being completely insane in a psychiatric hospital is being incompletely insane. The nurses smiled what looked like fangs and assured me it was good for me.

After I'd been in the hospital in that half-life for three months, Mum happened to see Mr Maitland out at the uni and she unburdened herself to him about what had happened to his brightest pupil. So he visited me, good old Maitland, with his theories of conspiracy. He sat by my bed and watched me for a few hours on three consecutive afternoons. Later, he told me he found me slumped in an easy chair, propped up with pillows, wearing a bib to catch any dribble. I don't remember him being there at all. I'm sure I agreed with any conspiracy he wanted to tell me about. But Maitland was smart. He took a few pages from my chart and rang Stella and said he was concerned they weren't helping me. She should do something about it, he said, and he sent her the chart. Stella had taken enough banned substances to know I was on some mighty doses.

Stella took the chart to a psych registrar she knew who enquired into my case. I was assigned to a new doctor, Dr Bain, who reduced my drugs immediately and said he'd see me when I woke up. I never met the doctor who'd put me on the drugs in the first place. I never even found out his name. I could have drifted on like that for my whole life. Pretty scary.

Slowly, I came back to the world and found myself almost as substantial as when I'd left it. I was put into Bain's therapy group that met every second day. The others were older men who didn't shave or bathe unless someone reminded them. The youngest was at least twice my age. Some of them had been there for thirty years, on and off. On the worst days, I wondered if that would be my future. I thought that giving up your sanity was like a bone fracture. It could happen again, and more easily next time, however much healing I did.

On the days I didn't have group I had private therapy with Bain, who peeled and ate an orange in each of our first two sessions. The sweet acrid smell of it filled his office. I told him a vitamin C supplement would be better; Manko was a great believer in vitamin C, said it cured cancer. Bain was supposed to be a grief expert and

I told him I wasn't grieving. He told me he thought I was depressed. 'If you could be depressed or mad, which would you pick, Jack?' I asked. I didn't know his first name but I wasn't going to call him Dr Bain.

'Not much of a choice. I'd probably do my work in therapy so I didn't need to be either.' He thought this was a good joke. 'My name's Max, by the way, but you can call me Doctor Bain.'

'Quite the comedian,' I said, without returning his smile. I wanted to be like Stella, hard and cynical. I wanted it to protect me from Dad the way it had protected her. I asked Max if the orange was strategic, like Mr Rebo's psychology, and if he ate six oranges a day, one for each patient, or if he selected the one he'd eat his orange with on a most-needs basis.

'You know what I think?' he said towards the end of our third session. I shook my head. 'I think you might be depressed because what you really feel is something else.' I nodded but didn't say anything. Bain had an orange that day but he hadn't started peeling it and we were nearly finished. He'd put it down on the table next to him carefully. 'I wonder if you're angry.'

'Nup.' My knee was jiggling and I felt edgy for the last ten silent minutes. I counted tassels on the rug on Bain's floor. I got to five hundred and twenty-six before I lost count. When Bain said it was time to finish I got up and left without saying anything.

It was Bain who decided I was sane enough to be discharged. At the end of one of our silent sessions, I said I didn't want to be there anymore and he said there was nothing wrong with me as far as he was concerned, and I could leave any time I liked, as if it had always been like that.

The next morning I came out into bright sunshine that made me think I'd been wearing sunglasses for a year. Stella took me home to Mum's. Jim came over. I said to the three of them that I was sorry for everything that had happened. I tried to sound normal but I started crying. Mum smiled and said it was okay. She was wary, I could tell. I kept reassuring myself in the way I'd learned in group, but it wasn't working particularly well with everyone else so cautious.

chapter**twenty-two**

Manko had told me to follow the body. A couple of days after I got home, when Mum had left for work, I caught a bus into the city and went to the Missing Persons Unit at police headquarters in Makerston Street. I said I was a uni student doing a sociology paper on people who go missing. They were as helpful as they were allowed to be. They gave me the public-access file which had the names of all the missing persons who disappeared around the time of Dad's supposed death. There were eight unsolved cases over a month-long period. Three were females. Within ten minutes, I'd narrowed five males down to one. Two others were kids, a third was Chinese and the fourth was only five foot two; Dad was five nine. I told the officer at the counter I wanted more information about one case. He shrugged and said he could show me the Misspers file if I liked.

Martin Sharpe was five years younger than Dad, but his height was the same. He was also lighter than Dad, which fitted with Marion's and Kerry's story about weight loss. The case was still open but not active, the file said. I asked the officer at the desk what that meant, and he said that sometimes if there are no leads quickly, they have to scale down a search. Martin Sharpe had a mental disability, coupled with serious health problems, including a heart condition. He also had a history of wandering, according to the medical report from the institution he lived in.

There was a photograph in the file which had been taken five to seven years prior to Sharpe's disappearance. From my wallet I took the photo I'd brought with me of the dead man in the coffin. To be honest, when I first looked at it, I thought just for a moment it looked like Dad. But I put that thought away and placed the two photographs side by side on the bench where I was working. The two pictures were similar enough to convince me, especially given the match in the dates and height.

On reading the file notes I discovered that Martin Sharpe had been reported missing two days after my father's supposed death. I took note of his next-of-kin, his mother, and her address in Brisbane. His residential address at the time of his disappearance was a hostel in Spring Hill. He'd been on a day trip to the Gold Coast when he'd disappeared.

I tried to put together a sequence of events. Martin Sharpe is admitted to Alloysius, dying or dead on arrival. Somehow, Martin Sharpe becomes Allan Goodwin. In order for that to happen, they needed someone inside the hospital system. I had no idea who it could be. It also

meant they waited for someone who looked enough like
Dad, someone who could pass the scrutiny of anyone
who didn't know Dad personally. Maybe they thought I
wouldn't go and see the body, or if I did, I wouldn't know
him well enough anymore to know it wasn't him. Maybe
they even killed Martin Sharpe. But there were still too
many holes, and the thing that bothered me most was
that even if I worked out how they'd done it, I still had
no idea why.

I was sure Kerry Vance was the key. Someone broke
in and stole the photograph of Dad from the funeral
home. It could have been Kerry. The mission to New
Guinea didn't add up. I checked the dates of Kerry's
newspaper reports in the State Library. There were some
hostages killed in New Guinea, but it was six months
before Dad's death. Kerry had lied about that, and
everything else.

The next morning I took a bus up to Oakey after
Mum had left for work. Kerry Vance didn't greet me at
all when I walked into his workshop. He just stared.
'Kerry,' I said, 'I reckon I know how you did it. What I
want to know is why.'

'Heard you'd been sick, Scott. You okay now?' He
looked around nervously, as if Dad was hiding in a
corner of the shed.

'I'm going to find him whether you help me or not,
Kerry. I know about Martin Sharpe.' He didn't react.
'You wouldn't like me to go to the police about him,
would you?'

He looked straight into my eyes and said, 'I don't
know what the fuck you're talking about.'

'You're a liar,' I said. 'Was it money? Did he pay you? Or is this the kind of thing you do for your Vietnam mates?'

'Listen, son, if you weren't my friend's boy, I'd have you, coming in here accusing me.' Kerry's hand rested on a big shifting spanner on the bench. 'I won't be generous twice. You don't call me a liar, not ever. And you better stop poking your nose round business you don't understand. Got it?'

'Why, what are you going to do, Kerry, hit me with a spanner?' I think I wanted him to; I wanted to make something happen.

Kerry looked behind me. I turned and saw what he saw, a middle-aged woman in a white pantsuit with white sneakers. She had blond hair which was almost black where it parted. 'Hello,' she said in a high, pretty voice. 'Darling?' addressing Kerry. She was holding a set of car keys in one hand. In the other she had a small suitcase, like the one Stella's Travelling Barbie had when we were little.

Kerry looked from the woman to me. He was blinking fast. I turned back to Barbie, who had an ID card pinned to her chest. 'Sweetie,' Kerry said.

'What a night. I'm dead. Well, aren't you going to introduce me?' she said, walking past me and over to Kerry, slipping her arm around his waist.

'This is Scott Goodwin,' Kerry said. 'Allan Goodwin's boy. We were just having a talk about his dad.'

The woman's face registered shock. 'Oh, Scott,' she said. 'Hi.' She smiled weakly. I moved closer.

'And you're …?' I was peering at her name tag. She pulled it off and put it in her pocket.

'Silly me. I always forget to take it off. I'm Kerry's girlfriend. I'm Helen.'

'You've been at work?' I said. She nodded. 'Where's that?' She told me she worked in a nursing home in Brisbane and she was on days off now, but I'd seen her name tag. Helen Barrett, Alloysius Hospital. The hospital on the Gold Coast where Dad had supposedly died.

Helen Barrett was the nurse who'd signed the form admitting the man they said was my father. I'd written her name down along with the names of the doctor and nurses involved in the man's care. For once, I thought, luck had been on my side. Her handwriting was neat and her signature was easy to read on the form. Helen Barrett had been the one to change the records. She'd turned Martin Sharpe, DOA, into Allan Goodwin, DOA. Suddenly, I had something more than assumptions. I had what old Manko would have called evidence. I decided it was enough.

chapter**twenty-three**

Martin Sharpe's mother was still living in the Coorparoo flat she'd been renting when her son disappeared. She was in her seventies, I guessed. I talked to her on the phone, told her as gently as I could that I might have information. Then I caught the train into the city and the bus out to her place. It was a nondescript pale brick building called Villa Del Rosa in a street full of nondescript pale brick buildings with similar names.

Mrs Sharpe's lounge room was fussy with lace and floral covers and photographs of a long-dead husband. It smelled of human and animal habitation, as if she hadn't opened the windows in a long while. We talked about Martin and what a blessing he'd been. More than several cats wandered in and climbed the furniture. I lost count after four. Mrs Sharpe told me a few more times it had been worth every minute she'd had with Martin. She kept talking, eager and not wanting to hear what news I might have.

'Mrs Sharpe, I'm afraid I have to tell you that your son died. He collapsed and was taken to hospital. Unfortunately, he never regained consciousness.'

'Why didn't they tell me?'

'He was mistaken for someone else. Another man who was also missing.'

She let out a breath slowly as she shook her head. 'Was it his heart?' she asked. I nodded. 'His heart was weak too, as well as his head.' I said the doctors had done everything they could to save him, because that's what the doctor from Alloysius had said to me and I would have been comforted if I'd believed him. I said how sorry I was and took her hand. She nodded gently for a while.

I made Mrs Sharpe a cup of tea before I left. We chatted about the weather, which was colder than normal, she thought. It was twenty-six degrees and balmy outside, but I didn't say so. She didn't ask how the 'mistake' had been made or whether anyone would apologise. As I was leaving, she said, 'Do you know where he is?' At first I thought she'd flipped, like people thought I had, but then I realised she meant his remains.

'Yes. He was given a Catholic funeral.' I'd seen a big crucifix in the hall. I was relieved my father's religion matched Martin's. 'His ashes are at the Eternal Rest Gardens in Yeronga, if you want to visit him.' Mum had stepped in and paid for the ashes to be laid to rest at Yeronga near the military cemetery. 'The name on the ashes is Allan Goodwin.'

'Will they change the name now?'

I didn't know what to say. 'I think they will, yes,' I said.

She asked me to wait a moment more. She went into what must have been the second bedroom, which still had a little porcelain plaque on the door that said 'Martin's Room', with a picture of a sports car, a Ferrari, I thought. I could see model planes, too, hanging from the ceiling over the made-up single bed. Mrs Sharpe came out, closing the door behind her. 'Could you get them to put this as the epitaph? It was his favourite.' She handed across a piece of lined paper, worn at the folds. I said sure, and put the piece of paper in my pocket without looking at it.

I don't know if Mrs Sharpe believed me. She seemed so calm about it all. But she didn't call the police, which is what most people would have done if some eighteen-year-old told them a story like that. I think maybe she wasn't quite all there, to be honest.

The next day I went to an engraver in the city. They didn't even blink when I made my strange request. I changed into jeans, a work shirt and boots, and took a taxi out to the cemetery. I drilled my holes like a good tradesman and put a new plaque over Allan Goodwin's name, enough like the existing plaques to pass. It felt satisfying. I looked at the result.

Martin Sharpe 1952–1987
*What would you do
If we picked you
To become a real Astroboy?*

I rang Mrs Sharpe and told her the urn number of her son's remains. I said they'd changed the names over now, along with the epitaph. I dropped off twenty dollars so she could get a taxi to go and see her son. I couldn't bear to take her myself and watch her grief.

chapter**twenty-four**

'Were you that sure?' Emily said. She'd stood up and was at the window facing the sea. She turned to me with a look of concern.

'No,' I said. 'And I'm still not. And even if I'm right, it doesn't tell me why. So it's hardly an end to the story.'

'But what about Mrs Sharpe? You told her you found out what happened to Martin. What if you were wrong?'

'It gets worse,' I said.

I tried to find Manko to thank him. I thought he'd made sense at a time in my life when I badly needed someone to make sense. I didn't know his first name so I went back to the hospital. The admissions desk in psych said they had no record of a Dr Manko ever working there, in any area, let alone psych. I went to the ward. The sister gave me the telephone number of one of the nurses I knew. 'Manko,' she said when I phoned. 'Yeah, I know Manko. Who could forget those ears? But he

wasn't a doctor, Scott. He was one of the patients.
Manic-depressive, wasn't he? Was he on your floor?'
I asked if she knew where he was now. 'He killed himself,
on the ward. Stole some pills. Must have been a couple
of weeks back. He'd been with us for years.'

Manko had been a policeman. I only found this out
recently, when the hospital deposited some records in
Archives. He became obsessed with a case in which a
young girl was raped and murdered. He was convinced
he knew the culprit but couldn't prove it. He shot the
unarmed man in a police raid and killed him. In the
inquiry that followed, it came out that Manko had been
following the man for a year. He'd organised the raid
after a tip-off no one could substantiate. No charges were
laid but Manko was retired on medical grounds, after
which he drifted into the hospital and my life.

Stella told me Tony Matthews had a copy of Dad's
will and that Dad had left half his estate to Marion and
half to Mum. Dad had a big lump of life insurance he'd
taken out in the last year of his life. That was the bulk of
the estate; he'd already drawn down on his Army
pension, probably for one of his hobbies. So he'd
provided for Mum to some extent. Marion had sent me
Dad's trunk, Stella said, which was in the garage at
Mum's. It was only much later that I dared look inside it,
and the only thing missing was the cardboard envelope
containing Dad's medals.

As an eighteenth birthday present, Stella and Mum
decided to take me to the Gold Coast for a weekend.
This was where guys from my school had gone when
they finished their final year. I'd been on the way to

Duntroon then and didn't feel like hanging round with other kids. Mum said it would be my own private schoolies weekend. I told her that having your mother and big sister there wasn't quite the same. She said it would be a gas, which proved my point.

We stayed in a high-rise overlooking Main Beach and it rained. On the Sunday, we went to a shopping centre, and Mum and Stella left me in a café while they went to look at clothes. Mum assured me they'd only be gone half an hour. It was Stella's idea, for sure. I doubt Mum would have left me alone for five minutes. She looked back at me and smiled nervously a couple of times as they walked away.

I was on a stool at a counter waiting for a Coke. I had storefronts behind me and a view of people going up and down escalators. At the base of the escalators they had a bird aviary and a giant green plastic imitation of Michelangelo's David, surrounded by frolicking dolphins. I wasn't thinking of anything, really. My eyes rested on one person, then another and another; I didn't register faces. I saw a woman all in white and, behind her, a man in a bright red T-shirt. Something made me look at the man more carefully, perhaps the newness of his T-shirt. I noticed that the rest of his clothes — dark blue jeans and white runners — were new too. It was as if he'd been created on the first floor and plonked on the down escalator to join the world. He had a navy blue baseball cap on his head and a K-Mart bag in his right hand. He stood straight with his arms out from his body. A Christmas tree.

As he descended further, I saw his face. I found myself moving off the stool. I walked around the coffee bar and toward the escalator, calling his name. He looked at me, and so did several other people. He saw me and our eyes met, and I was absolutely sure. He turned and pushed past the people behind him on the escalator. It took him a while to get to the top because he was travelling up against both the escalator and the tide of people coming down, but his body moved swiftly and confidently, just as I remembered, dodging pedestrians like a dancer. I watched him disappear into the crowd at the top as I leapt onto the up escalator after him. I saw his baseball cap come off as he turned left. I figured he was heading towards the fire exit on the first floor. I could see its green light. Without being able to see him anymore, I headed that way.

I pushed through the crowd clumsily, knocking a woman with a stroller and stopping to let a little kid by. By the time I opened the fire exit door, I had my camera from my coat pocket. I looked up then down the fire exit stairwell, saw a bare arm on the rail, the red T-shirt sleeve. I lined up a shot, took one. I called out, 'Dad!' He looked up the stairs as I took a second shot. 'I've got you,' I called after him. 'I've got you in here now, you bastard.' I was breathing fast through my mouth. He kept going down the steps. I took off after him. By the time I reached the basement carpark, he was nowhere to be seen. He could have got out anywhere.

We went home later that day and Mum said it was such a shame it had rained because we hadn't had a chance to swim. I agreed. She kept asking me if I was all right. That night I slept with the film under my pillow.

The next morning, after Mum left, I caught a train into the city and waited at the processing place for the two hours they needed. Before they were even properly dry I used cotton gloves and flicked through the prints until I came to the stairwell. In the first shot I could see the top of a head, dark hair, the shoulders in the red shirt. In the second shot, where he'd looked up, a face. It wasn't Dad. It wasn't anything like him.

I walked the streets and looked at the photograph again and again. A guy with grubby clothes and yellow hair who smelled strongly of sweat and urine asked me for money. I gave him everything in my wallet. I was so sure I'd seen Dad in the stairwell, but it hadn't been him. The man might have had a reason to run away from a pursuer — maybe he was a shoplifter, or a father who'd left a son, or maybe he was just a guy who saw this mad kid coming at him and panicked. The expression on his face in the photograph was one of complete surprise. If I'd been wrong about it being Dad when I was so sure, then I could be wrong about everything. The only person who believed me was Manko, and Manko was a psychiatric patient, like me. Everyone else — my mother, her partner, my sister, my uncle and auntie, my grandparents, the doctors, Marion and Kerry Vance — told me my father was dead.

When I told Stella what had happened, she took leave from work and hung around with me at Mum's. 'What a way to spend your holidays,' I said.

She wanted a simple solution. 'I wondered if it was the gun,' she said.

'What gun?' I said.

'You remember. The day you were playing with a gun. Dad went spare.'

'No.'

'Yes you do. You locked yourself in the car, and you were playing with the Magnum. When they got you out, he told you he'd kill you if you ever did it again. Don't you remember? I was so scared of him that day. Mum was in tears. It was horrible.'

'No, I don't remember that,' I said. I was lying. I remembered him yelling, just like Stella said, and pushing me away from the gun. I remember him pulling me close, hugging me tightly, then holding the gun to my head, his eyes vacant. But what had frightened me wasn't his screaming anger. It wasn't even the gun, which I didn't understand anyway. It was the second part of the story, when he told me that his father had done the same to him, had held a loaded gun to his head. It wasn't what he said, either — it was the way he told me, in a soft little voice just like a child, like me, a voice I'd never heard from him before and didn't hear again. That voice terrified me. It was as if I had seen into his insides and had found him wanting. I looked up at Stella. She was staring at me. 'Must have repressed it.' I smiled.

Stella didn't respond for a while. 'Fair enough.' But she put her hand on my shoulder as she got up to clear the dishes. I flinched at her touch. 'He fucked us up, didn't he?' she said.

I fell into a depression again, and didn't realise it until I admitted myself to hospital and the doctors told me I was depressed. I was voluntary this time, so they didn't use as many drugs. I didn't want drugs. I wanted surrender. I wanted sleep. I felt hands on my body like safety. He'd throw me up in the air and catch me when I was little. I could hear his heart in his chest, beating fast, pumping blood through his great body. I'll never let you down, he'd say. I'll always be here to catch you. I could feel the warm dryness of his safe hands in the nurses' hands. I could see the bright sun beyond us. Up up up in the air, flying, feeling as if I'm light as the air itself, the horror of slowing, stopping, the terror of flipping over and back down fast, then the safety of those big big arms.

I came out of hospital after two weeks, convinced that even if he was alive, it was better he was dead. It wasn't worth it, I told myself. He wasn't worth it. I didn't have the courage to find him, I'd go mad if I kept looking. I've lasted all these years. And I've done okay.

chapter**twenty-five**

I looked at the clock. It was nearly three pm. We hadn't
been out of the motel room or eaten since breakfast. I was
still sitting on the floor in the corner. My leg had gone to
sleep. Emily had come back from the window and was
lying on her stomach on the bed again. I stared at the
clock a while more, as if I might find courage there.
Finally I looked over towards Emily, but she was looking
down, studying the sheet. After a moment more, I said her
name, softly, almost a whisper. She looked up, and I
expected disbelief, or embarrassment, or even a wry smile.
What I didn't expect was tears. 'Jesus,' she said, 'you poor
bastard. I never realised it had been like that.' She wiped
her eyes and nose. 'And after that you've never wanted to
find out for sure what happened? Or why he did it?'

'No,' I said, emphatically. 'Never. Not now. When he
left…' I didn't finish the sentence. I sighed. 'I've still got the
photo I took of the guy in the coffin. Martin Sharpe.' I stood

up; my legs were stiff and I was exhausted. I took my wallet
from my knapsack. 'Even I can see that it doesn't look like
anyone.' I walked over and handed it to Emily. I could see
my reflection in the mirror behind her. I was glaring like a
madman, but I couldn't look any softer. I went back and sat
in my corner on the floor. She studied the photograph.

'You're right, it's very blurry,' she said. 'But I don't
know your father, so I can't help in that way. I can help,
though, Scott. I can be a good friend.'

Emily put the photograph down on the bedside table
carefully and got up slowly and walked over to me. She
stopped halfway. I nodded to let her come further.
'Whatever you want', she said. 'Whatever.' She sat next to
me, without touching. She put her hand on the floor near
mine and I didn't take it, not at first. She just held it there
anyway and said whenever you're ready, and then I was.
We sat in that corner of the room holding hands while
kids dived into the pool and yelled beneath our window.

And then I'm back with him, lifting me up above his
head, swinging me round, laughing and laughing and
throwing me upwards, I'm flying higher and higher. Until
I scream with laughter, I scream and squeal, and he's
laughing still, and I'm screaming not laughing. Stop, stop,
but he doesn't know I'm serious. And he throws me higher
this time, so high I'm out of his reach for seconds, hours.
I'm flying, my ribs come free, they're wings, I take off like
a jet in the sky, leave a pink jetstream behind me that leads
me back to him. And he's there to catch me in his big big
hands and I hear that voice: 'Don't cry, I've got you, I'll
never drop you, you hear me?' And I'm sobbing like a
baby, and I've pissed myself. I can see the line of piss on

his shirt. It's across his hair too, and his face. And he says, again, 'I said I'll never drop you, Scott, didn't you hear me?' And he throws me again, not so high. Only this time he doesn't catch me. I land in a jumble on the grass. Later, I realise I've cut my cheek on a little stone. But there and then I'm thankful for the softness of the grass. I lie there. It's cool and the sun's warm on the bare nape of my neck. He's walking away. 'I don't drop you unless I say so, Scott,' he's saying. He's walking away.

And I'm sobbing like a baby, back with Emily. And she holds my hand and knows not to ask questions.

We spent the afternoon and evening doing nothing much. We had coffee and burgers at the Byronian Café and drove up to the lighthouse. Emily was convinced we were going to see whales, even though it was too early for them to be heading home to Antarctica from the warmer north with their new calves. I kept telling her this and she kept saying, 'You wait.' We didn't see whales, but we did see a pod of dolphins. They were surfing waves, standing up on their tails and flipping over. 'See,' Emily said, 'I told you we'd see them.'

'But those are dolphins,' I said.

'Same difference.'

We had a pizza at Earth 'n Sea and went to bed and made love. I could hear the waves like they were in the room with us, and my love scared away any demons that might have been left. The next morning, I got up early and watched Emily sleep for an hour. Later that day, we drove home quietly. I felt like my real life had just started and the pretend life, the one that other guy had been living, was gone forever.

chaptertwenty-six

Two weeks after we got back from Byron, I moved out of Mum's unit at Toowong, where I'd lived since she and Jim had bought acreage west of Brisbane, and into Emily's flat on the river at West End. By then West End was booming. All the old buildings were being replaced by new apartment blocks that were like dolls' houses for the children of giants, or by smaller, squatting imitations of the old wooden Queenslander house, featuring corrugated iron and blue panels and ochre timber. They called them new Queenslanders, but I bet nothing about them came from Queensland.

Emily's place was in a mercifully untouched seventies rendered brick block. I brought with me my herb collection, a satellite dish chair that took up so much space we had to give it away, a filing cabinet full of neatly labelled files of my research, mostly into my father's life and death, and a few history books and CDs. It wasn't much for a life, I said. Emily said I was unencumbered. Unencumbered is good, she said.

Emily, I quickly learned, is a bower bird. She collects difficult-to-acquire things, especially food-related things, like I collect information. She loves shopping for provisions at hard-to-get-to places and coming home and spending all afternoon preparing a meal. Within a week of moving in, I learned about a Brisbane I'd never seen in all the years I'd lived there. A Greek deli and Vietnamese bakery at West End, Merlo's Coffee in the Valley and Sol's Organic Breads in Highgate Hill. Emily took me to a butcher at Woolloongabba for whom every sale was a negotiation. You had to prove you were worthy of his meat by telling him what you planned to do with it. He'd correct your recipe, offer alternatives and finally agree you could have the meat. It took half an hour just to buy steak for a barbecue.

Emily coaxed me back into a swimming pool, which I never thought would happen. For years even the smell of a pool had made me queasy, and yet in a strange way I missed swimming — the early mornings, the trees next to the pool, Mr Rebo, Jennifer. When Emily suggested we go swimming at the Spring Hill baths one Saturday, I decided to see what it would be like. The baths were built in 1890 and still had the original change cubicles, now painted with brightly coloured doors, that Emily liked. A sign on the Ladies' side said Gents weren't to loiter there. Emily didn't take swimming seriously. It was something she did for fun. I found I liked the feel of water, the way I could glide through at a slow pace and not really care about times and goals and objectives.

Emily had done journalism and had worked for a few years at *The Australian* after she graduated. She quit to write freelance because she wanted to be an investigative journalist and to do that you had to be independent. Emily's father had been a photographer who made a difference, she said, and that's what she wanted to do, make a difference. When we met, she was working on a story about a private hospital that had mistreated patients in the seventies but had never been investigated. Emily had become involved when she met the daughter of one of the patients on another story. She used to get calls in the middle of the night from a guy I christened Deep Throat. He'd worked at the hospital as an orderly, but was still terrified of what might happen if he talked.

Emily was scrupulous about work ethics. She advocated truth no matter what the cost. We had those moral discussions you have when you're checking each other out: 'What if someone tells you something off the record and you have to go to court to prove ...' Emily was emphatic that she'd always go for the story, no matter what. I admired her conviction. I was much more flexible.

Emily was so convinced of her own moral rhetoric on the truth that the first time I caught her lying, I assumed it was an honest mistake. It wasn't a big deal. We were swimming together at Spring Hill as we often did on a Saturday morning before we did the hours and hours of shopping we needed for the week's meals. The sun streaming through the open roof hit the middle of the pool and made it look brand new instead of a hundred years old. I'd done a mile or so, and had lapped Emily half a dozen times, but when I asked how far she'd swum she said it was a mile too, which was impossible. I didn't say anything. I thought she mustn't have a good sense of distances.

The next time was when Colin Rawlins visited Brisbane. After he left Duntroon, he left Defence as well and got a job with a big software firm. Now he has his own company, operating out of Sydney. They do business security software. When I visited their offices overlooking the harbour at Balmain, I noticed that the staff all looked like Colin had the first day at Duntroon — long hair, jeans and T-shirts. He was more like their big brother than the boss.

We had Colin over for dinner on the Saturday night. Beforehand I'd been worried he and Emily might not get along. Colin is quiet and I thought Emily's questioning might frighten him off. I hadn't said anything to Emily, though. I figured she'd only think there must be some undiscovered secret she needed to unearth. I was cooking that night, baked fish with coconut rice. I could hear them from the kitchen, Emily's questions, Colin's answers. He seemed relaxed enough.

'So where are your family from, Colin?' I heard Emily ask.

'Well, that depends which family you mean,' Colin said. 'I grew up in Sydney but my father's people are from out west in Queensland. Dad was a property manager for a while after his family sold their own farm, but the property he was managing went belly-up in a drought. Then he was a clerk in the shipping industry in Sydney. My mother died when I was a baby. I have a wicked stepmother who lives in Sydney.' While

I prepared vegetables I learned more about Colin than I had in the ten years before, that he'd been a freak as a kid in terms of maths ability, and that his school had wanted him to sit university exams. His father said no. 'He wanted me to grow up normally,' Colin said. 'And I'm glad he put his foot down. I'd have been even more of a geek than I am already.'

They talked too softly for me to hear then. 'And are you seeing anyone at the moment?' I heard Emily say.

'No,' Colin said. 'I work hard, and I don't really meet any girls in my industry.'

'We'll have to see about that,' Emily said. 'Won't we, Scott?' she called to me.

I came to the kitchen door. 'I suppose we will.'

In bed later, I said to Emily that I felt like Colin and I were creatures from different planets, that until that night we'd never really had a conversation, and that Emily was our intergalactic translator. She didn't understand what I meant. Now, she calls where I come from Planet Scott.

On the Sunday, the three of us went for a walk. Emily drove us up into the Gold Coast hinterland past rolling hills and dairy farms to Binna Burra on the edge of Lamington National Park. Emily had understood from the start that the rainforest had become an important place for me. The two of us can be terrible cynics who make fun of most things, but there are those few sacred cows we respect in one another. My photographs, Emily's wanting to be an investigative reporter. We don't make fun of those things.

I first went to Binna Burra from school, on a biology camp, the one where Mr Maitland was trying to crack on to Miss Tyquin, the biol teacher. After I got out of hospital I used to catch a bus to Binna Burra on a Friday afternoon and set up a tent. I'd walk both days, and take the bus back late on Sunday. I found the rainforest soothed me. I always walked alone, and I thought about nothing more complicated than light and shadow for photographs and where I might stop for lunch. For a while it was the only good thing about my life. Colin and Emily were the only other people I'd taken there with me.

We did a long walk that day. I was after shots of wildflowers so we took a track along a narrow ridge and picnicked on a precipice in front of a bower of orchids that weren't yet in flower. On the way back to the car Colin pulled us up, pointing to a squawking speckled bird in the undergrowth.

'That's a noisy pitta,' Emily said when Colin asked, and before I had a chance to answer.

'A what?' I said.

'A noisy pitta. Haven't you ever heard of it?' she said, dismissively.

I smiled. 'Yes, I have.'

'You can tell by the call,' Emily said to Colin, ignoring me. 'That unmistakable squawk.'

On the way home, after we'd dropped Colin off, Emily asked me why I'd looked at her strangely when we'd seen the bird. 'No reason,' I said. 'But why did you say it was a noisy pitta?'

'It was.'

'It was a bower bird. Noisy pittas are green and yellow and violet, not speckled brown. And their call is a high-pitched whistle, not a squawk.'

'Perhaps I made a mistake,' Emily said, without hesitation.

'Perhaps you did,' I said. Liars are the worst form of people, he'd say. In my mind, I told him to fuck off.

If Emily was a liar, it was about things like this that didn't much matter, or at least I thought it was. It was like she wanted to be involved, to help with the answer, even if it was the wrong answer. It was more facilitating than mischievous. So while her lying was an imperfection, it was part of what made her perfect for me. I think Emily wanted more than anything to connect with people. She was the optimist to beat my pessimism. To her, the glass was overflowing, where I was always running on half-empty. It was good for me. I've always had a tendency to become maudlin, to expect the worst. Emily simply doesn't tolerate maudlin. Shit or get off the pot, she'd say. Just do it, like the Nike ad. Just do it.

Emily didn't question my conviction that Dad was alive either. I didn't know if that was because she believed me or because she didn't want to offend me. But despite Marion, Stella, Mum and all the rest, she never wavered in her support of me. If she was interested in how and why he'd cheated death, I didn't notice, not at first. I was just relieved someone believed me. But over time it seemed to eat away at Emily. It was as if she took over that part of my psyche, and the better I got, the worse she got. 'I'd want to know what really happened if I were you,' she'd say, often enough that I knew immediately what she was talking about. 'Well, you're not me, so drop it.' I'd say this with a smile, but a grumpy smile. The conversation would hang there between us until she raised it again.

Mum and Jim came to the flat for lunch that Christmas. Mum was prone to worrying about me, especially when I did what she thought were rash things like starting a relationship or moving out of home. Even buying a loud shirt could make her look sideways at me. Stella was in the US for Christmas, on an extended honeymoon, as it turned out. She'd moved to Canada the year before with a forest ranger she'd met when he was on holiday in Australia. He'd been struck with appendicitis and Stella had nursed him. They married in Vancouver, they wrote and told Mum. In the photo they sent, Stella was bending over and laughing. She looked so happy. They were in Banff National Park, next to a sign that said 'Caution! Aggressive Elk', and Mark, her new husband, was throwing his head back, imitating an elk, I suspect. 'I guess you had to be there,' I said in Stella fashion when I saw the picture.

To prepare for Christmas Emily and I painted the living room lemon and bought a round dining table. Emily said round tables were cooperative and lemon was calming. She was taking Christmas pretty seriously. We had to have a proper tree too, and we drove for an hour towards Ipswich and then spent another hour at the nursery finding the one that was ours. We must have talked about the menu a hundred times.

When the day itself dawned cold and drizzling, uncharacteristically Brisbane, I thought it was a good omen, because Emily had settled on hot turkey with gravy, bought after a full hour's consultation with Hans, the Woolloongabba butcher, and sweet potato mash and greens. She even cooked a cake, a proper Christmas cake, from a recipe that included a truckload of fruit and eight eggs. Emily made a double batch, she told me, to be sure we had enough, as if I had an army of mothers. She mixed the cake with her hands, in a borrowed baby bath. I hated getting mucky, to the extent that when I chopped garlic I used a knife and fork, and wouldn't touch raw meat if I could help it. Killer cake, I called it. I threatened to tell them how she'd mixed it. 'So?' she said. She couldn't see the problem.

In the first few weeks after I moved in, Emily did all the cooking if we weren't eating out, and I let her because there didn't seem much room for me. One night when she had the flu, I cooked up a spaghetti with chilli and garlic, which was the closest thing to a chicken soup that I knew. I don't know that it hastened Emily's cure, but she was pleasantly surprised. 'A man of hidden talents,' she said. From then on we've shared responsibility for meals. We never cook together and although we've never discussed the idea, I'm sure she'd know, as I do, that it wouldn't work. I'm neat, preparing everything and cleaning up carefully as I go. I love to watch sushi chefs. Emily's the opposite and says she can't stand all their fiddling. After she cooks, the kitchen looks like it's still under construction.

Mum and Emily got on so well I was sure some disaster was about to befall us. Mum smiled politely from a distance at Emily's fussing but said to me, quietly, that I looked well, with that knowing, Jennifer Rebo kind of smile. I was afraid she was going to ask me was I getting some. Jim and Emily were like two kids, laughing out loud at whatever they were doing in the kitchen. I suspect they drank a little brandy when they were supposed to be flaming the plum pudding. Back out with me and Mum, they were quite giggly. Jim gave Emily a big hug when they were leaving. He was like a bear going off to hibernate.

On Boxing Day we went to see the rerelease of *Apocalypse Now*, and afterwards Emily got back to her favourite subject. 'He was in Vietnam, wasn't he?' I agreed he was. 'Did he talk about it?'

'Only to say it was the worst thing he'd ever been through. He was pretty young when he went over there. Mum was pregnant with me.'

'That's doing it tough. How long was he there?'

'Only six months. He busted his leg.'

'How?'

'To be honest, I don't know, Emily. It was when he was awarded the Victoria Cross. I told you about that.'

'I know, the reconnaissance operation that went wrong. How many others were with your dad when he was injured?' she said.

'As far as I know, six Australians were killed, and Dad was one of the three who survived. The others were his CO, Kerry Vance, who I've talked about, and a bloke named Jarratt, who I've never met.'

'Your dad stayed on in the Army. Did the other two?'

'Kerry's the one who made up the bullshit story about the mission Dad was on. He left the Army after Vietnam. He'd done three tours all up, one at the start and two later, when he and Dad met. As for Jarratt, I've got no idea.'

'Scott,' she said, and smiled a little-girl smile that let me know what was coming. 'Aren't you just a bit curious about why he faked his death?' I started to tell her no, I wasn't curious, I was happy, but she went on. 'Why don't we just find out? You're a researcher. If anyone can do it, you can. I'll help.'

'I said no!' Emily dropped the subject that day, but talking about him again, and the way she kept bringing it up, had started me thinking. Even though I knew I should leave it alone, I took out half a dozen of my files and went through them. I wish now I never had. My perfect seventeen-year-old's handwriting, pages and pages of neat notes — the funeral home meeting, Kerry Vance, the library, the hospital, the Archives. It seemed ridiculous now, my adolescent 'investigation'. It was like it was a different me who'd done all that, and yet I knew it was the same me.

I took out the photograph of the dead man in the coffin too, which I kept in my wallet but hardly ever looked at. I sat at my desk at work and stared at it. Next to it I put the photograph of Dad from the Gold Coast. I looked at the two shots and had trouble remembering what was different about them. Not for the first time, I wondered if the rest of them had been right and I'd been wrong and this was Dad and he was dead. I returned the photographs to my wallet and turned instead to my screen and information I could rely on.

chapter twenty-seven

Emily's mother had given Emily a fountain pen for Christmas, a Waterman 'Diamonds' she'd bought in Paris. 'For your journalism,' Marie Duval had said.

After Christmas Emily got it into her head that we should go overseas. At first, it was something she wanted more than me. Having moved around so much as a kid, I never wanted to shift again if I could help it. More than that, I didn't want to take any risks when it came to me and Emily — not that I knew what we'd be risking by travelling, but I wanted to dig in where we were and make it home.

'I have to get an international perspective,' Emily said to me. 'I'm in a cultural vacuum,' she said, with considerable drama. So I applied for leave and she finished off her hospital story. We were set to depart early in March.

I'd never been out of Australia, and getting a passport and putting together a packing list made me feel I was

finally grown up. Emily was over the moon, and used
the Internet to find accommodation and things to do in the
ten places we were planning to visit. I found myself getting excited about the idea of travel with Emily, as if this
adventure would finish some cleansing process for me.

When I told Mum we were going, she said it was a
sudden decision and asked was I all right. I grinned and
said I was fine. It's almost impossible to prove you're not
crazy. 'Emily's a lovely girl,' Mum said, 'but what if you
get sick?' I hadn't told Stella I had a girlfriend now, and
I'd asked Mum not to mention it. When I broke up with
Cecilia, Stella phoned Cecilia and told her she was a
fuckwit who didn't know what she was giving away.
I didn't want Stella putting all her he's-my-brother
expectations on Emily. I didn't want Mum fussing over
me either. I just wanted to get away with this great girl
and forget about all that past. 'We'll be fine, Mum,'
I said. 'Emily's a journalist.' She looked at me quizzically
and I realised this probably hadn't helped.

I told Emily about Mum's worries. 'I think she
wanted me to take Dr Bain with us, just in case,' I said.
Emily laughed. 'It's a bit new for her, me having a life.'
I couldn't blame Mum and Stella for their worrying.
Even though it had been many years since my last visit
to the hospital, I worried about myself at times, at least
until I met Emily. I was so easily defeated by the smallest
things in life. 'I'm sure once we get back and I'm still
normal, they'll settle down,' I said to Emily. She asked
me if I'd mentioned her to Stella yet and I said I hadn't.
She said that was probably good and we might meet
when Stella came home from the US.

Emily took me to meet her mother who'd been away at Christmas, visiting her sister in France. Marie Duval lived in Bardon, in a little cottage with a cottage garden that reminded me of photographs of European houses I'd seen in travel brochures. She came out to meet us with her dog, Ruffles, who jumped all over me and got a little pink dick of excitement that we were all too polite to mention. Inside, the house was perfect, with carefully placed pieces of antique furniture in the living room and artwork on every wall. There were flowers in a vase on the table and a collection of family photographs over a small fireplace. Emily and I towered over her mother like giants in the small space.

Marie made us tea in a floral tea service. She sat forward in a high-backed chair and watched me carefully without saying much, her legs crossed at the ankles, her hands in her lap. She played Bach records, and I mean records. She had Emily's eyes, only her gaze was more intense. I imagined Emily would look at me like that when she was sixty, but it would bother me less.

Marie told me, when Emily had left the room for something, that Emily was excitable as a child and had gone to several schools before they'd found one that was suitable. Emily's version was that she'd been thrown out of the first three. 'Do you have any pictures?' I said. This was something Emily told me I wasn't to ask about. She couldn't stand me to look at her baby photographs, she said. By the time Emily came back into the room, her mother and I were ensconced on the lounge, going through the album. I don't remember many of the photographs. I kept wondering which ones had been taken when Emily's father was still alive. I wanted to see if she changed. Marie didn't mention her husband and I didn't either. There were hardly any of Emily and Marie together, and none of the three of them.

The photograph I liked most was one of Emily as a toddler at the beach. She's in the shallows sitting between what I assumed were her father's legs, with an ice cream in one hand. His hair has flopped into his face, and he's curling around his daughter, with his hands clasping his ankles, as if to protect her from the waves. You can see hair on his chest. He looks fit and bronzed. Her hand, the one not holding the ice cream, is placed tenderly on his forearm, as if she can keep him there with that lightest little touch. Marie only mentioned where the photographs had been taken, not who the people in them were. That one was taken in Cannes, she said. They met in Paris, Emily had told me, where her father was photographing student protests in the sixties. Marie was one of the protestors. They'd settled in the south of France for a couple of years before deciding to move permanently to Australia, where Emily's father had spent his childhood.

A guy in the hospital, another patient, had a neurological disorder which caused facial tics that made him look like a wind-up toy winding down. The funny thing was that, despite all his jerky movement, or maybe because of it, being with him made us all feel calm. Marie Duval didn't have his tics, but she seemed to elicit the same calm feeling from me. Emily said she'd become religious after her husband's death. She'd tried every kind of organised religion and had finally settled on her own

brand. She believed in auras, Emily told me, and mine
was probably bright purple, whatever that meant.

Marie treated Emily more like a friend than a
daughter, and it reminded me of the way Mum and I
used to be when we were alone together. It was something I rued bitterly after I got out of the hospital. When
Emily talked about her work, Marie pursed her lips and
tilted her head as she listened, asked careful, perceptive
questions, and added encouragement and praise. A strand
of her long grey hair fell out of its bun and over her face.
She blew it and pulled it behind her ear, just like Emily
does. Occasionally she looked from Emily to me. I wasn't
sure if she was gauging my reaction or simply felt proud.
As we were leaving she held my hand in both of hers for
a long moment. She gave me an asessing look and this
time there was no ambiguity; I wasn't to mess with her
daughter. I smiled my most dependable smile.

'You didn't tell me your father was in Vietnam,' I
said on the way home. I'd picked up a photograph of
Jack Duval from the mantelpiece and had been about to
ask Marie where it was taken when Emily came back into
the room from the kitchen. She snatched the photo from
me and put it back on the mantelpiece. I looked at it again
as we were leaving, when Emily was in the kitchen with
her mother. Jack Duval had his arms around two guys,
one in nothing but shorts and boots, the other in uniform. Duval was wearing jeans and a T-shirt. His camera
and press pass were slung around his neck. The man
on the left also had a pass around his neck. You couldn't
see Duval's face very well, just the thick hair like Emily's
and the smile. He looked a larrikin. It was unmistakably

Vietnam — the palm trees, the kids in the background, the huts and, of course, behind them the helicopters on legs, like giant preying mantises.

'So?' she said. 'He wasn't a soldier.' She said it so defensively, I thought she must have been offended at the suggestion that he could have been.

'My father was a soldier,' I said. 'It's not that bad.'

'I didn't mean that,' she said quickly. But she didn't go on to say what she did mean. 'He was only there for three months. He took one of those famous photographs. Not *the* famous photograph, but one of them. He was very brave, you know.'

'So was Dad.' I realised I sounded defensive now.

I had this sudden awful feeling then. I remembered when Emily first came to see me in the Archives, she'd been a bit flustered about what she was searching for. What if we were mirror searchers, I thought, and her father was the dead body in my father's coffin? But Emily's father had died years before, I assured myself. And there was Martin Sharpe. I dismissed the thought almost as soon as I was conscious of it.

'You should find him,' Emily said suddenly, as if she'd been reading my mind. 'Find out where he is now.'

'Don't you ever give up?'

'Nup,' she said. 'You know what would be great? If you knew what a gutless bastard he was, not seeing you for all those years. If you could see that he's just a bloody guy, probably not even as good as you are. Definitely not as good as you are.' I sighed as loudly as I could. 'I'm serious. All that stuff you say about him,' she said. 'How good he was at swimming, how courageous, how strong.

He was probably a big cowardy custard. I bet he wasn't gentle like you. That takes real courage. I think I'd dislike him, to be honest. I'm sure I would.'

'It's not that simple,' I said.

'Why not?'

'What's it to you anyway?' I said. 'Why are you so obsessed about me finding him?'

'For God's sake, Scott, anyone can see you're not finished with him. It's as if you're two people and one of them isn't real. Every now and then I see it, the real you, when you laugh or get mad at me like you just did. Or when we make love. But then you switch it all off and go back to being only half here. He gets the other half.' She paused. 'I'll tell you one thing. If I were you and I had the option of finding my dead father, you couldn't stop me.'

'I know, but you're not me,' I said with some energy. 'You don't know when to leave things alone.'

'What do you mean by that?'

'All these questions. Why can't you just let it die?'

'Because you can't. I even know how we could do it. Why don't you let me?'

'Please, Emily,' I said, and the conversation ended there. But a few days later I said, 'How would you do it?'

She looked at me. 'I'd start with his service record.'

'I already did that, with Colin. The file was closed.'

'That was over a decade ago. I bet you could get more info now you work in the Archives.'

'Because I work in the Archives, Emily, I know what I can get and what I can't. There's no thirty-year rule on personnel files; they're closed forever. And at any rate,

even if more information was available now, what difference would it make? It wouldn't tell us why he did what
he did.'

'I wouldn't be so sure if I were you. When you and
Colin broke into the Army computer system, Colin said
your father might have been discharged a month before
his so-called death. If that's right, you never found out
why. Now, you probably could find out.

'Call it a journalistic hunch,' she said, slipping into
investigative mode, 'but I reckon you could have missed
something about your dad's service that you might notice
now that you've got a bit more distance. You're really sure
the body wasn't his, aren't you?'

'Yeah.'

'Really sure?'

I hesitated. 'It was a long time ago.'

'Well, the body's gone, so you can't start there anyway.
And you've looked through Missing Persons, and all that's
turned up is Martin Sharpe as a possible. But the one
thing you never looked into properly was your father's
service, except for the nonsense story Kerry Vance fed you,
and the stuff with Colin.

'Think about it. Even you and Colin, two boys,
managed to get as far as the termination note on your
father's computer file. The Army never chucks anything
out. They would still have paper records, for sure. What
you need to know is how come the last month of his
record is missing and why he was discharged, if he was.

'Another thing,' Emily said. 'You implied that when
you rang your dad's corporal, Peter White, he hinted at
something.'

'What do you mean?' I'd once thought Peter White was part of the Army cover-up. It seemed ridiculous now.

'He mentioned rumours in relation to your dad's Army service. What were the rumours? And when you got back to Duntroon, the Commandant went to great pains to tell you his own father was a drunk and you'd be judged on your merits. Why would he say that? There has to be something they know that you don't.

'Maybe he lied about more things than just his Superman-dangerous job,' Emily said. 'If someone faked their death, they'd have to have good reasons, wouldn't they? He had to be running from something.

'But maybe you're so scared of the truth, you'd rather not know.'

I was annoyed at Emily for saying I was scared of the truth, I was annoyed she even thought it, but mostly I was annoyed because I knew in my heart she was right.

chapter twenty-eight

The next day I rang Peter White. He was a sergeant now, in Canberra. 'Scott Goodwin. Yeah, I remember. How you doing, son?' I said I was doing well. He asked about Duntroon and I told him I'd left because I wasn't cut out for the life. 'Don't blame you,' he said. 'It's a tough bloody place, Duntroon. I don't reckon I could hack it.'

'I'm just a bit confused about something, Peter,' I said. 'Mum got a letter the other day from someone in Veterans' Affairs,' I lied. 'They got Dad's years of service wrong. The termination date was a month before he died.'

'Yeah, that's right, after his discharge.'

'I didn't realise,' I said. 'We thought he was in the service when he died. So he left the Army?'

'Yeah, he had his twenty years and more, which meant the full pension and all the other benefits. Why not, I say. And your dad wasn't like a lot of them. He'd served in a war. He had every right to take his money and run. It was just a shame that ...' He didn't finish the sentence. 'Anyway, that's all water under the bridge.' I asked what was a shame but he wouldn't say more.

I told Emily what Peter White had said, everything except his final comment, hoping that would close the matter. Instead she offered to check newspaper library files and her government contacts to find out where we could go next. I was sure she wouldn't turn up anything and then she'd drop it. But she sat me down after dinner the next night and said she'd found something. I was in a good mood, full of travel fever. I'd made Emily practise packing twice. Just in case it doesn't fit, I said. She rolled her eyes but went along.

'I went back through the morgue files at *The Courier-Mail*,' Emily said. She'd been working part-time for the Brisbane daily to save up for the trip. 'There was a dead story in the year your father died. It concerned something that happened in Vietnam.'

'A dead story?'

'That just means it was dropped before it ran. Sometimes it's because the journalist hits a dead end. Other times, like in this case, there's a threat of legal action.'

'What was the story about?' I said.

'Indirectly, it's about your dad,' she said slowly. She looked at me. 'And it's only the journalist's notes, not a finished story, so there are big gaps.'

'Tell me,' I said, wondering what on earth she could have found out and why she was being so uncharacteristically hesitant.

Emily sighed. 'I guess there's no easy way to say this. It was the story of what happened at Bien Duh when your dad was injured, the story of what really happened. You told me he got the Victoria Cross for his courage.'

'Yeah, he did. So?'

'Theses notes are those of a US journalist named John Webster, who was doing some work for Australian Consolidated Press. He was also in Vietnam when your dad was there, working for Reuters.

'Webster is quite well known, one of those go anywhere, do anything for a story types. He wrote up the original story of the Bien Duh operation for the Australian media.

'It was published pretty widely here, of course, including in *The Courier*, which had a local angle with your mum being in Toowoomba. They interviewed her after your dad got home. Did you know that?' I didn't. 'The *Women's Weekly* ran a pic story. She never told you?' I shook my head.

'Anyway, Webster was at the base at Bien Duh at the time. He went out with the choppers to pick up the three survivors the morning after the operation, so he saw what had happened first-hand. In his notes he says he and the photographer were pretty sure there was some sort of cover-up. They weren't allowed to take some of the pictures they wanted, and Army Press Liaison didn't want them to interview anyone.

'Webster fixed it so that he rode back in the helicopter with your father and Kerry Vance. In his notes he says something didn't gel in Kerry's story. He tried talking to them all again later, but by then your dad and Jarratt had gone home and Kerry wouldn't talk.

'It bugged Webster for years that he'd failed to get to

the bottom of it. He came back to Australia in 1987 and while here decided to look into the story again. Some papers from Vietnam had been released that year in the US, although it looks like they only confirmed the story you've already been told.

'Webster's notes go through the chain of events that night. He says your dad's unit was ambushed in the hills above the US Army base, just as you've always thought. Six Australians were killed. Your father and Kerry Vance were two of the survivors. There was a third, Dick Jarratt, who you've mentioned. Your dad, who was badly injured, was awarded the Cross. The other two got Distinguished Conduct Medals.'

'I've told you all this before, Emily.'

She nodded but didn't go on straight away. Then she said, 'Webster didn't ever get to interview the third survivor, Jarratt, back in Vietnam, or your dad. So in 1987, when he came back here, he interviewed all three of them. The notes are here in the file. Jarratt wouldn't talk about what happened at first, although after a few drinks he claimed that Kerry Vance had done something wrong. He wouldn't say what.

'Webster went to Melbourne and met with your dad. He was nervous, Webster said, and wouldn't talk at all. He walked out on the interview when he knew what Webster wanted.'

'Dad was always like that about Vietnam,' I said. 'It's pretty understandable.'

'Webster interviewed Kerry Vance last. He was so sure Vance was hiding something, he flew back to Western Australia to see Jarratt again. I think he bluffed

Jarratt into telling the true story. I think he managed to
find out whatever it was that Kerry Vance and your
father were hiding.'

Emily was going through the file as she spoke. I was
having trouble taking her words in. I was having trouble
taking Emily in. She'd put her glasses on, rectangular,
black-rimmed, trendy but harsh on her soft lovely face.
She looked like someone else, the hard-hitting
investigative journalist she wanted to be. I asked to see the
file. She gave me a manilla folder of notes held together by
a metal clip. I spent a long while opening and closing the
clip before I did anything else. There was a pocket with
pictures — poking out was a shot of steamy churned-up
earth, broken trees and bits of men, not recognisable as
Australian or Viet Cong, or even as men. I couldn't put my
father in the scene, no matter what. I couldn't look
through the rest of the photographs yet.

'Go to the back,' Emily said, as if she knew how I
felt. 'Before he went back to the States, Webster started
his second story.'

The last page of the file was one sheet of yellowing
copy paper with a typewritten paragraph.

Duh 1 Webs
###
Almost twenty years ago, three young soldiers were awarded
medals for courage shown in a bloody ambush in Vietnam,
except that two of those soldiers are cowards and the third
was bullied into protecting them.

That was as far as the story went.

'This is bullshit, Emily. Dad was forward scout. He saw the enemy before they saw him, which meant they managed to radio back for help. He and Kerry Vance and the other guy managed to hold back a Viet Cong battalion into the night, for godsake. Then the US gunships came in. Dad and Kerry were rescued. Kerry saved Dad's leg.'

'Webster's no slouch, Scott, and the only dirt he digs up is dirt that's already there. The thing is, the dates match. Webster interviewed your dad two months before his discharge and then your dad left the Army and apparently died. It's too bloody neat.' I scowled. 'All I'm saying is, the two things could be related. Webster's story might have uncovered something about Bien Duh that scared your father enough to make him fake his own death.'

Emily sat opposite me while I read the rest of the file. When I was finished, I didn't speak. 'How do you feel?' Emily said, finally.

'I don't know yet,' I said. 'There's no details here.'

'No,' she said. 'I didn't know whether to tell you or not.'

'So you think he faked his death because Webster was going to do a story. But there was no story, was there?'

'There's a second part to the file here, from the Legal Department.' Emily handed me another, much slimmer folder. There was a letter from a solicitor denying any wrongdoing on Kerry Vance's part in relation to the matter of the 'Incident at Bien Duh Base or any other matter in the Vietnam conflict'. Vance threatened a defamation action if the paper published the story. 'The law favoured plaintiffs back then,' Emily said. 'And unless there's something he didn't put on the file, Webster had no proof of whatever it was Jarratt told him. It was all hearsay. *The Courier* backed off the story. Webster gave up and went home. I just wish he'd left his last interview with Jarratt,' she said. 'I've looked, but it's not on the file anywhere.'

'But if there was no story, why would Dad fake his own death?'

'I don't know. I'm sure Webster's probing was enough to get the Army interested. Maybe there was going to be an official inquiry. If your father was court-martialled, he'd lose his pension, wouldn't he? The point is, there's almost certainly something in it.'

'You're drawing a long bow,' I said. 'Webster's saying my father was a coward.'

'I don't know what he's saying, but if I were you, I'd find Dick Jarratt. He and Kerry Vance are the only ones who know, and Kerry's never going to talk. What have you got to lose?'

Emily was right. What did I have to lose? I'd spent half my adult life looking for a shadow superman, and now I might find out who my father really was.

chaptertwenty-nine

Two weeks ago, just before we left Australia, I went to
Perth. Emily had offered to give me a lift to the airport.
No, I said, this is my journey. I caught a cab in rain of
monsoon proportions to make the five-thirty am direct
flight. I checked in and went upstairs to watch jets
waddle round the slick tarmac.

We took off swiftly and lifted above the clouds to
silver blue that filled me with hope. At cruise altitude,
thirty thousand feet or more, the sun near my horizon
burned into my retina and remained there for minutes.
I stared and stared and felt completely unaffected.

From the little flat airport in Perth I took a cab to
Leederville in the inner city. I arrived at the top of a steep
drive and looked down to a plain brick building with all
the hallmarks of an institution — a row of bins like
soldiers, community washlines, a visitor carpark, a van
parked near the front door. I arrived just after ten am. It

was a hot, dry day and as I walked down the drive,
I wished I hadn't come.

The woman who came to the door wore a white
nurse's uniform with a watch pinned to her chest, but
I didn't think she was actually a nurse; I couldn't say why.
'Can I help?' she said, and the way she said it annoyed
me. I couldn't say why that was either. I told the mock-
nurse who I'd come for. She led me into a community
kitchen that had a cold room on one side and a long
green laminated bench on the other. The room was filthy
and smelled of boiled eggs and rotting fruit. There were
no windows. A television above me in the corner showed
the mid-morning news, with the sound muted. Someone
named Tracy was standing with the sea behind her and
the wind whipping up her hair.

A tall thin man came into the kitchen. He wore
badly faded black jeans tucked into long canvas combat
boots, and a T-shirt with a faded Smurf on its front. His
frame was large, as if he'd once been fit, but his hair
looked as if it had never been cut and the skin around his
mouth was yellow with either nicotine stains or jaundice.
He looked not long for the world.

'Who are you?' the man said. 'And what do you want?'

I was sitting at the large green laminated table in the
centre of the room. I got up. The man stood on the other
side of the table with his arms folded.

'Dick Jarratt?' He didn't respond. 'My name's Scott
Goodwin. You knew my father.'

A hint of a smile crossed his face and disappeared.
'Clarky,' he said. 'You the son of Superman?' He laughed
harshly. He lit a cigarette. The tips of his first two fingers

were dark yellow and his hand was shaking as the flame reached the tip. He took a long draw and continued to look down at his other hand on the table.

'Can we sit down?' I said.

He took a chair opposite me and motioned me to sit. 'Clark's dead,' he said.

'Yeah,' I said. 'I want to know about Bien Duh.'

He almost smiled again and said, 'No you don't. Boy like you. You don't want to know anything about it.' His smile was nasty. He made as if to get up.

'Please,' I said, 'he was my father.'

Dick Jarratt sat for a long moment staring across at me without looking away. His gaze was so intense I couldn't hold it for long. 'You seen Vance?' he said.

'No,' I said, 'but I know about the journalist, Webster.'

'He came to see me.' I nodded. 'Vance is a cunt.'

'Yeah,' I said. 'But he and my dad were pretty tight.'

'Had to be,' Jarratt said. 'Your dad had no choice after Bien Duh. They were tied like blood after that.'

'Tell me what happened, Jarratt,' I said. 'I've got a right to know.'

'You want to know,' he said, 'you buy me a drink.'

We walked down Oxford Street, passing a grocer, a newsagent and a closed café before arriving at the pub on the first corner. We sat at the bar, which was covered in a sopping towel, and ordered beers that were served immediately in fat glass mugs. It was dim inside the pub compared to the brightness of the Perth morning. Jarratt was known by the two or three others at the bar. I wasn't a beer drinker and hardly touched mine while Jarratt downed his first three. He smoked constantly, roll-your-owns from a tin he kept in his jeans pocket.

Jarratt's wife had left him. Three kids. The eldest had killed herself. The wife blamed Jarratt. He said this matter-of-factly, with less sentiment than he gave to ordering another beer. He showed me pictures of the kids, taken years before, which he kept in a cheap wallet. There was no money in there. He said he'd had a job driving trucks 'over east' for a bit when he first left the service, but that fell through. Too many pills to take, he said.

Then he started on Bien Duh. I could tell he didn't want to talk but couldn't stop either. I wondered if it would cleanse him to tell the story, or make it worse. Probably both, I figured. 'It was a fucking nightmare,' he said. 'We were kids, all of us, but especially Clark. Jesus, he'd only been in-country a couple of months. Vance should have known better.

'I was 2IC, this was the last bit of my tour and I was due for promotion to my own command, but Vance didn't like me, didn't like anyone who crossed him. He'd given me a bad report the month before. I didn't have a hope of getting my own show after that.

'Clark had come in from Canungra looking keen as hell. Like all the new blokes, he looked up to Vance. Vance loved that, loved being the man.

'Eight guys on a night op and Vance puts the new kid in charge. Superman, he called him. Super fucker.'

'But Kerry Vance was in charge,' I said.

Jarratt ignored me. 'I was pretty shitty. I figured I'd let Clark fuck up and then come in and save the day and prove Vance wrong. The 'Nam had a way of twisting

your mind, making you think things like that. I can't
believe I put all those guys at risk, just to prove a point.
And your dad; he was just a kid. I should have been
looking out for him, not doing him over.

'Early in the night we had a bit of fire, which was
pretty rare in that area. I said to Clark maybe we should
go back. The Yanks didn't want Aussie casualties on their
books, so they wouldn't care if we didn't finish. I reckon
they were just filling in our timesheets anyway. We never
seemed to face much fire, to be honest.

'If we'd turned back, the Yanks could have just
napalmed the whole area to smoke old Charlie out. And
we'd have been safe and sound tucked up in our beds. I
had it figured. We'd double back the way we came and do
an early rendezvous with the choppers. We were clear
behind. Managed well, it would have been a piece of piss.

'But Clark wouldn't hear of it. Looking back, I can
see he wanted to impress Vance. He wanted Vance's
approval more than anything. You know what he said to
me? "Back into line, soldier," like we were in a movie.
What a fucking nightmare.

'So, I did what Clark said. I got back into line and
let him walk us into disaster. I always think back to that
moment when I could have done differently. I just said
fine, it's up to you, you're the boss. I should have done
something. I should have ordered him to stop there and
go back. I had the rank and the experience. And we'd all
have come home.'

'But what about Vance?' I said. 'He was the CO.'

Jarratt smiled harshly. 'Vance? Vance was where he
always was, getting himself laid.'

'What do you mean?'

'He had it all figured. He'd done his two tours, he reckoned. It was time for a holiday. What he'd do was, he'd arrange for us to get dropped right outside this village the Yanks were supposed to be protecting, one of the new settlements they tried to establish with no VC infiltration.

'Kerry was fucking some thirteen-year-old in the village. He'd stop with her and we'd do the patrol and pick him up when we were finished.

'He used to send this Gook kid with us, the whore's little brother, and the idea was, the kid would run back and get Vance if there was trouble. After Clark refused to turn back I sent the kid off to get Vance, but it was already too late.

'Clark was a disaster, needless to say. Sorry to speak ill of your old man but, first up, he stayed in front, the big-man forward scout. Then he didn't radio our position back to the base. I did that, just before they hit us.

'As soon as they opened fire, I knew we didn't have a hope. They were all over us. I did take over then, told Clark to get back with the others, but it was way too late for any kind of strategic moves. And then Clark panicked. He just lost it completely. Not that I blame him for that. We all did things we wouldn't have done if … It tested you, Vietnam, too much.

'So Clark falls over and starts sobbing. Then he runs. Not much point in that, I could have told him; they were all around us by then. I dug in with the other guys as best I could. We came up with a plan to get out but, one by one, the VC picked us off. It's not much fun watching your men get shot.

'Clark got hit right at the start. I didn't see it but I heard his yells behind us until he passed out. He found a Claymore, poor bastard. Fucked his leg.

'The VC left him for dead. They left us all for dead. They had richer pickings in mind, getting the Yanks where they slept. We didn't know it at the time, but they had a fucking battalion out there. They were planning a hit on Bien Duh.

'Vance arrived with the kid from the village. I don't know how he got past the VC. He was pretty good, old Vance. He found Clark first, then me. He had some morphine and bandages for Clark and we packed his wound as best we could. I'd been hit in the head by shrapnel, but not badly. My helmet saved me. I was just a bit concussed.

'Vance and the kid and me crawled back to the village. We heard the US planes come across and then that sweet sound as they bombed the shit out of the VC. By morning, when the dust-offs arrived, we'd agreed the story; Kerry was there. He was CO. I was 2IC. Clark was forward scout. We did our best.

'You're thinking I could have refused to go along with Vance. He'd already fucked me over, so what did I owe him?

'Vance was the CO, and as far as anyone else was concerned, I was just a soldier with an attitude problem. Who would they believe, do you reckon? And to be honest, I thought Clark was going to cark it and it would be my word against Vance's anyway. When Clark pulled through and went along with the story, I didn't have any choice.

'I'm sure Army Press knew something was up, but those guys are complete snakes. They kept any journalists away from us and made us into heroes. Six KIA, they needed a win, I reckon.

'So they gave us medals and none of us ever said what really happened. Vance never would have, of course. His arse would have been on the line. He'd lose his pension, his status, everything. And Clark was never going to do Vance in, specially when he'd fucked up so bad himself. The story suited him as much as it suited Vance.

'As for me, I didn't like Kerry Vance. I thought he was a power-mad shit. But you don't dob another soldier. First rule. The other blokes would have killed me if I'd done Vance in. I shut up and let them give me the fucking medal. Why not, I thought. It seemed to fit just right with Vietnam.'

chapter**thirty**

Mum and Jim had moved onto a small farm at the base of Mount Barney. Mum wrote for science magazines and Jim grew things. Mum and I sat out on the back deck, which had a view of Mount Maroon. Emily and Jim were picking wild strawberries.

'Did you know what happened at Bien Duh?' I said.

At first Mum looked as if she was going to say no. Then she saw my face and sighed. 'I was so relieved when he said he was coming home. They told me he'd been injured and that he might not walk again. Then when he finally got to call me, from Saigon, he said it was just a little graze. He was in tears. I told him I didn't care that he was injured. I was just relieved he was coming home. I thought that whatever else happened, they couldn't kill him now. He didn't mention the medal. Kerry Vance talked about it constantly. He came home before your father and hung around like a bad smell. He kept telling me it was all guts from Dad.

'And then Dad came home and he was like somebody else. It ate at him, whatever they'd done. I knew war affected men horribly, so I assumed it was that. I tried to be patient. He couldn't even walk for a long while, so it was pretty frustrating for him.

'I took him to see his father because I thought George, being a soldier, might understand. He so much wanted George's approval. But George called him a coward, not for what had happened, which he couldn't have known about, but for coming home at all. George got this idea your dad had injured himself to get out, which was ridiculous. He couldn't wait to get over there. The last thing he would have wanted was to come home. Perhaps if he'd stayed on, he'd have redeemed himself in his own eyes. He didn't get that chance.

'The newspapers wanted to interview us. Kerry talked to them, of course, but it was your father they wanted. He was young and handsome, and here we were, the perfect family. Stella had just started kindy. You weren't even born. This was when the marches against the war were in full swing. He was the Army's golden-haired boy, they thought, and they didn't do much to stop the papers. I knew he didn't feel he'd done anything to deserve the medal, but I thought that was normal.

'The *Women's Weekly* came out to the house. They took a picture of Stella and me in the front garden. Stella was in her best dress, the navy one with the red and white sash, and she looked so pretty. She just adored your father, but he didn't even know you kids existed, not for months after he came home. In a way, it was you who saved him.

'The *Weekly* did their story. They used the photo of him setting off from Sydney. You know the one, on the steps of the plane, waving like mad. I told them how proud I was, how wonderful he was. I hoped it would bring him back to us.' She sighed and looked at me, but her eyes remained dry.

'I didn't tell him about the story. I wanted it to be a surprise. I wanted him to know how proud I was. Maybe I liked the attention too, like he said. I don't know. When he saw it, he came home from work and threw the magazine across the room. He was still on crutches. He hit me, punched me so hard I fell on the floor. He fell too, off balance on the crutches. Then he cried but nothing would change what he'd done.

'He never hit me again, but he didn't have to. We were finished. Whatever else happened, we were finished. You just can't come back from there.

'That night, as his way of saying sorry, he told me what had happened. His voice had this awful chill, flat and hopeless. There was nothing I could say to help him. And I wasn't sure I wanted to by then, anyway.

'He said that he'd been really stupid and had got a medal for it. He laughed that awful hollow laugh he had. He said men had been killed, good men, because of him. He said the Victoria Cross was what he got for killing his men.'

'Do you know why he thought it was his fault?'

'I asked him that, what he'd done wrong. He said they were on a patrol and he was in charge. They were up on top of a hill that had been cleared and they'd been fired at but no one had been injured. He said they could have gone back then, because they were a small group, and they should have gone back, according to their procedures, but he wanted to keep going. He wanted to be the hero, is what he said.

'I tried to tell him that it didn't matter, but it was like a bandaid on an arterial bleed. There was nothing I could say, nothing I could ever say, that would help. This was our life.'

'Did he mention Kerry Vance?'

'Only that Kerry came in and cleaned up after him.'

'And you believed that?'

'I knew the man I married was gone forever. I didn't much care about why.' She took my hand. 'Don't ever ask me again why I hate the Army,' she said.

We sat together a while more in silence. Then I said, 'You remember how I thought he wasn't dead?' Her lips, which had been set tight in anger, parted now and I saw fear in her eyes. I realised for the first time that she needed him to be dead almost as much as I'd needed him to be alive. 'I know how silly that must have seemed,' I said. She relaxed again. 'Thanks for sticking by me.' And she had stuck by me. They'd all stuck by me, all except for him.

chapterthirty-one

Emily and I flew into Rome first. We had three days of history, pizza and streets I couldn't believe could be so wonderful. We took the train from Rome across Italy and into France and the Côte d'Azur and Nice. I lit a candle at the chapel in Vence, the one Matisse designed to thank the nuns who healed him. I don't know who I was thanking, or for what, but it seemed right.

Last night I rang Stella. I knew she was going home to Australia from the States, and she and Mark were in Paris. I thought we might be able to meet up somewhere. I had a hankering to talk to my silly sister. 'You sound great, Scott,' she said. She suggested they could fly to Nice the next day, today. So I said that would be wonderful, because there was someone I wanted her to meet. She asked me who I wanted her to meet, and I said never you mind, and I got off the phone and ran back to our little apartment to tell Emily what a great surprise we'd have the next day.

Emily was quiet through dinner, and I didn't know what was wrong. She'd made the ratatouille with loin of lamb that left such a mess this morning, and I said it was a feast. She didn't respond. 'Don't you think it's a feast?' I said.

She opened a second bottle of wine. 'I have to tell you something,' she said.

She sat back in her chair and said there was no easy way to tell it. 'I knew everything about your father before you and I met,' she said.

'Come again?' I said.

'I haven't been honest with you. That day I came into the Archives, I knew about you. I knew who you were. I was doing a story, on Vietnam veterans. I was finishing John Webster's story, all these years later. It was such a good story, and I knew if I could just find out what had really happened, I could use it.

'I didn't expect to meet you that day. I knew you worked there but I thought I'd just go to the counter and ask someone for your father's records. Maybe I hoped you'd find out that someone had been asking and then you'd contact me. But you were there, at the counter, the first person I met, so I had to make it up as I went along.

'Once I'd started with a lie, it got harder to tell you the truth,' she said. 'I would have, at Byron, but I couldn't when I saw your face. I thought you'd feel betrayed.

'But you see, it will all come out now, because Stella knows me. She knows my name. I emailed her at the start. I asked if I could interview her over the phone. I asked for your contact details.'

'So, me and Stella, we're a story?' I said, taking it in.

'No. There's no story, not now. I dropped any thought of a story after Byron. Or at least, after you moved in.'

'But you knew that I'd been in hospital, that I didn't believe Dad was dead? That he'd been a gutless bastard. You listened to me rant on and didn't say.' I sat there for a few moments in silence. 'That's why you wanted me to find him.'

'It wasn't personal for me, Scott, not like it is for you. It was the kind of story that could launch my career. John Webster was a friend of my father's. He's in that photo you saw of Dad in Vietnam. Dad was the one who took the photographs at Bien Duh.

'Webster came to see my mother when he was in Australia in 1987. I was a teenager. He told us about the story. Mum gave him the negatives for the pictures you saw in the file. Later he wrote to Mum and told her they'd canned the story. I didn't think about it again until I was freelancing. There was one of those welcome-home parades for Vietnam veterans and I was covering it for *The Courier-Mail*. I remembered Webster's visit, so I went and found the file in the paper's library.

'I wanted to do a profile piece on your father, the kind of man who could do what he did. First I tried Webster, but he died a few years ago. Then I called Jarratt, but he wouldn't even see me, then Stella, who wouldn't talk to me either. I didn't even bother to try your mother. I knew she wouldn't talk. I traced you through Duntroon and then Archives.'

'Did you know I thought Dad was still alive?'

'Yes. I'd done my research. I thought you were right

at first. It was just too convenient that he died. And the timing smacked of something amiss. So, when I started, I did most of the things you did, went to the hospital, went to the funeral home. And then I came to you.'

'So, I suppose now you're going to tell me that you know where he is as well?' She nodded. 'Where?' I said.

'He's dead, Scott. He's been dead all along.'

chapterthirty-two

'It seemed far-fetched to me that Kerry and your father could wait for someone dead to come along who looked like your father. I wondered if they'd killed Martin Sharpe, but that was pretty out there too.

'I did what you did, went to Missing Persons. To me, the photo of Martin Sharpe in the file looked nothing like your father's photo which I got from *The Courier-Mail* file. Actually, I think the shot of your father at the beach does look like the man in the coffin, although I couldn't say for sure.'

'Why didn't you tell me that?'

'You'd had people telling you that. You didn't believe them, so why would you believe me?

'A few weeks ago, when you found out about your dad's discharge, I told you what I knew about what happened in Vietnam. I could see you still believed your father was alive. I wasn't convinced.

'Two weeks ago I went to see Marion. She still lives in the Coast hinterland. It's years now and I thought I could get her to talk. At first I tried to scare her. I told her I knew everything, which was a bit of bluff. I didn't at that stage. I mentioned John Webster and she knew what I was talking about, I could tell.

'But she still wouldn't talk, not until I told her about you, what's happened in your life, how much it's hurt you. I should have started there, I suppose, because then she told me the truth. Your dad really did die.'

'But how?' I said.

'He killed himself.' I was shaking my head. 'Scott, he was about to be exposed. Kerry Vance was pressuring him to stick to their story. *The Courier-Mail* looked as if it might publish. Marion was pressuring him too. She wanted him to tell them the truth. She thought it would allow him to move on.

'And more than that, there was an Army inquiry. Your dad had been questioned. He resigned his commission and left the Army to avoid a possible court martial. But he still couldn't see a way out. If they carried out the investigation and found out the truth, his pension would be cut off. He'd be shamed. He killed himself.'

I looked at the floor. I wanted to hit something. I dug my nails into my palm, hard.

'He left a note. Marion gave me a copy.' Emily went into the bedroom and was gone for what seemed like hours. I listened to the drip of the kitchen tap, which was out of synch with the clock on the wall behind me. I counted twenty-seven yellow and twenty-nine red tiles in the splashback.

Emily came back into the room and sat down. She put a piece of paper face down on the table between us. I turned it over. His writing, the date in digits and the time according to the twenty-four hour system in the top right hand corner, just like all his letters. Dear Marion, he started. There was none of the crappy sentimentality he'd normally have saved for talk of his own death. He listed insurance policy numbers, contacts, bank accounts and the Army Staff Office number. He said all the things Marion asked for at the funeral home, that he wanted a Catholic funeral, no Army involvement, even that he wanted the cheapest of everything. He said he felt at peace, that he was leaving his families well-provided for, that she mustn't tell anyone he'd killed himself because then the insurance wouldn't pay up. It was so pragmatic, so like him in one way, so unlike him in another. At the end, he told her he loved her and he'd see her 'up there, or in the other place (only kidding)'. He said to call Kerry Vance, who'd know what to do to fix things so it looked like he died of natural causes. He said for what he'd done, for everything he'd done, this might in some small way atone.

'Marion found him in the shed behind her house. He'd hanged himself. She did what he'd said, called Kerry Vance, and it was Kerry who concocted the story of the asthma attack and the bushwalking. He organised his girlfriend, Helen Barrett, to falsify the records. That's why they went to that pokey little hospital instead of Southport. Helen got Dr Johnson out of bed. Dr Johnson declared your father dead, with cause of death as heart failure, without seeing the body.

'They didn't want you to see the body because there was bruising on his neck from the rope. That's why he was wearing a polo-neck sweater. Kerry was the one who arranged for those local boys to destroy the funeral home records because the home had the photograph and description of the bruising. And Shirley Stapleton was probably weird with you because she thought you hadn't been told the truth she knew, which was that your father had taken his own life.'

Emily sat quietly while I took it all in. Finally I said, 'You. You knew and didn't tell me.'

'I knew, yeah.' She looked almost proud of herself.

'So now you've told me, you can launch your great career,' I said. 'You've got better than him. You've got his mad son.'

'No,' she said quickly. 'I can't write anything anyway. It wouldn't be ethical.'

'Ethical? What the fuck would you know about ethical? You lie about what you ate for lunch, Emily. Ethical, now that's a good one coming from you.'

'No,' Emily said. 'Please, Scott, let's not be like this. I couldn't bring myself to tell you, and then it seemed like it could just go on. I didn't set out to deceive you. I'm not like that.'

'Aren't you?'

'No,' she said. 'I'll admit it wasn't the nicest thing I've ever done. But you were a stranger when I first did it. I didn't know you. And your sister did her block at me when I asked her about your father. I just thought I'd let you get to know me a bit first. See how good I am.'

'You should have told me all this, Emily. It's too big.'

'That's nonsense,' she said. 'Every relationship starts with lies. You didn't tell me everything about yourself the first time we met.'

'Yes I did,' I said.

'Well, you didn't have to,' she said. 'My point is …' She couldn't think of a point at first. 'My point is that it's not a lie if you intend to tell the truth. I wanted to tell you so many times, but you kept saying how much the fact he lied to you made it so bad. I thought if you knew I'd lied to you, you'd hate me.'

'Well, that's the bit you got right,' I said. 'We're finished, Emily. We're so fucked.'

chapter**thirty-three**

Bain told me I needed to be wary of any occasion when people I had reason to trust suddenly seemed untrustworthy. It was probably me, he said. I probably needed a top-up visit. Emily was the only person other than Manko who'd believed me unconditionally. Or at least she'd said she did. She was the person I'd trusted. Learn to look for the warning signs, Bain said. If I found myself not believing loved ones, if I became deceitful, hid behaviours, it was a good indication I was heading for an episode. All I had to do was call the hospital and check in. Bain never mentioned betrayal as something real. The last time I'd seen him, he tossed a green orange over to me. When I asked him what it was for, he said, 'Don't you know what that is?'

'It's an orange?' I said.

'No, it's green kryptonite. Use it wisely.'

The Promenade des Anglais is busy now. The lovers

have left me, the fishermen too are off home to sleep, and the old woman is probably on her way to the markets for some salad for lunch. Those early risers have been replaced by at least a hundred tourists who've come to Nice so that something of the Mediterranean will rub off on them. The jetstream has become the sun. The only remaining members of our pre-dawn group are you and me, you gliding through the water with the grace of a dolphin, me up here like a lone seal.

I walk along the promenade towards you. The sea, which before the sun came up was like smooth black glass, is azure now, the colour this coast is named for, and choppy. The trick with a tide is not to fight it, you used to tell me. You're swimming in towards me, fighting a tide that wants you to stay out there forever.

I used to think my story was unique and tragic. Stella says I'm maudlin. But now I've told it, I wonder if I'm different from other sons. We get bigger, they get smaller, until we can barely remember the giants they were. They might matter less, make fewer decisions that bind us. But somewhere inside us they're there still, as voices or fears. Or Supermen. And whether my father was dead or disappeared or living and breathing, it was Superman inside me I had to accommodate. And that's what I've been doing.

My images of him shift like the colour of the water here. Right now I'm thinking of a boy of ten holding a snake that's nearly as long as him, a dark slick curl of thick hair falling into those bright eyes. His right foot is turned in, toe pointing, digging into the dirt. He looks uncomfortable, as if hesitant about being in the world at all. He who hesitates is lost. I don't know who took the picture.

I can see you on that hill too. You'd have taken
charge in Kerry's absence, just like that. Sure mate, no
worries. My new scout's a bonza, Kerry might have told
the other non-coms. Smells the Nogs before they smell
him. Clark, they call him, and this guy really is
Superman. And afterwards, how easy it must have been
to go along with Kerry. I was there, Kerry would have
said, or I'll be charged. I was there, and you were there,
and we did our best.

You once said to me, about killing, that you just do
it. But you didn't just do it. And then the rest of life
wanting. Mum told me that when I was doing well with
swimming, you used to say, 'Looks like things worked
out for the best, doesn't it?' She didn't know what you
meant. What a life.

Mr Maitland always reckoned I had courage. He was
talking about Plato's definition. For Plato, courage was
wise endurance. Not just enduring, but enduring with
wisdom, with full knowledge. What would a man of wise
endurance make of Emily Duval?

As you emerge from the water, I step down onto the
pebble beach and walk towards you. I hear the rocks
scrape together under my feet, the waves hitting them
with a dull roar. We pass one another. You say nothing.
Do you take a second look, tilt your head and keep
going? Close-up, you're young, no more than fourteen.

I look beyond you to the blue. I think of my warm
bed, of pain de montagne and strawberries with strong
milky coffee. I think of Emily. I turn away from you and
set out on the short walk home.

acknowledgments

Heartfelt thanks from the author to the members of the Australia Council Literature Fund who provided a grant and a shot of confidence; to readers Belinda Dangerfield, Jo Fleming, Michelle de Kretser, David Mayocchi, Sasha Marin and Rosie Scott who provided helpful comments on various drafts; to the staff of Banff Centre for the Arts who provided a residency and especially to faculty member Audrey Thomas who commented on an initial draft with just the right measure of stern and kind words; to Paul Stewart and Terry Mayocchi from the Queensland Police, to the Funeral Directors' Association and to medico Nick Earls who provided technical advice; and to Peter Forster who told me about fast cars, among other things.

For a beautiful place in which to write, thanks to Christa Neumann.

For support in all those ways that matter, thanks to Lenore Cooper, Cherrell Hirst, Robyn Sheahan-Bright, Cathy Sinclair, Theanne Walters and Kim Wilkins.

The publishing team at Allen & Unwin, headed by Annette Barlow and Christa Munns, have cherished *Killing Superman* and me in equal measure. They are treasures. My agent Rachel Skinner acquitted herself brilliantly in the wrangling phase. The editor of the manuscript, Jo Jarrah, did an absolutely superb job; any remaining errors are mine. For another stunning cover, thanks to Ellie Exarchos.